Praise for Laura Wilson

'Plausible and ... ne, fluent writer, followin ... tch'

... ry Review

'The building of ... and as the story unfolds, so the chilling menace creeps up on you and increases with every new revelation. This is a brilliant piece of writing and highly recommended' *Mystery Women*

'Wilson's prose is clear, her pace fast-moving, at times even terse. Alice is a triumph' *Good Book Guide*

My Best Friend

'All the personalities are sharply drawn and the sense of inevitable doom slowly builds up as the story unfolds. The writing is spare and without a wasted word. This book has real class' *Sunday Telegraph*

'What's most impressive about this dark, disturbing book is the considerable skill with which Wilson tells the story through several voices. Her portrayals of flawed and dysfunctional people are skin-crawlingly real' *Observer*

A Little Death

'This is a deceptively simple and compelling tale where the pathos is the fuel for real suspense'

Frances Fyfield, *Sunday Express*

Laura Wilson was brought up in London and has degrees in English Literature from Somerville College, Oxford, and University College London. She has worked briefly and ingloriously as a teacher, and more successfully as an editor of non-fiction books. She has written history books for children and is interested in history, particularly of the recent past, painting and sculpture, uninhabited buildings, underground structures, cemeteries and time capsules. Her first three novels were critically acclaimed, and the first, *A Little Death*, was shortlisted for both the CWA Historical Dagger and the Anthony Award for Best Paperback Original. She lives in London.

By Laura Wilson

Hello Bunny Alice
My Best Friend
Dying Voices
A Little Death

Laura Wilson

Hello Bunny Alice

ORION

An Orion paperback

First published in Great Britain in 2003
by Orion
This paperback edition published in 2004
by Orion Books Ltd,
Orion House, 5 Upper St Martin's Lane,
London WC2H 9EA

A CIP catalogue record for this book is
available from the British Library.

ISBN 0 75285 885 8

Typeset at The Spartan Press Ltd,
Lymington, Hants

Printed and bound in Great Britain by
Clays Ltd, St Ives plc

To all those who walk their dogs in Lincoln's Inn Fields –
and the dogs themselves, of course.

ACKNOWLEDGEMENTS

I am very grateful to Jane Barlow, Roxy Beaujolais, PC Tony Cassidy, Laura Darby, Broo Doherty, Tim Donnelly, Ruth Gavin, Jane Gregory, Peter Guttridge, Barbara Haigh, Marilyn Lownes, David Mann, Christine Moodie, Tristan Oliver, Nigel Osborne, Lisanne Radice, Giles Radice, Derek Rimmer, Ann Sturley of the BT Archive, Liz Tillings, Pandora White, June and William Wilson, and Jane Wood, for their encouragement, advice and support. I am also grateful to my fellow Unusual Suspects, Natasha Cooper, Leslie Forbes, Manda Scott, Michelle Spring and Andrew Taylor; to my favourite redhead, for services above and beyond the call of duty; and to Freeway, who provided the model for Eustace.

THE DAILY MIRROR
Monday May 18, 1970

LENNY MAXTED FOUND DEAD

Farewell Note: Please Forgive Me

The man once voted Britain's top comic has been found hanged – just three days after announcing his engagement. His fiancée discovered his body, surrounded by sleeping pills and empty gin bottles, in the Wiltshire cottage where he was staying. Maxted, 40, had been dead for several hours. Police do not believe anyone else was involved.

With his partner, Jack Flowers, Lenny Maxted became one of the nation's best-loved funny men following the brilliant success of the TV series *Please Turn Over For Jack and Lenny*. Often praised for his faultless timing, Maxted's languid manner was a perfect foil to Flowers's machine-gun delivery. But viewers caught a glimpse of his personal torment when he broke down during a guest appearance with Jack Flowers on the TV show *Close Up*. The interviewer, veteran broadcaster Geoffrey Wallace, was criticised for encouraging a tearful Maxted to tell the audience about his alcoholism. Flowers commented afterwards, 'Lenny isn't a happy man. He's been overworking and he needs a rest.'

Maxted had not been seen in public since he announced his engagement to Alice Conway, a 24-year-old former nightclub hostess. He left a farewell note addressed to Miss Conway which included the words 'I love you, please forgive me.' Their agent and close friend Donald Findlater said last night, 'I don't know how I'm going to break the news to Jack. There may have been artistic differences, but they were the best of friends.' Jack Flowers is currently on holiday in the Mediterranean.

Maxted's Battle with the Bottle – Page Five

PROLOGUE

**Maynard's Farm, Duck End, Oxfordshire
Thursday 19 August, 1976**

I had the dream again last night. I'm at the bottom of a lake looking through the window of a car. Everything's gin-bottle green, murky, and there's a skeleton sitting behind the wheel, dressed as a bunny girl. The ears are perched on the skull, jaunty, the collar and bow tie are hanging round the neck vertebrae and the body's dressed in the satin costume, black, the colour we all used to want because it was slimming, with two empty cone-shaped cups sticking out in front of the ribcage.

Someone comes up behind me and rubs my face with a trail of waterweed. At first I don't mind because it's pleasant, sensual, even – but then they start to twist the weed round my head and neck and it's choking me so I try to grab it, pull it away, but I can't do it. I lean forward to bang on the window of the car to get help but I can't reach and I'm being dragged down and I can't escape and I think I'm going to die.

Then I wake up with the sheets tangled round my neck, feeling guilty, and I can't make the feeling go away. Because I know who it is, all right. The skeleton in the car.

It's replaced the Lenny dream, the one where I find his body. Ever since I got that newspaper cutting in the post, three days ago.

2

CHAPTER ONE

BODY FOUND IN LAKE

Falling water levels led to gruesome revelations yesterday when a car containing human remains was fished out of a lake on the Ivar Park estate in Wiltshire. A police spokesman said that the skeleton, which has not yet been identified, may have been in the water for several years.

I don't know who sent it. There wasn't a letter, just the cutting, with the date, *Sat 14 Aug '76*, scrawled across the top. Don't recognise the writing. London postmark. Could be anyone. But why send the cutting to *me*? That's what I don't understand.

I remembered the girl who disappeared. Another bunny. Kitty. Lenny'd slept with her. Mind you, he wasn't the only one, not by a long chalk. It was in the summer, 1969, during our bad patch. Seven years ago. I thought I'd left all that behind. Well, I'd tried to. That's why I came down here.

Nobody even noticed Kitty was missing. It wasn't surprising, really. There must have been a couple of hundred people at that party, and from what I can remember, most of them were so out of it they probably didn't know what planet *they* were on, never mind anyone else. I don't think it was actually reported for a few weeks, but I'm pretty sure the police never found anyone who'd seen her after that night. At least, that's what everyone said.

Ivar Park House was down near Salisbury Plain. Massive.

Stables, gardens, woods, the lot. And a lake. Definitely a lake. Kitty'd been wearing her bunny costume. We weren't meant to take them out of the club, but someone – maybe even Lenny, because he was the one who brought her along – must have slipped the security guard a few quid not to look into her bag. I remember her coming down this huge flight of stairs at Ivar and people cheering, but that's all.

It was weird, though, because they couldn't find anyone who'd given Kitty a lift or seen her leave the party or anything, and she didn't exactly blend into the background, dressed like that. Nothing about the costume in the paper, though, but then it's probably rotted or been eaten by fish or something after this long. I suppose it would have stayed underwater for ever if it hadn't been for the drought. There must be somebody out there who wishes it had.

To be honest, I didn't pay much attention at the time. Me and Kitty were not what you'd call the best of friends, but in any case, our whole – well, our whole world, if you like – was pretty free and easy, people coming and going. Even Kitty's flatmate thought she'd gone off to stay with a boyfriend, but she didn't know who. Not surprising, because Kitty wasn't exactly famous for saying 'no', if you see what I mean.

If I'd had to guess, I'd have said she'd hooked up with a rich punter and gone abroad somewhere. You could get yourself very well taken care of if you played your cards right, and she was always pretty good at looking after Number One.

I don't *know* that it's her. It just says remains, skeleton. But if I'm supposed to know – well, there's no one else it could be. I didn't like Kitty. With good reason, I might add, because she was a real bitch, what my granddad would have called 'a right piece of work', and I was pretty glad – no, more than glad, I was delighted – when she didn't come

4

back to the club. But you wouldn't wish it on your worst enemy, dying like that. It doesn't bear thinking about. And now I can't stop thinking about it. Some things you can't. You try, shut the door, but they're always there, waiting to jump out at you. Like finding Lenny. I mean, usually, when I think about Lenny, it's Lenny when he was alive, but if I wake up in the night or it catches me off guard or something, that's when it all comes back.

The anniversaries are the worst, and the week before. Just dreading it, knowing what it's going to be like. Each year, when it comes up, I think, it has to be better this time, but it never is.

I walked into Lenny's body. The room was pretty dark and I didn't realise what it was, but when I looked up all I could see for the first couple of seconds were these bulging eyeballs looking straight at me. His head was like a balloon, up by the ceiling, dark red, and his body just hanging down from it like a sack or something. He'd done it with a belt. Wide leather belt. But I didn't know that till later, because I just took one look and ran straight out again. The guy who was with me – the taxi-driver – he got the police. He said I was screaming, but I don't remember. I just recall a dull feeling, as if my brain needed sharpening – they'd given me a tranquilliser or something – and when I tried to sleep, later, I saw those eyes again, straining to pop out of his face. And I kept telling myself, that isn't my Lenny, my Lenny's gone.

That was why I married Jeff, really. I kept saying to myself that I was getting on with my life and getting over it, but really it was because I was trying to keep hold of Lenny, or at least keep the feeling of closeness, the life I should have had with him. I was trying to re-create it, somehow. I didn't realise, until it all fell apart, that that was why I'd done it, and perhaps . . . oh, maybe there was a bit of me that always knew it wasn't going to work, but after what happened with Lenny I was in a mess and I needed someone and he was *there*.

I don't mean it could have been anyone at all. Jeff was great looking, glamorous and talented – he's a photographer, that was how we met in the first place. He told me he'd look after me and God knows I needed it. I wasn't exactly pretending he was Lenny, but I think that's sort of what I *expected* from him, which wasn't fair. Jeff didn't have that much of a sense of humour and he was quite a closed person. Tough. More like Jack than Lenny in that way, now I come to think about it. Quite hard, in a way I wasn't used to, and I thought it meant he was strong, because Lenny'd been so . . . not weak, but . . . Well, you looked after Lenny.

It wasn't just women, everybody did it, even Jack. People always did things for him, and because he was charming and kind and terribly grateful, it made them feel they'd done something useful and good. He used it to his advantage, of course, played it up, but he really could be pretty hopeless. I mean, I'll never forget watching him trying to open a tin of baked beans, and that was when he was sober. But Lenny *connected* with people, that was the point, and Jeff didn't. Not in that way. He liked to get one up on them, and I could never understand that. Actually, I think that's what his affairs were about, it was the secrecy he liked more than the actual sex. You know, being able to chat away to someone knowing that he was knocking off their wife or girlfriend and they had no idea. I kept telling myself it didn't matter – not the affairs, because it was a couple of years before I found out about those, but just the way he was. I mean, you can't be down on someone because they're not someone else, can you? And we had a lovely home and a nice life, but it never really came together. I'm not blaming Jeff, it was my fault as much as his. The timing, apart from anything else, because it was less than two years after Lenny died when we got married and I just wasn't ready for it.

I had a calendar once, with quotations on it, and there was one that said, 'Life is lived forwards but understood backwards.' It's true, isn't it? If you ever understand it at all, that is. I'm starting to wonder. I mean, I've been over and over Lenny's death in my head, but I've never come up with any real answers. Except that I failed him. It always comes back to that. It's like those words you sometimes see on gravestones, *If love could have saved him, he would not have died.* But you can't save people with love, can you? You should be able to, and it happens in books and things, but you can't, not in real life.

The cottage where Lenny killed himself was on the same estate. It belonged to the bloke who'd had the party. Marcus's father was the Earl of Ivar. He died a few years ago. Marcus, I mean, not his dad. Drug overdose. He can't have been more than thirty-five.

This cutting's from the *Mirror*. That's the paper I get, if I get a paper at all. Even if I do, I hardly ever get round to reading it. Just use it for lining the guinea-pigs' hutch. You'd have a job lining a matchbox with this little scrap. Might as well chuck it away. Concentrate on routine. Looking after the animals, riding – *life*, really. Roll up your sleeves and keep pedalling, as my granddad used to say.

But it's hard when you're on your own a lot. I wish there was someone I could talk to – someone I trusted enough – but there isn't, really.

I thought I'd made myself safe here, but I don't feel safe any more.

I'm frightened.

CHAPTER TWO

Since I came here, I've tried not to think about the past, but sometimes you can't help it. Even with little things. Like yesterday, I was looking for a pair of socks and the drawer wouldn't shut, and when I peered down the back there was this grey furry thing wedged in there. I thought it was a dead mouse, but when I got the rubber gloves on and fished it out, it was a bunny tail. Filthy, with a big black mark across it where it was jammed against the back of the drawer. I stood there with it in my hand, and I thought, I can't believe I used to have a job where I had to pin this on my bum.

Mind you, if you'd gone to the Bunny Mother with a tail like that you'd have got what-for. She used to inspect us before we went on the floor, check your nails were painted, no ladder in your tights, no bits of loo paper sticking out of your top. You'd wrap it round your hand, stuff it down there, give a little shove, and Bob's your uncle: beautiful cleavage, and it looked all real. They fitted the costumes individually, but they only came in two bust sizes, 34D or 36D, and most of us couldn't fill that without a *bit* of help. We used to use old tights, too, and the spare tails, stick them in there. When I told that to Lenny I thought he was going to die laughing. He had a real *thing* about my tail. He even bought one from the gift shop. It was mounted on a plaque with 'Caught at the Bunny Club' or something written underneath.

The one I found was my special tail. I'd written my name on the back. I used to take it home myself and wash it and fluff it up with a dog-grooming brush to get it looking really smart. I can't believe how long I used to spend getting ready. Nowadays I spend more time on the horses than I do on me – I hardly bother with mascara, let alone two sets of false eyelashes. I suppose I must have a few pairs of those left over somewhere. Hate to think what they'd look like now – like having two old spiders crawling across your eyelids. Actually – confession time – I kept a whole costume when I left the club. That was naughty, because they didn't belong to us, but I wanted a souvenir, and I'd been there the best part of three years so I thought I'd earned it. God knows where that went, probably in the attic. I haven't looked at it in years.

Lenny didn't know I was a Bunny when we first met. It was on the motorway. I didn't have my own car, I'd sort of borrowed one. When I say 'borrowed', I don't mean stole because I put it back afterwards, but it belonged to this guy called James Clarke-Dibley who used to come to the club. This was in 1967, when I'd just started working there. Anyway, he was quite keen on me. First time I met him was at a photographer's studio. I was modelling swimsuits or something, and he came in and asked me out. I went once but then said I couldn't because I was working in the evenings, so he started coming to the club.

He was very rich – from what I could make out his father owned half of Scotland – and quite good looking, but for some reason I just couldn't fancy him baked, boiled or fried. They had a rule that you weren't allowed to date customers, so I used that as an excuse. But he paid for me to have driving lessons, and when I passed my test I didn't have a car so he used to let me drive his, but only if he came with me. I tell you, if I'd been him, I wouldn't have let me drive my car in a million years, because I used to go like a mad thing, and it was this beautiful white Mercedes Cabriolet which cost a fortune.

There'd been a party at his house. I'd gone there after my shift – in my own clothes, of course, not the costume – and I'd stayed the night. Not in his bed. He wanted me to, but he was too plastered to do anything about it, and I don't drink much so I was all right, I just went up to the top of the house and found a nice little room and made myself comfortable.

The next morning, everyone left was sleeping it off, so I tiptoed downstairs and took the keys out of his jacket. I thought I'd go and visit my mum. Well, that's what I said to myself, but really I just wanted the chance to be in that car on my own and see what I could do.

It was a beautiful day. July, with bright blue sky like on a postcard, and I was flying along with the top down and my blonde hair streaming out behind me and my bare arms and the sunglasses and all the rest of it. It was perfect. I was like a girl in a film with the music playing along in my head and this lovely warm gooey feeling inside my stomach and the tops of my legs and this sensation of being so *alive*, so sexy, and able to do whatever I wanted.

There wasn't much else on the road so I put my foot right down, ninety miles an hour, it didn't matter, I just wanted to go *fast*. I was in the middle lane, and I suddenly noticed this car come alongside me, a gunmetal blue Aston Martin Coupé. I thought, that's funny, because it wasn't overtaking, so I looked across and there was this gorgeous man sitting behind the wheel.

I saw black hair, tan, sunglasses, open-necked shirt, all in a blur, and then he gave a little nod and accelerated past me. I thought, *right*, because the way he'd done it was like a challenge, and I went after him, a hundred, a hundred and ten, we were neck and neck and I couldn't take my eyes off him. I nearly drove into the back of some old man in a Ford Anglia and I screamed and put my hand up to my mouth and he went zooming in front, and when he turned his head to look at me I saw he was laughing. So I got into the outside lane after him, then back into the middle lane and overtook him – naughty – then he did the same to me and cut someone up and of course they sounded their horn, so it was my turn to laugh at him. Then he swerved in front of me, so I had to stand on the brake not to bang into him. We went on like that for a bit, waving and laughing at each other, and then he grinned at me and motioned with his arm towards the side of the road. He cut straight across me into the slow lane and indicated that he was coming off, so I followed – didn't think, just did it. He turned off the motorway and down another road, and in a minute we were in these twisty country lanes with all the trees and hedges, going seventy miles an hour with me right behind, almost nudging his bumper, and him glancing in his mirror every few seconds to make sure I was still there. God knows what would have happened if anything had come the other way, because the road was only wide enough for one car, but nothing did.

Just as I thought I'd better ease up a bit – I mean it was James's car, after all – he disappeared round a corner. I thought I'd lost him, but then I saw the back of his car going off up a track into a field. I pulled the wheel round so fast I nearly ended up in a ditch – thank you, Guardian Angel – and went bumping across all these ruts to where he was pulled up. It wasn't a proper farmyard, just a big old barn with straw piled up inside and a bit of concrete out the front.

I drove up right next to his car and stopped. He didn't get out, just leant over the seat.

'Hello.'

He *was* really handsome. A bit older than me, with thick hair so black that it was almost blue, and a lovely wide mouth, broad shoulders and strong brown arms – he had his sleeves rolled up – big hands. I couldn't stop looking at him.

He took his sunglasses off – lovely deep dark eyes with crinkly lines from laughing. 'You're not going to go all shy on me, are you?'

'No . . .'

It was like a film: two sports cars side by side, the bonnets shining in the sun, all the colours so bright and perfect, and the way he was looking at me. I'd no idea who he was. It was just at the time when he and Jack had their first television series, but I hadn't seen it because I was always at the club, and I never read the papers in those days, either.

'You're quite a driver. What else can you do?'

I said, 'That's for me to know and you to find out,' and I hopped across the seat and out of the passenger door and ran over to the barn.

There was a big door, open, and I stopped just inside but so he could see me. I waited until he'd got out of his car and then I kicked my shoes off and ran up the ladder into the loft. He chased me but I was too quick, I was jumping over all the bales, twisting and turning, giggling, and all the time I had the film running in my head, him and me, my hair across my face and the dusty sunlight coming in through the door. I was in love with all of it, the *idea* of it. Then he caught me and held me tight so I couldn't struggle and kissed me.

It wasn't the first time I'd done it, but it was the first time it had meant anything. Afterwards I felt so happy I lay there and laughed.

He said, 'You liked that, didn't you?'

I said, 'Yes, so did you.'

'Yes.' And he laughed, too. Then he got out his cigarettes and I said, 'You'll start a fire with all this hay.'

'It's straw, not hay.'

'It'll burn just the same, won't it?'

'Who bought you the car?'

'Nobody.'

'Did you beg, steal or borrow?'

'Borrow.'

'I stole mine.'

'I don't believe you.'

'I could buy you a car.'

'I don't believe that, either.'

'You don't believe very much, do you?'

'I believe I'm here with you.'

'You're not here. Neither am I. We're just an idea in the mind of God.'

'Then God's got a dirty mind, hasn't He?'

He laughed and stroked my hair and said, 'You shouldn't do this, you know.'

'Do what?'

'What you're doing. I could be anyone. I could have done anything. I could have killed you. I could kill you right now.' He wrapped the ends of my hair round my neck like a rope.

'But you won't, will you?'

He let go of my hair and kissed me on the forehead. 'No.'

I was so happy I almost couldn't have cared if I had died right that minute, as long as it didn't hurt. I said, 'You've got a nerve, telling me I shouldn't be doing this. Whose idea was it?'

'You were the one who came running in here. You led me on.'

'Why, did you have something different in mind?'

'I was going to instruct you in the rudiments of hay-making.'

'You just told me it was straw, not hay.'

He laughed again and said, 'You're not frightened of much, are you?'

'There's nothing to be frightened *of*.'

He raised his eyebrows, then rolled over and pulled his clothes on. He went down the ladder and I thought he was going outside to have a cigarette, but after a couple of minutes I heard his car start. By the time I'd straightened my clothes and found both my shoes there was no sign he'd ever been there, except tyre marks and a note tucked under one of my windscreen wipers: *I'll find you* xxx.

I thought, *you'd better*. Because I've just had the best day of my life and I don't even know your name.

CHAPTER THREE

Next time I saw Lenny it was in the Playmate Bar at the club, about a month after our 'encounter'. It was Saturday night and packed, and I was weaving my way across the floor with a tray of drinks when someone pulled my tail. It gave me a shock and I spun straight round because that was a real no-no, a customer touching you. I'd been doing what we called a 'high carry' with the tray up by my shoulder, and I nearly lost the lot. I was too busy doing a juggling act with the glasses to look up and see who'd done it. I could hear these guys laughing, which annoyed me, but I wasn't going to give them the satisfaction of showing them how furious I was. Anyway, I'd just got it all under control and I was about to call the floor manager when I heard one of them say, 'Well, look what's hopped out of the haystack.'

I knew straightaway who it was. As soon as he'd said the first word I was staring at him.

'Uuh?' Ladylike or what, but I couldn't stop myself. There were three of them: Donald Findlater and Jack, although I didn't know that then, with Lenny in the middle, all laughing their heads off.

I don't think I've ever felt so on-the-spot in all my life. My heart was thumping and I was sure they could all see it. Lenny was smirking as if he knew I'd been thinking about him ever since, because it was true, I had been. He leant over to see my name – we had them on rosettes pinned over one hip.

'Hello, Bunny Alice.'

I said, 'Don't you Bunny Alice me. It would have served you right if I'd tipped this lot straight into your lap.'

Lenny said, 'But you won't, will you?'

It struck me that that was my reply when he'd said he could strangle me in the barn, and I wondered if he remembered it. But I was still pretty angry so I said, 'Don't bet on it' and stalked off.

I spent the rest of my shift ignoring them. It wasn't too hard to avoid going near them because they weren't on my station, but I was so aware of them that I couldn't concentrate on what I was meant to be doing for more than a few seconds at a time.

You had to set up the tray with the right glasses and garnish – olive for a Martini, lemon twist if it was dry, cocktail onion if it was a Gibson, and some drinks had cherries or other bits and pieces – before you took it up to the bar. I knew the call-in order backwards, still do: Scotch, Canadian, Bourbon, Rye, Irish, Gin, Vodka, Rum, Brandy, Liqueurs, Mixed, Blended, Creamed, Beer, Wine, One for the money – the bottles were arranged in the same sequence so you called and the barman poured, except yours was right to left and his was left to right, if you see what I mean.

Anyway, that night I was all over the shop – not a good thing to be, because you needed to keep on the right side of the barmen. They were like a Mafia. A lot of them had been on the cruise ships so they were very slick, and they expected us to be the same. If they decided you were no good or they didn't like you, they could make your life hell. I usually got on well with them, but *that night* – there was one bloke who must have been working a double shift because he'd had a few, and he kept shouting at me, 'What's got into you, you silly cow?'

That made it worse, and every time I happened to glance

in Lenny's direction, he seemed to be staring straight at me, and I felt so self-conscious.

Then when I was on my break I was talking to one of the other girls, and when I told her what had happened she said, 'You know who that was, don't you?'

I said I hadn't got a clue and she said, 'Lenny Maxted and Jack Flowers, that's who.'

I said, 'What, those comedians on the box? You're pulling my leg,' because I thought someone like that would be in the VIP Room, and I wouldn't believe her till a couple of the others backed her up.

Then I asked which one was which, and when she told me I realised – that little tumble in the haystack, it must have been Lenny. I didn't go into details, just said, 'Oh, really?' or something, as if it was no big deal. So I went back in and carried on, and then at one point I looked over to where they were sitting and they'd gone. I felt relieved and disappointed at the same time but I thought, well, that's that.

Except it wasn't, because when I came out of the club at four, there was this bloke sitting in a car. I didn't see who it was immediately because it wasn't near a street light, but he'd got the window wound down and when I walked past he leant out. 'Alice?'

I recognised the voice immediately. It was all right because we were by the back entrance, not in full view or anything, so I went over. He was by himself.

'Hello there.'

I said, 'You've been here a while,' because they'd left around two o'clock.

'Get in, I'll drive you home.'

'No, thanks.'

'Got your car, then? Want a race?'

'No.'

'It'll be fun. I'll even let you win.'

'The only reason you won last time was because I let you. Anyway, I told you, it doesn't belong to me.'

'Put it back before he noticed, did you?'

'How do you know it was a he?'

'Well it was, wasn't it?'

'Yes . . . anyway, I think you could at least tell me your name, now you know what mine is.'

All he said was, 'Lenny.' Not, 'Oh, don't you know who I am,' or anything like that, just 'Lenny' as if he'd come to fit a carpet or something. I liked that, although I thought afterwards, he probably knew I knew his name already.

'Are you a Keyholder?' That's what the club members were called. They could bring in guests if they wanted, but you had to see the key before you took the order for drinks.

'Only recently.'

'I've never seen you in the club before, that's all.'

There was a pause, and then he said, 'Look, I'm sorry about what happened.'

I said, 'It's all right.' Well, I couldn't really do anything else, could I? But I wasn't going to let him off the hook that easily, so I said, 'I suppose you told your friends what we did.'

He said, 'No,' and he looked a bit surprised, but I thought, don't come the innocent, so I said, 'The bunny in the haystack – I bet you all had a good old laugh.'

'No!' He looked quite hurt. I thought, oops-a-daisy, but there was something about the way they'd been laughing and looking at me in the club that made me not feel so sure I believed him.

He said, 'Are you sure you don't want a lift home?'

'Positive. Thanks.'

'What about dinner? Would you have dinner with me?' He sounded quite humble, as if he thought I was going to turn him down. I thought that was sweet. That and the fact he must have waited for the best part of two hours, so I said I would.

Then he got his diary out and started going through it saying, can you come then, can you come then, and I kept saying no, I'll be at the club, or, no, I'm doing something else. Most of it was true, but also I wanted to show him that I wasn't just, sort of, there for the taking, if you know what I mean.

We fixed up something eventually and Lenny wrote it down on a piece of paper. When he leant out of the car to tuck it into my pocket I jumped about three feet into the air.

'Don't do that!' The management were obsessed about keeping their gaming licence and if anyone had seen him right outside the club giving me something that looked like money, they might have reported that it was a knocking shop, which would not have gone down well, I can tell you.

'Are you trying to lose me my job or something?'

'Sorry, sorry . . . no, of course not.' He put his hands up like 'I surrender' with the note between two of his fingers, so I had a quick look up and down the street before I grabbed it from him and stuffed it in my pocket. I said goodbye and headed off. Every time I looked back he was still sitting there in his car, looking after me, and all the time I had my hand in my pocket, clutching his little piece of paper.

I've still got it. In a shoebox under my bed, where I keep special things. I don't look in there, not often, but it's nice to have them. Just stuff like birthday cards from my grand-dad, my wedding ring, from when I was married to Jeff, and Lenny's last note to me. The one he wrote before he killed himself.

CHAPTER FOUR

I was excited about the dinner. It was the *Mirabelle*, which I'm pretty sure was Lenny thinking, *let's impress her*. But I'd been there before with James Clarke-Dibley, so I wasn't totally bowled over. I didn't expect to see Jack, though. Well, I didn't know I was *going* to see Jack until the *maitre d'* met us at the foot of the stairs, all smiles – Lenny'd picked me up from my flat so we arrived together – and said, 'This way, Sir. Mr Flowers is already here.'

So we went over to the table, and there was Jack with his feet well underneath. He obviously wasn't going anywhere, and Lenny was clearly expecting him, because he said, 'You beat me to it,' and Jack said, 'Only to the table,' and they both laughed. Well, I thought, so much for Mr Injured Innocence, but I didn't say anything, just sat down.

In fact I don't think I said more than about ten words the whole time we were there, because the minute we'd ordered, Lenny and Jack went into their double act. I was sitting between them with my head going back and forth as if I was watching a tennis match, and half the restaurant watching, too, but pretending they weren't, because the *Mirabelle* isn't the sort of place where you go up to someone and ask for their autograph.

Lenny'd introduced me, 'Meet Jack. I know you'll get on like a house on fire, you're just his type,' but it sort of felt like . . . I don't know, as if I could have been a new car he'd just bought and not a person at all. I wasn't thrilled about that, but it was exciting sitting there with them in this luxurious restaurant, and I was enjoying myself because they were very, very funny and I was getting my own personal show.

I can't remember much of what they said. A lot of it went straight over my head because they were talking about people I didn't know, not then, anyway, and it was hard to concentrate because they were both playing footsie with me. I kept wondering how the evening was going to end, especially when Jack started going on about this Polaroid camera he'd just bought, and saying how it was good for taking sexy pictures. I wasn't sure about that, so in the end I tucked my feet under my chair and let them play footsie with each other. It took about ten minutes before they noticed, but they both wound up looking under the table-cloth.

Jack said, 'I thought your legs were a bit hairy,' and I said, 'Well, what do you expect? I'm a bunny.'

Which made *them* laugh, and that made me feel a bit more confident, so I said, 'How did you two meet, anyway?'

They both started laughing again. 'National service,' Lenny said. 'We were in some godforsaken dump in the West Country, on a training course, men from all different regiments, and there was this RSM who'd been through the war, and he thought we were a right shower. We'd had it up to here with being shouted at and all the rest of it, so we were pretty fed up.'

'He kept ordering these bloody fire drills. He used to sound the siren, and you had to drop whatever you were doing and charge over and parade outside the guardroom. We were meant to assemble in three minutes but nobody could be bothered, so we'd come ambling up five, ten minutes late and he'd start shouting. "You're a cretin! What are you?"' Jack bellowed in a strangled voice. I ducked my head because the whole restaurant was looking at us.

'I'm a cretin, Sir!' yelled Lenny.

'Anyway,' he continued, more quietly, thank God, 'we'd had enough of it, so Jack – I didn't know him then – Jack decided he was going to do something about it.'

'What this RSM used to do,' said Jack, 'was he always went to the local town on Friday nights. He'd have a few drinks at the British Legion Club, and then he'd come back and set off the fire alarm. So one night I was on guard duty, and a few of us climbed up on the roof of the guard-room with a plank of wood and stuck it through the siren. Because it used to rotate, you see, to make the sound, and we jammed this great big plank in there and lashed it with rope so it couldn't move . . .'

'And then the RSM comes back,' said Lenny, 'and he tries to set off the alarm and nothing happens. So next morning he goes up on the roof. When he saw what was causing it he went mad. So Jack owned up. Well, he had to, or we'd all have been in the shit, and he got put on jankers.'

'Jankers?' I asked.

'Punishment,' said Lenny. 'After that, of course, it was fire drill every other minute, and he kept on at us about how it didn't matter what we were doing, we'd only got three minutes to get down there.'

'We knew damn well,' said Jack, 'he'd always do it midday Saturday because it was a free afternoon, so every-one wanted to get their skates on and down to the town as fast as they could. So Lenny said, "Right. We'll take our clothes off, like we're in the showers, but keep your boots on, and when the siren goes we'll all rush down there stark bollock naked and line up." So we got there in two minutes flat, and the RSM came out on the steps to inspect us.'

'He didn't say anything,' said Lenny, 'but you could see

his eyes light up, and he made us form up and marched us down the road to the parade ground, still in the buff, and of course the NAAFI girls' quarters were on the other side of the road and they were all cheering and whooping. And then the fucker only drilled us for an hour. Oh, dear . . .' Lenny wiped his eyes. 'Then he called it quits.'

'Lenny and I were standing next to each other in the line-up, and he turned round and gave me a wink, and I thought, *nice one*, because I'd been told it was his idea. So we shook hands, and I said I'd buy him a drink.'

'And that was it, really. But it still makes me laugh, us standing there with our tackle blowing in the breeze, and this bloke never batted an eyelid. He was all right, though, wasn't he? Remember when he retired, we had a whip round for a cigarette case, and he made a speech.'

'Yeah,' said Jack. 'He took it pretty well, when you think about it . . .' He raised his glass, and Lenny raised his, too, and they said, 'The sum of our parts!' I thought I'd better join in, so I raised mine, 'The sum of your parts!' Then I asked, 'Why do you say that?'

'It's silly, really,' said Lenny. 'But it's what Don Findlater says. He's our agent. He's always telling people that the act works because we're greater than the sum of our parts.'

Jack gave a schoolboy smirk. 'Don's in love with Lenny. Besotted with him.'

'Pack it in, Jack.' Lenny looked uncomfortable. 'She doesn't want to know about that.'

'Don't worry,' Jack said to me, 'Don knows Lenny's normal so he contents himself with longing from afar. That's how he likes it. He's the sort of queer who can only get a hard-on if he's paying for it. Thinks it doesn't count, poor sod.' Jack rolled his eyes. 'He only comes to the club with us because he's got his eye on one of the busboys.'

It was a combined effort at seduction, really, although

they didn't ask me anything about myself, which is what men often do when they're trying to get you into bed. Actually, I got the feeling that they were trying to impress each other as much as me, which was quite weird, and the fact that Lenny was sort of showing me off to Jack, 'Isn't she great?' and all that. It made me feel a bit like I was on parade, or something, but it sort of intrigued me, as well – probably for all the wrong reasons.

I've always thought Jack was attractive. If I was being completely objective I'd say he was better looking than Lenny, and he's definitely sexy. They were quite similar, both tall and dark, but Jack had this sort of wolfy look to him, narrow eyes and pointy incisors, and something very physical, a really strong sexual presence. More than Lenny did, I think, but Lenny was *the one* and that's all I can say about it. I don't know if that happens to some people more than once in their lives, but that's the only time it's happened to me.

As soon as we'd finished our coffee, Lenny said, 'Shall we go back to my flat?' It was obvious that Jack was included in the invitation so I made some excuse about having to get up early. They were pretty fed up but they didn't press it, and Lenny said he'd drive me home. Jack left before we did. Lenny went with him to get his coat and I saw them standing at the other side of the room. Lenny said something and Jack shrugged his shoulders. Then they both glanced over at me and I had to pretend not to notice. Lenny came back after about five minutes. 'Let's go,' he said, abruptly. 'I've paid the bill.' I thought, *Ouch!*

He hardly said a word all the way home and I thought, I've really blown it this time, now he thinks I'm a spoilsport. I was sure he wouldn't contact me, but two days later, just about the time I was starting to think I'd made a real

24

mistake saying I didn't want to go back with them, he rang up. I was so astonished to hear his voice that I couldn't think of anything to say, but it didn't matter because he launched straight in with, 'Will you come out with me again? Jack won't be there.'

I said, 'I didn't know he was going to be there last time.'

'But you liked him, didn't you?' I was surprised by how anxious he sounded. 'I wanted you to meet him, that was all.' He sounded so hurt that even though half of me was thinking, pull the other one, it's got bells on, the other half was thinking, did I get the wrong end of the stick? That made me feel a bit embarrassed, because it's not as if I go about thinking I'm God's gift to men or anything. There was this long pause, and I was embarrassed because it felt like he could hear what I was thinking, so as soon as he mentioned a date I said, 'Yes, fine, whatever you like,' just to get him off the phone. Then, of course, I looked at what I'd scribbled down and realised I'd have to ask if I could swap my shift. It never even occurred to me to ring him back and change it.

Somebody asked me once, if Lenny hadn't been so famous, would I have said yes? Which annoyed me, because I didn't know he was famous, did I, that first time? And I still fancied him like anything. But I suppose that was part of the turn-on, although I don't think I realised it, back then. There was something about him. Well, it was power, really, because Lenny and Jack, they did have a lot of power. They were very successful, they earned a lot of money and people wanted to be around them and do what they said, you know?

But I noticed that quite a few times at the club, when someone important came in. With those men, the rich, powerful ones – some of them were nice, good manners, and some of them were pretty vile, really, but they all had one thing in common: they thought they could just have anybody. Whether they were going to charm the girl into bed or just snap their fingers – although, of course, they weren't doing any of that in the club because it was very controlled – they behaved like they'd got it all laid out on a plate, with an apple in its mouth and a feather up its bum.

Mind you, the last few years . . . I don't know if I just met the wrong men, but they all seemed to *expect* that you'd go to bed with them, even one or two while I was married to Jeff, although that really only lasted about three years. It was this constant pressure that it was just *the thing you did.*

It seemed so ridiculous, and half of them I couldn't have fancied if my life depended on it. I wasn't interested, and I wasn't getting anything out of it. After a while I started to think, what sort of person does it make me if I'm doing this? It all seemed so pointless, as if I didn't have a compass anymore, I was just sort of drifting about with no idea what I was doing, or why. That was when I came to live here.

I miss it, though. Not sex so much – well, a bit – but *being* with someone. I mean, it's great with my dog and the horses and everything, but the talking, and . . . you know. All that stuff. I thought it was wonderful at first, being alone after everything that happened, but with something like this newspaper cutting, you suddenly realise: you're on your own.

Whoever sent it knows where I live and they know I was at that party, so I suppose they know about Lenny. It wouldn't be hard to find out that I'd left Jeff, that I'm here alone. I've told myself a hundred times that they just forgot to put a note in with the cutting, but I can't make myself believe it.

The nights are the worst. I keep expecting a phone call, or a knock on the door, a tap on the window. I'm even afraid to go to sleep, because I don't want to have the dream. The really stupid thing is, I'm terrified something's going to happen, but I've got no idea what, or why.

It's the way it brought everything back, what happened between Kitty and Lenny, and how unhappy I was, and he was, and then the way he died. It's just . . . horrible. I was on the point of ringing a friend in London last night to ask if I could stay with her, but then I thought, the animals – I can't just leave them. There'd be no one to look after them if I wasn't here, so I'm stuck.

CHAPTER FIVE

With Lenny, the fame was part of him, who he was, but I wasn't looking to hook myself up with a rich man or anything. In those days I just thought about enjoying myself. That sounds shallow, doesn't it? But I was twenty, twenty-one, and I thought that was what life was all about. I didn't come to London because I wanted to get rich and famous and be the Big I Am. I came because it was exciting and I wanted to be part of that.

One of the best things about the club was that you could be whoever you wanted to be. We only knew each other by our bunny names, you see, and they weren't always the real ones. Everyone had to have a different name, and if there was already a bunny with your name, you picked something else. I started life as Alison. I didn't change because there was another one, but because 'Bunny Alison' just didn't sound right. I chose Alice because it was close, but with a bit more class. I got used to everyone calling me Alice at work and I liked it, so if I did a bit of modelling or made a new friend I'd always tell them my name was Alice, and it stuck. Honestly, if I went down the street tomorrow and heard someone shouting 'Alison!' I'd never think it was me they wanted. The only person who calls me Alison now is my mum.

I don't think I ever knew anybody's surname at the club. Well, only Suzanne Palmer. She got a bit part in a Hammer film, and I asked so I could look out for her when the credits came up at the end. It was a Dennis Wheatley thing, and she had about three seconds as one of the virgins they sacrificed, ha, ha.

Oh, yeah, and Candy Knight, the porn star. I don't know if that was her real name, but she was always Candy, Bunny Candy. When I was in London a few weeks ago I went past the Eros Cinema in Piccadilly, and there was a poster for one of those smutty comedies she does. I can't remember what it was called, *Knickers Must Fall* or something stupid like that. But anyway, *Jack*'s name was on it! I couldn't believe my eyes. I know he hasn't been on TV recently, but honestly. He'd never have been doing that if Lenny was still around, I'm sure of it.

If they'd stayed together, that is, because Lenny did most of the writing. They did use other people from time to time, but mainly it was the two of them. They'd spend hours in Lenny's flat just talking, bouncing things off each other, tape-recording it all. Then Jack would go home to Val, and Lenny would sit down at the typewriter and spend all night bashing out a script, and that would be the basis of the act or the series or whatever it was. It really was like Don Findlater said, together they were greater than the sum of their parts. Just *brilliant*. That's why I was so astonished to see Jack doing rubbish like that.

The only other girl whose full name I knew was Bunny Kitty. Her real name was Gail McClintock. Everyone at the club thought she'd just jacked it in without telling anybody, because quite a lot of girls did that, but we found out later that she'd never picked up her cards or anything. I did hear something about her flatmate coming home one day and finding some of Kitty's stuff gone, but it could have been a burglary because there wasn't a note or anything. And that was it, really. Well, so far as I know.

I didn't know much about Kitty's background, or any of

the other Bunnies', come to that, because nobody really talked about their families. I mean, most of them probably went home for the odd Sunday and ate roast beef and tinned peaches and drank orangeade, like I did with Grandma and Granddad. What I mean is, once you were in the club you could leave all that behind and be a new person, and wearing the costume gave you this great feeling of confidence. Power, even. Mind you, those costumes, if they nipped you in a certain place, down the side, you'd get the most terrible stitch, and your *feet* . . . Of course, you had to be the right type to start with. I mean, you couldn't take just any girl and make her into a Bunny – there were masses of them who didn't make it through the training.

But the point is, we were all into what was happening in the here and now, not talking about the past. There were one or two quite posh girls when I was there, but I never felt looked down on. From what I could make out, they were doing it to get up their family's noses anyway – but of course they did know more what the drinks were, and things like that. I mean, I'd never tasted champagne or gin or Scotch before I went to work at the club.

I remember the first time I walked in there, I couldn't imagine there was anything more sophisticated in the world. And then I met Blanche, the Bunny Mother, and she was a vision of perfection and glamour and all the rest of it, and I thought, she probably *lives* in a place like this. God, when I think of it now, I was *so naïve.* But all I knew was my mum's caravan and my grandparents' semi in Horsham. All my friends at school had the same, although not so much the caravan, because my mum – well, let's just say she wasn't quite like the other mothers. I didn't have a dad, for a start. I wasn't aware of that at first, but then I heard a few remarks and the kids in my class would talk about, oh, my dad did this or that, and I'd think, well, where's *my* dad? I asked her, I suppose I was about seven, and all she said was, 'Oh, you can forget about him, he's dead.' I don't know if that was true but it could have been, because I was a war baby. I think a lot of kids like me were adopted, and I don't really know why I wasn't, but it might explain why I often had a feeling of being on probation, if you know what I mean.

I remember once my grandma told me about shopping in the olden days, how you could get things 'on approval'. I don't mean like a leg of lamb, but a dress or a hat or something, and then if you didn't like it, you could take it back. I thought it was sad for the things if people didn't want them and they had to go back to the shop – well, I was only little, but I think it was because of feeling a bit like that about myself.

My mum's always been a difficult person. She prefers living alone and she likes animals better than people, including me, so most of the time I stayed with Granddad and Grandma. Mum didn't get on with them, so when I was born Granddad bought a field and put a caravan in the middle of it, and she moved in there. He couldn't afford to get her a house and anyway, she wanted the grass because she had a sheep and a goat. Not for milk or anything, they were her pets – the goat had a collar and lead and she used to take it for walks up and down the lane. I think that's one of my earliest memories, picking flowers and trying to stop Maisy eating them . . . that and lying in bed in the caravan and listening to the rain on the roof.

A lot of people around us thought Mum was off her head. There'd be the odd funny remark about me not being born on the right side of the blanket, but my granddad was the stationmaster and everyone liked him, so it was more a case of 'Poor old Mr Conway, his daughter's a bit touched,' and wondering behind their hands if I'd go the same way. I can't say Granddad was thrilled when I told him what job I'd got. I hadn't gone to live in London with the intention of becoming a Bunny – just as well, because if I'd told him that he'd probably have locked me in my bedroom for good.

One of my friends showed me this ad for the club in the *Stage*, and she said she was going for the audition and asked me to come with her, and I thought, Why not? I only did it for a giggle, but she'd told me the money was good and on the way there I started thinking maybe I could do this, because I'd done a bit of waitressing, you know . . . But when we got inside the door there was this stunning girl there, just gorgeous, and I said, 'Well, if they all look like that, we might as well turn round and go home,' but my friend said, 'Oh, rubbish,' and pushed me in front of her . . . I don't remember much about it. You had to wear a swimsuit, and there was an interview, and that was about it, really.

But I remember next time I went to see Granddad, I was on the train and all I could think of was, How on earth am I going to tell him? Like I said, he wasn't exactly delighted; in his mind, the club was some sort of bordello, and nothing I said could persuade him it wasn't. I think that was mainly because of Mum – the shame of having a baby when you weren't married, and he was bothered about it happening to me, but in the end he said, 'Well, if you're happy . . .' Which was quite progressive of him, really, because I know he used to worry about me. He never wanted to know anything about my work. The only question he ever asked me was whether I'd remembered to look at my pay packet to check they'd given me the right money. I never dared tell him I was making more in tips than I got in wages . . .

He didn't tell any of the neighbours, either. The first time I came back visiting I was determined to show him how well I was doing and that I was looking after myself and all the rest of it. I got dressed up in all my new clothes – showing off, really – and put my face on because I'd hardly worn make-up at home, Horsham not being exactly the height of sophistication. I'd been getting tips from the other girls, watching how they did it, and of course it was a very made-up look then, very artificial.

Anyway, I went to Granddad's house and walked up the front path in all this clobber, and I was standing in the porch feeling like the cat's whiskers when I heard 'Will you look at that? Now we know what *she* does in London . . .' It was Mrs O'Shea and Mrs Cooper from up the road. Granddad almost pulled my arm off dragging me inside.

'What have you done to yourself? Talk about the dog's dinner.'

I felt about an inch high, but I wanted him to see that I was still the same person, so I said I'd come down to his allotment and give him a hand, like I used to when I was little. I didn't have anything to protect my dress, so Granddad wrapped a bit of sacking round me, but it must have been dirty, because when I took it off there was mud all down my front. My grandma was clucking over it. 'Why did you let her do that, Bert? She's spoilt her new frock. They don't grow on trees, you know!' as if I was about six.

But Granddad just winked at me and said, 'Well, it looks better like that, if you ask me.' It was from one of those boutiques in the King's Road, all swirly and garish, so the mud toned it down a bit. I suddenly thought, you old . . . *whatever*, you did it on purpose. I suppose I should have got angry with him, but I was too busy trying not to laugh.

It's a shame Granddad's dead now, because he would have loved it here with the chickens and the vegetable patch and everything, and I could do with some advice. I'm glad he died before Lenny did, though. He always got on with

Lenny and he would have hated all the stuff in the papers, but I do miss him. Not Grandma, because I always felt I was a bit of a nuisance to her. Mind you, from her point of view, there she was thinking her child-rearing days were over, and I had to come along. She told me Mum was no good at it, she was always leaving me on my own in the caravan and forgetting to change the nappies, so she'd taken over.

I've got a film of them that Lenny made. He was trying out this 16mm cine camera he'd just bought. It only lasts a couple of minutes, but it's Granddad in the garden, looking after his sweet peas, and then you see Grandma come out the back door and start cutting flowers with her big sewing scissors. Granddad hated cut flowers, there were no vases in the house and normally he'd never let anyone touch his garden. I've never been able to work out if Lenny'd suggested it so Grandma would have something to do in the film, or if she was doing it deliberately to wind Granddad up. But either way, he doesn't say anything. Then my mum's old spaniel, Tinker, comes trotting down the path and wags his tail at Granddad, so he looks up to see if Mum's coming too. She's obviously standing just out of shot because he's saying something and beckoning, but she doesn't appear. That's all it is, really.

Lenny's projector must be upstairs somewhere, but I don't know how to work it. In any case, it would only make me cry, so what's the point? Typical of Mum that she wouldn't join in, even to please Granddad. He wanted to be friends with her but she wouldn't let him. She's like Grandma, closed off from people. They hardly ever saw each other. You can see on the film, when the dog comes in and Granddad starts talking to Mum, Grandma doesn't even look up.

Not that I can talk, because I've never been close to

Mum, either. I've been trying to go there more often because her health hasn't been so great, although I get the impression that she's not really bothered one way or the other. She won't come and stay with me because she doesn't want to leave her animals.

To be honest, I'd been starting to wonder if it was worth the effort, but last time I saw her I was telling her about the farm and she suddenly said, 'I'd always thought you might turn out like me.' When I asked what she meant, she said, 'Well, you're about twenty-six, aren't you?'

'Thirty.'

'Oh, are you? I'd had enough of it by the time I was twenty-six. You must be a bit slow on the uptake.'

'Enough of what? What are you talking about?'

We were sitting on either side of the caravan table and she waved her hand at the window. 'People. *Men*.' And I suddenly thought, she's right. But then I looked at her, sitting there like a scarecrow with her jumper covered in dog hair, and I thought, *I don't want to be like you*. So I said, 'How can you like living here? You've got water running down the walls every time it rains.' I've offered her the money to fix it enough times, but she won't take it.

'There's nothing wrong with it.'

'It's falling to pieces.'

'It's fine. I like it. Doesn't matter what anyone else thinks. That's something I've learned. Animals are the only ones that don't let you down.'

I'm never very relaxed around my mum and I find it quite hard to talk to her, but I thought, what the hell, she's not getting any younger, so I said, 'Did my father let you down?'

'Oh, that's all mumbo-jumbo. He's got nothing to do with it. Or with you. He was barely there when you were conceived, never mind afterwards.'

'What do you mean?'

'He was drunk.'

'Why didn't . . .'

'He was married. Married as well as drunk. Anyway, I like being on my own.'

'You sound like Greta Garbo.' She shrugged. 'You've never minded what people thought, have you?'

'That's a bit rich coming from someone who went to work with a rabbit's tail stuck on her backside.'

'You never told me you didn't approve.'

'I neither approved nor disapproved. It's your life. Come on, it's time for me to see to the animals. You'd better be on your way.'

She tipped the cat off her lap and opened the door. I wanted to carry on talking but I knew she wouldn't, so I got up and went down the steps. When I turned to say goodbye she was standing in the doorway with her two Jack Russells, tying plastic shopping bags over her shoes to keep off the mud. She looked so self-contained I thought, she doesn't need me, so I said, on the spur of the moment, 'Do you want me to come again? It's just that I'm not sure if you want me here, that's all.'

She looked surprised. 'Of course I want you here. I always look forward to your visits.'

I thought, you could have told me, but when I thought about it later I realised that she must be lonely, too. She always seemed to me like some sort of impregnable fort – no, wrong word, because I'm here, aren't I? I used to think my father was the great love of her life. Not that she ever said so, I'd just pretended – hoped – but at least it could have been a dashing young soldier, not some married, middle-aged letch out for a night on the tiles, which is what she made it sound like. At least, it didn't sound as if she'd fancied him very much. She said he's dead, anyway, so

36

I couldn't go and find him even if I wanted to, which I don't.

I've wondered recently if people see me like that. Self-contained. I've thought about it a lot, though, why I came here. All my friends thought I'd gone mad. They kept ringing up and asking if I was OK on my own. But it's been nearly nine months now, and I still think it was the right decision. I would be lonely without Eustace, though.

That was one of the weirdest days of my life, getting him, and believe me, living with Lenny, I've had a few of those. I wanted to get a stray, or a dog that nobody wanted, so I went to the shelter and walked down the row of pens, and all these lovely dogs rushed up to the wire and wagged their tails and stood on their hind legs, and tried to lick my hand. I couldn't begin to choose, I wanted to take them all. But right at the end of the row there was one dog that didn't move. A basset hound, brown and white. He just lay at the back of the pen on his stomach in a perfect straight line, with his back legs tucked in neatly like a sugar mouse, great stubby front paws stuck out on either side of his chops and big velvet ears spread out on the ground like pools of gravy. He'd got his eyes closed, but he must have heard me coming because he looked at me from under his eyebrows, stretched, yawned massively and ambled over to the front of the pen. I thought he was coming to say hello, but he didn't, he just lay down again with his nose pressed right against the crack of the door as if he was pointing to it with his whole body. Then he sighed, and it sounded like, 'You took your time, didn't you?'

They said I could take him for a walk to see if I liked him, but I already knew I'd be taking him home, because *he* had chosen *me*, and I wasn't about to let him down. We were about halfway down the little track when he stopped and looked up at me with these huge, serious eyes. It reminded me of Granddad. I don't know what happens to your soul after you die, but if there is such a thing as re-incarnation . . . The dates fit, anyway. That's why I called him Eustace – it was Granddad's middle name.

Lenny bought this place a few months before he died. We were going to live here together. I'd been looking at houses while he was away in the States, making a film, and as soon as I saw Maynard's Farm, I thought, *that's it.* I should think it was quite something in its heyday, but the farmer who owned it was long retired. His wife had died about thirty years before, and he'd sold off most of the land and let the place fall to pieces around him. He'd even pulled up the floorboards in a couple of the upstairs rooms to use as firewood. But it was big – five bedrooms – and it had a garden, a stable yard and ten acres of paddock.

It was all pretty ramshackle, but it was like a dream come true: wisteria on the front, and the big oak staircase, ivy on the stone walls in the garden and the beautiful old barn. I fell in love with it straightaway and I knew that Lenny would love it, too. He was still in the States, but I phoned him and as soon as I told him the name of the village, Duck End, he said, 'We'll take it.' It immediately became Duck's Arse, then D. A. for short.

The first weekend we were here was like camping, because the place was a complete mess, with puddles on the floor and lumps of plaster falling off the walls, the lot. The dining room, that's in the front bit, which is Georgian, the rest is Tudor – it's two houses stuck together, really – had its walls covered in brown hessian with all these little pins sticking out that they'd used to tack it on. When we pulled them out we discovered they were old gramophone needles, hundreds of them, and underneath was a beautiful wall-covering, china blue watermarked silk. It was very old, completely shredded in some places, but Lenny said, 'It's beautiful, let's keep it,' so we took down all the hessian and had dinner in there by candlelight. Lenny had a favourite toast he always used: 'Champagne for your real friends, real pain for your sham friends.' He was so happy, he didn't get drunk, for once. The usual pattern was that I'd come home from the club and find him passed out on the sofa.

That night, I'd made up a bed on the sitting room floor. There wasn't any electricity, so after dinner we took the big silver candle-holder in there, and lay on my mattress with all the windows open because it was warm. May, I think. We giggled and talked and made love, and I thought, I really did think, *this is the beginning*. I thought if we could live down here, away from London, Lenny would be happy and I could help him get better. Well, I was a romantic. I believed in love. How stupid can you get? Because I had no excuse, not by then.

The first time he'd promised to stop drinking was if I moved in with him. I believed it, but after a couple of months we were right back to square one. Then he said it was the flat, so we found a house. That didn't work, so then he said it was living in London and he'd be fine if he got some peace and quiet. That's why he wanted this place.

But it wasn't only that. He blamed people as well. He used to keep a list of names pinned up by the fridge. He called it his Shooting List, and every so often he'd cross off one name and replace it with somebody else. I didn't know who half the people were, but it never stopped him talking to them, it was all business as usual and he'd invite them round to dinner. I'd be frantic to keep them out of the kitchen so they wouldn't see 'People Who Deserve To Be Shot' with their name scrawled underneath it in black biro. My name was on there a few times. I never made it into the top ten, but Jack was a permanent fixture after they came back from the States. Not that there was any chance of him being invited to dinner – by that stage they couldn't even agree about the time.

But even after that I still thought that all Lenny needed to get well again was love, and that if I loved him uncritically and gave him security, I could save him. I must have been off my head, because the only thing I was doing was making it easier for him to drink. But I felt guilty, too, because I thought their splitting up was partly my fault. Lenny'd never talked to me about it, and Jack always swore he'd never breathed a word – about us, I mean – but I don't know.

The wall-covering, or what's left of it, is still in the dining room. I've never changed it because Lenny liked it, and it was the only comment I remember him making about the decoration. He left me the house. Money as well, otherwise I couldn't live here. We'd had most of the major repairs done before he died, but it was just too soon, and I couldn't face being here on my own. I didn't want to sell it because it was Lenny's, so I hung onto it. Then I married Jeff, and I was living in London and hardly ever came up here. I only moved in properly last November.

It was *unbelievably* cold. The boiler broke down after a week, and I was freezing for a fortnight because that's how long it took the plumber to get the part. It was probably warmer outside the house than in it. I slept with all my clothes on and Eustace tucked in beside me like a hot water bottle, otherwise he would have frozen too. I remember some nights waking up because I was so cold and thinking, what the hell am I doing here? But when I thought about it again in the morning, I knew I didn't want to leave. For one thing, I couldn't face going back to London, and for another, it was my decision so I wanted it to work. It was like being a Bunny, in a way, something I was doing for *me*. Because I was always the one who got chosen. Lenny, Jeff, even the dog. Lenny and Eustace I didn't mind, of course. Jeff wasn't so great, but as I say, it wasn't his fault, really.

He was older than me, as well. Ten years, something like that. Don't think I don't know, the older man, the father I never had, that's what a psychiatrist would say. All I can say about that is, if that's what they get up to with their fathers, then frankly I don't think I'm the one with the problem. But it's easy to look at somebody else's life and trot out pat answers about why they do this or that. In my case, I don't know whether it's true or not, and what's more I couldn't give a monkey's, either.

Lenny and I hit it off from the word go. He took me to *The Ark* and ordered *boeuf en daube* for both of us – I still ate meat in those days – and two bottles of wine, straight-away. I felt a bit uncomfortable at first because I wasn't sure where it was all going – which was ridiculous, really, when you think we'd had it off before we were even *introduced* – but I was half-expecting Jack to be there, and there was a touch of, you know, this man is a famous comedian, what's he doing with me, what are we going to talk about? Which was unusual for me because I've been chatted up by the best of them, and turned quite a few down too. But . . . well, I wouldn't go as far as to say I was in love with Lenny, not then. Let's just say I already knew that whatever happened was going to matter a lot.

When we first got into the restaurant I couldn't stop staring at his head. He had two great lumps of hair cut out at the side. I hadn't noticed in the taxi, but it looked bizarre, because there was all this lovely wavy black hair with two socking great bald patches just above his ear. I wasn't going to say anything, because I thought he must have done it for a film or something, but he was obviously a bit self-conscious because he kept putting his hand up to his head.

Then he said, 'Sorry about the barnet. I hope you don't

41

mind being seen in public with me looking like this, but it got singed.'

I said, 'Was it a gas ring or something?'

'No, nothing like that. In fact, I was hit on the head by a burning dildo.'

I thought he was joking so I said, very straight faced, 'Well, each to his own. Spoils your hair, though.'

'No, that's the truth. It was thrown over a fence.'

'A *fence*?'

'Yes, a garden fence. Jack and Val have got this place out in Cuffley, you see, huge great garden, and there's a woman who lives next door, eighty-five and made of tweed, pillar of the community. Anyway, it was her granddaughter's 21st birthday, and someone had given her this thing as a present, so she took off the wrapping paper and waved it about, "Hey, look at this," but then she suddenly realised what it *was*. The old girl had no idea. They tried to tell her it was an African votive object, but she'd knocked about a bit in the colonies, and she didn't believe them because it was made of rubber, and apparently African stuff is usually wood. Well, she cottoned on in the end, and she said, "Oh, we can't have such a thing in the house, I'll take it down to the long paddock at once and set fire to it." Which she did, in a dustbin for burning garden rubbish. She got a big can of petrol, poured it over, and threw in a match.

'Well, there we were, playing tennis without a care in the world, and suddenly we were enveloped in this evil-smelling cloud of smoke, and this great black thing came whizzing out of nowhere and thumped me on the head. The smoke was getting out of control and the old dear had panicked, lobbed it over the fence and legged it. Jack ran up to the fence and saw her going hell for leather back to the house, walking stick and all. He rushed over to the barbeque for a pair of tongs, picked this thing up, saw what it was, bellowed "Jesus *Christ!*" and marched straight round and rang the bell.

'Val put me out by dipping her jersey in the fishpond and wrapping it round my head, then we rushed after Jack because we could hear all this shouting and bawling coming from next door, and Val was convinced he'd done the old girl a mischief. We got there just in time to see him plunging the dildo into one of the ice buckets – they were having champagne. The granddaughter was hiding in the downstairs cloakroom, and the woman was in a terrible state, choking and rushing round opening windows because of the smell.

'At first she denied all knowledge, but of course her guests knew and there I was with this sodden jumper round my head, dripping on the Axminster.

'Jack said, "Madam, you should have the decency to restrain your depraved urges until you get to the privacy of your own bedroom," so of course she said, "How dare you," and her son came in, "Don't speak to my mother like that," so Jack said, "Well, she's the one who's been throwing burning dildoes at complete strangers, not me."

'Then she got even more upset, because she's a magistrate and people usually say your ladyship, and offer her cups of tea and all the rest of it, and there was Jack telling her what a pervert she was.

'Then, when she did own up, he pretended not to believe her. Val was terrifically embarrassed. She said afterwards she thought the old dear was going to keel over with a heart attack and Jack would be blamed, so she started being conciliatory and saying we'd remove the offending object for her.

'We practically had to carry Jack out of her house, and he kept shouting at Val, "Why did you offer to get rid of it? I don't want her smouldering marital aids in my dustbin.

43

Why can't she use her own? What happens if the dustmen find it? I tell you what'll happen, we'll have to pay them to keep quiet, that's what. I can see it now: Jack Flowers's red hot night of love melts sex toy . . ."

'He made Val wrap it up in so much newspaper and tape that we almost couldn't get it in the dustbin. She told me afterwards that he'd made a point of asking her which day the binmen came, so he could hide behind the curtains and make sure they'd pitched it into the dustcart without looking inside . . . Are you all right?'

'Yes . . . fine . . . sorry . . .' I was laughing too much to get the words out.

'Here, let me help . . .' Lenny got out his handkerchief, 'wipe your eyes.'

When I finally got my breath back, I said, 'You said . . . Val . . . is that Jack's wife?'

'Yes, why?'

'He doesn't behave as if . . . Are *you* married?'

'No . . . *No!* Don't wrinkle your nose like that. You don't believe anything I say, do you?'

'Bits of it. I want to ask you something. When you took me to the *Mirabelle*, and Jack was there . . .'

'Ye-es?'

'Did you intend for the three of us to end up in bed together?'

'*Together?*' The expression on Lenny's face was so priceless I started laughing again.

'What, then?'

'Well, you know . . .' He wouldn't look at me.

'You meant . . . both of you, didn't you? *Ménage a trois?*'

'Not at the same time! Just, you know . . .'

I shook my head. 'Not till you tell me.'

'More, sort of . . . take turns.'

I said, 'Oh, take it in turns, I see,' all sarcastic. 'What do you do, toss a coin for who goes first?'

Lenny looked embarrassed, then he got all defensive and said, 'Well, you'd be surprised how many women go for that sort of thing,' and he named a couple of well-known actresses and a model. I can't tell you who they were for obvious reasons, but I was very surprised about one of the actresses, because she always looks terribly prim and plays these very strait-laced parts. The other one I'd have been able to guess, if I'd thought about it.

'*Really?* Is that true?'

'Well, they get twice as much out of it, don't they? Twice as much attention, twice as much . . .'

'I've got the picture, you don't need to colour it in. What do you get out of it?'

Lenny thought for a moment, and said, 'I suppose it's a habit. When we were playing the halls, touring . . . Well, we were always skint and we had to share a room, so we'd pool our cash and take one girl out instead of two, but we never . . . not *both* of us. Have you done that?'

'Done what?'

'Been in bed with two men at the same time.'

I said, 'No, do you want to try it?'

'Two birds, I would.' He rolled his eyes. 'Two blokes and a girl sounds a bit poofy to me.'

Lenny was so different to how he was at the *Mirabelle*, and I found myself telling him all about . . . Well, all sorts of things. It made a real change from sitting there nodding away, yes, yes, oh how interesting, while some guy bored the pants off me. Or tried to. I hardly ate anything, too busy talking, and then we had coffee and Lenny started telling me about his dad.

'He never said much because he had this problem where he could never remember the word for anything, what it

45

was called, and when he got angry about something, that made it worse. The best one was when I was called up for national service. I thought you could pick the service you preferred, which you could, in *theory*, but most people ended up in the Army. I told Dad I wanted to be in the Navy, and he looked at me and his mouth started working, and then he said, "What do you want to join that lot for? It's all . . . all . . . *ram, jam and buggery*!" '

'He meant rum, bum and concertina. I've never forgotten that – ram, jam and buggery . . . it sounds like what would happen if the W.I. gave the homemade wine a thrashing . . .'

'What did he do, your dad?'

'He used to do cleaning at an industrial chemist's. They used a lot of phosphorus, and they gave you more money if you'd work with that, because it was dangerous. If you don't keep phosphorus underwater it bursts into flames, and they had to deal with it when it was out of the water. All the workers had to wet their hair and clothes before they started, and when they finished work they had to shower and change into other things.

'My dad was mad about cowboy films. God knows why, I shouldn't think the old boy had ever ridden a horse in his life, let alone kissed one. But if they had a western at the Rialto he'd move heaven and earth to get there.

'One night they had a Tom Mix, but the problem was, it started at six o'clock, and he couldn't think of any way to get there on time. In the end he decided to skip the shower and jump on his bike just as he was, with the clothes still wet. So he pedalled like hell and got there just in time to get his place smack in the middle of the front row, where he always sat because he had bad eyesight, you see.

'So he watched the film, and of course all the time his clothes were drying out. Well, the climax of this thing had

46

Tom Mix behind the boulder, one arm round the girl, blasting away, and the redskins chucking these burning arrows at him . . . you can probably guess what happened next. Dad's clothes were covered in little flakes of phosphorus, and they started to ignite. Not all at once, but more like matches, flaring up. They'd positioned the camera so the Indians appeared to be hurling these fire-arrows straight at the audience, and that was the point when Dad's arm burst into flames.

'Of course the audience thought the film had come alive, everyone screamed and there was a stampede out of the cinema, with Dad running after them shouting for water. Some parts of his clothes were still damp enough to be all right, but different bits of his jacket and trousers kept igniting as they dried out, and all these people just took one look at him and . . . I don't know if they thought it was witchcraft or something, but they all scarpered.

'Eventually he got to a butcher's shop and the man was flinging pails of water at him, but it wasn't enough. In the end, the butcher went and called the chemist, "We've got a man here keeps bursting into flames, can you come and put him out?" '

There was a pause, and I was sitting there with my hand up to my mouth, and then Lenny said, 'You've got that disbelieving look on your face again.'

'No, no, it's not that . . . but . . . your dad, didn't he get burnt?'

Lenny frowned. 'Do you know, I don't think anyone's ever asked me that before. They usually just take it as a funny story and leave it at that.'

'Sorry. But, did he? Get burnt?'

'Yes, his arms. He was all right, though. They patched him up. Don't look so worried, Bunny Alice. Tell you what, why don't we go back to my place and forget all about it?'

47

So that's what we did. It was lovely. Not quite as exciting as the first time, slower, but in some ways it was even better. Lenny kissed me right down the middle of my stomach, and then he said, 'Now I'm going to find out . . . exactly what it takes . . . to make you blush.' No one ever did that to me before, and it was wonderful.

Afterwards I said I was hungry so we went down to the kitchen. I made sardines on toast and Lenny found some champagne in the fridge so we took it all back up to bed and had it there. We were licking our fingers – well, licking each other's fingers really – and I said, 'You didn't, by the way.'

'Didn't what?'

'Make me blush.'

'Well, if at first you don't succeed . . .'

'Have a sardine kiss.'

'We must smell like two cats who've just raided a dustbin.'

'You know in cartoons, when there's a dustbin, they always draw a fish-bone, don't they? Always very big . . . as big as . . . as a cat . . .'

'Alice?'

'Mmm . . . ?'

'Shut up.'

The second time was even better. Lenny said, '*Now* you're blushing.'

'I'm not.'

'Yes, you are. See?' He handed me a very small mirror.

'Hardly. You nicked this from a budgie, didn't you? Did you get the little bell to go with it?'

'Ha, ha.' Lenny took it out of my hand and tried to look at his hair. 'It's not too bad, is it? We're filming next week.'

'Can't you position yourself so the camera won't see it?'

'I can hardly do the whole thing in profile, can I? Well, not the whole show. Maybe we could do something with it.'

'You mean, what you told me?'

'My dear child, can you imagine what would happen if one of us went on television and told a story about a dildo? We'd never work again. We'd certainly never get Mrs Whitehouse off our backs.'

'I am not your dear child. I'm twenty-two.'

'As old as that? I never would have guessed.'

'Oh, stop teasing me. How old are you?'

'Thirty-four.'

He peered into the mirror again. 'If the worst comes to the worst, I could always get Wardrobe to find me an Irish.'

'Eh?'

'Irish. Irish jig. *Wig*, you fathead. It'll all fall out soon, anyway. That's what happened to Dad.' He stopped grimacing in the mirror and turned to face me.

'He told us he had to put his arms in a basin of water while they scraped out the phosphorus, and then they took him in a dark room to see if his arms were luminous, because that's how you tell a phosphorus burn, it glows in the dark. Must have been agony. It was phosphorus that killed him, being exposed to it all those years. Poisoned him.'

'Oh, Lenny . . .'

A week later I realised from something Jack said that Lenny'd lied to me about his age. He wasn't thirty-four, he was thirty-seven.

I didn't care, though, because I'd already fallen in love with him.

CHAPTER SIX

I meant to do some weeding after I'd seen to the animals, but I spent the afternoon sunbathing instead. I've got no excuse because it's so hot that I'm browner than I've ever been, even from holidays. I always take everything off. Any unexpected visitors can just get an eyeful, can't they? I don't care.

When I was married to Jeff I used to sunbathe topless on the roof of his studio, until one day he came up to talk to me, and spotted this bloke's binoculars glinting in the sun. I thought it was funny, I stood up and waved to the guy, but Jeff did his nut and practically dragged me down the stairs. He kept losing hold of me because I was all slippery with Ambre Solaire and wriggling like mad. In the end he had to let go and I ran down the corridor and straight into a guy from an ad agency that was one of his biggest clients. That's when I realised Jeff really didn't have a sense of humour, because he refused to speak to me for about a week. But in the end he had to admit it was good for business, because the ad man gave him even more work after that.

I was trying to read – Harold Robbins – but it was useless because I wanted to lie on my back and I'm so slow with books that by the time I've got halfway through I've forgotten what happened at the beginning, so I gave it up and thought about how it would be if my life had gone in a different direction. Not just with Lenny, but if I'd been any good at school and stayed on and taken exams. I'd like to have been a veterinary nurse, or . . . I don't know, something to do with animals. I might have been quite good, but I went to a secondary modern and there wasn't much encouragement. It never occurred to me at the time about needing exams and anyway, my marks were always so bad that the teachers would have thought I'd got a screw loose if I'd asked to stay on.

But I don't mind, really. Like I said, I may look like something I'm not, but I don't mind being what I am, if that makes sense. That was something I could never understand about Lenny: he made millions of people laugh and they all adored him, but he didn't want to be the person he was. He was very . . . what's the word? Inward-looking. Introspective, that's it. Much more than Jack. About the act, as well as himself. I mean, Jack would just go on, do his stuff and come off, and that was it. Lenny never thought anything was good enough. He was always jotting things down, how to improve it, and Jack just let him get on with it. If he thought it was a good idea he'd say, 'Fine, let's do it,' but he never really got involved. Lenny always felt he had to *test* everything, as if . . . I don't know. As if he was trying to make sure it was real, somehow.

I used to say to him, 'Don't be stupid, I love you *because* you're you,' and he'd say, 'How can you?'

Some of the things he did almost made me think he was behaving that way so I'd get fed up and leave him, and then he'd be able to turn round and say, 'I knew you didn't love me really.'

But I thought it must be my fault, so there I was trying to be the perfect girlfriend, and the harder I tried, the worse he got. I gave up in the end. Looking back, I think what it comes down to is, either you're the type of person who can be happy, or you're not. And if you're not, then you can have the whole country roaring with laughter at your jokes, and it won't make a blind bit of difference. So there you are. Hop on the couch, Doctor Alice will see you now.

But that's how people like comedians to be, isn't it? Miserable underneath. When Tony Hancock died, that really got to Lenny.

'Poor bastard,' he kept saying. 'Poor bastard.'

Then he waved the paper at me and said, 'That's how they want us to die.'

I thought I'd better make up for the afternoon by spending the evening cleaning the horses' tack in the kitchen. It's where I do everything. That and the bathroom are the only rooms I use downstairs, unless I've got people to stay. I don't need the others, because the kitchen's so big it's got a table and a sofa, as well as all the normal stuff.

I'd been putting off cleaning the tack over a week, but actually it was really satisfying. I'd got the radio on, and Eustace was snoring away on the rug, and I was just putting the second bridle back together when the front doorbell went. Eustace leapt to his feet and shot out into the hall, skidding on the runner like he always does. I grabbed his collar before I opened the door, because most people's idea of a warm welcome doesn't include a pint of dog slobber, so I was bending down. The first thing I saw was a suitcase and, next to it, feet and legs. Male.

'It's all right, he doesn't bite,' I said automatically, as Eustace lunged forward to sniff the shoes. I couldn't stand straight because that would have meant letting go of him, so I squinted up at the man through my hair and saw legs, crotch, chest, neck, and then—

'Hello, Bunny Alice.'

It was Jack. Standing on my porch under the light, holding a bunch of roses.

CHAPTER SEVEN

'What are *you* doing here?'

'Admiring your tan.'

Totally deadpan. A few more lines on his face, perhaps, but he was as handsome as ever. More, if anything. It threw me completely, I couldn't think what to say.

'Just hang on a sec.' Eustace had started making huffy little woofing noises, which is what he does when he's not sure whether he ought to bark or not, so I bundled him back into the kitchen and shut the door before he could make up his mind.

'What was *that*?'

'My dog. Why . . . I mean, what are you doing here?'

'I've come to see *you*, of course. Aren't you going to ask me in?'

I heard myself say, 'Oh, yes, sorry. Please, come in,' and I stood back and let him bring his suitcase into the hall. 'Are you . . .'

'I thought I'd stay a few days, if that's all right with you.'

He looked straight at me. I dropped my eyes first. It was pathetic. I was totally flustered, and he could see it.

'I don't recall inviting you,' I said, trying to pull myself together.

Jack held out the flowers as if I hadn't spoken.

'I bought you these.'

'That's very kind of you,' I said, automatically.

'Now then. Where do I go?'

I watched Jack look round the kitchen and saw it through his eyes: the dirty lino, the dishes in the sink, the saddle in the armchair, the dog shedding hairs on the sofa, and me with my bare feet, grubby T-shirt and jeans cut off at the knee. A drip from the drying rack landed on his head. He looked up.

'What's that thing hanging down?'

'A girth.'

'Oh. What's a girth?'

'Keeps the saddle on the horse. How did you get here?'

'Train. The taxi dropped me at the gate. I thought I'd stay a few days. I'm sure you could use a bit of company. I've been worried about you, out here by yourself.'

I stared at him.

'Jack, I haven't seen you since Lenny's funeral.'

'You haven't thought about me at all, have you?' he asked, aggressively.

'Yes, of course I've thought about you,' I said, taken back. 'Actually, I was thinking about you the other day, wondering if—'

'You don't have to pretend, Alice. There's someone else, isn't there?'

'What are you talking about, someone else?'

'Another man.'

'What do you mean, *another* man? Even if there was, I don't see . . .'

'It was a *joke*, darling.'

'It didn't sound like one.'

'Well, it was. You never did like hurting people's feelings, did you? Was that why you went to bed with me, all those years ago?'

'No! Jack, stop it! I don't understand what—'

Jack cut across me. 'Lenny bought this place, didn't he?'

'Yes.'

To my dismay, my eyes filled up with tears. I turned my head away, but not quickly enough.

'Never mind, darling. But I'm here now.' As if I'd begged him to come. Before I could reply, Jack said, 'Does he always do that?'

'Who?'

'Your dog. Does he always fall asleep with his arse hanging off the sofa like that?'

'All the time. Jack, I still don't . . .'

'You'd think he'd slip off, wouldn't you? I don't see how it can be comfortable. What's his name?'

'Eustace. Jack, why are you here, actually?'

'I'm here, actually, because I wanted to see you, actually. And London's like a bloody furnace. Anyway, now you've got me, you might offer me a drink. I wouldn't mind something to eat, either. Actually.'

'I can make you a cheese sandwich, and I think there's some Scotch . . .'

I put the roses in the sink and started pulling things out of the fridge. 'Cheddar?'

'Anything. This is a nice old place.'

He went over to the table and picked up a snaffle bit while I concentrated on cutting bread. 'Wouldn't fancy that in my mouth. Have you got a horse of your own?'

'Two. Pickle?'

'Why not? Where's the booze?'

'Oh, sorry. Try the cupboard in the corner.'

Jack stuck his head in and reappeared holding an elderly bottle of Johnnie Walker. I was hoping he'd go and sit down but he leant against the worktop and watched me. 'You're still gorgeous. Dishevelled, but gorgeous.'

'Thanks. By the way, does Val know you're here?'

'Still cynical, as well. You haven't given me a kiss yet.'

'So I haven't.'

I said it as flippantly as I could and kept my eyes on the breadboard.

'I've thought about you a lot.' Jack put his hand on my arm. I jumped. I couldn't help it. He let go and blew on his fingertips as if they were on fire. 'Whoa! You've been on your own too long, I can see that.'

'Sorry. It's just . . .'

'You never used to react like that. Rather the reverse, from what I remember.'

I took a deep breath, 'Jack, please don't.'

'All right.' He gestured towards the loaf. 'What's that, a dog biscuit?'

'Bread. I made it.'

'Made it? What do you think shops are for?'

He looked at the oozing doorstep I'd prepared. 'Not exactly gourmet fare, is it?'

'Sorry. It falls apart if I cut it any thinner.'

Jack pulled a piece off the top slice, chewed it, and looked surprised. 'Not bad. It certainly tastes *brown*, anyway.'

'*Does* Val know you're here?'

'In a manner of speaking.'

'Which manner would that be?'

'Well, she knows I'm not at home, so I must be some-where else, but she's not too bothered where.'

'I bet she *is* bothered. Did you have an argument?'

He shook his head. 'Not really. The thing is, she's a bit preoccupied at the moment. It's Rosalie. She's doing another degree. Art this time. She and her boyfriend have cooked up this so-called project, where they have to buy one thing from every page of one issue of the *Exchange & Mart*, and take photographs of them, the places they came from and the people who sold them. There's stuff all over the place: prams and bedsteads and ski boots, all sorts of junk. We might as well be living on the set of *Steptoe & Son*.

There's a car, too. Filthy old rust bucket. Broke down in the middle of the drive. Val's livid. Not with Rosalie, mind you. She says it's my fault for lending her the money.'

'Why did you?'

'I thought it was for paints and things. I said to Rosie, "This isn't art, it's shopping," and she said, "Yes, that's the point." At the end they're going to put all this crap on a conveyor belt somewhere, and film it so it looks like prizes on a game show.

'I said to Val, "Who's going to want to see that? I'd rather look at the test card."

'I only lent Rosie the money in the first place because I wanted her home for the summer, not hitch-hiking off to Christ knows where with her revolting boyfriend. *Covered* in pustules, you've never seen anything like it. And he dresses like a raving poof.'

'She's old enough to know her own mind, surely?'

'Yes, but she's my daughter and I'm not letting that . . . *troll* . . . maul her about.'

'All women are somebody's daughter, Jack. Even me. Believe it or not. Why don't you sit down?'

'In a minute.'

I began stripping the bottom leaves off the roses and arranging them in a vase. Jack moved behind me – too close. I could feel his breath. I bent over the flowers and tried to ignore him. He kissed my neck. This time, I was prepared. I didn't jump or move away, just stood there and let him do it. I didn't mind. In fact, it was rather nice to have someone touch me again, and I'd always been fond of Jack, and it was good – reassuring – to have someone around, even if I wasn't sure why he was here . . .

'It's good to see you again,' he murmured. 'So good to see you . . .' He put his hands on my shoulders. I put my head back and closed my eyes and suddenly, I saw Lenny's face in my mind, his eyes looking down into mine, as if he was on top of me, about to—

'Don't tense up, Alice.'

'I'm not, it's just—'

Before I could stop him Jack's hands shot down my arms and he grabbed my hands in his and yanked them behind my back. 'Are you ever going to relax?'

'Jack, you're hurting me.'

'You're resisting.' He sounded as if he was enjoying himself.

'Of course I'm bloody resisting,' I said, through gritted teeth.

'Aren't you pleased to see me?'

'Jack, *don't.*'

'Say you're pleased to see me.'

'I'm pleased to see you,' I gasped. 'Now please – let go.'

He dropped my hands and stepped back. I turned round to face him, rubbing my wrists. 'What did you think you were doing? That hurt.'

'Sorry,' he said. He didn't look it. His voice was mechanical, his eyes blank.

I pushed past him to the dresser. 'You need a glass.'

Jack took the whisky and sandwich over to the table, and sat down as if nothing had happened. I followed him with a glass, and then returned to the roses.

'What's up?' I asked, hoping I didn't sound as shaken as I felt.

'Well, I've been trying to learn lines for this play I'm supposed to be doing, but what with all the banging and crashing, and being *persona non grata* with Val, I thought it would be best for everyone if I decamped. So I said to myself, I'll go and see my old friend Alice, she'll be lonely all on her tod.'

'It was a kind thought but I'm fine. Honestly.'

'You know I've always been fond of you, sweetheart. I felt sorry for you. I heard about whatshisname. Your husband.'

'Jeff Jones. What about him?'

'Are you going back to him?'

I sighed, 'We're divorced.'

'Sensible girl. Once a Welshman, always a cunt, in my book.'

'Jack! That's a horrible thing to say.'

'Sorry. It's only because I'm so fond of you, darling. I won't be in your way. I can sit in the garden. And I can help you bringing in the sheaves or whatever it is you do. It'll be nice to spend some time in the country.'

I gave up. 'Look, I'm tired. You can stay the night and we'll discuss it in the morning. There's a spare room. Why don't you finish that while I get some sheets?'

Jack pushed the half-eaten sandwich away.

'I'll come with you. I'm not used to this level of mastication.'

'OK.'

Without thinking, I leant forward to pick up the Scotch and put it back in the cupboard, but Jack was there. Our eyes met above the bottle.

'I wouldn't mind a drop more,' he said, taking it from me. After a moment, he said, 'Don't worry, I'm not . . . I'm OK. Long day, that's all.'

I didn't answer. Jack looked irritated. 'Alice, for God's sake . . . I'm fine.'

'Are you?'

'Yes!'

He didn't try and touch me again, just sat in the spare room armchair, pouring Scotch into his glass while I made up the bed. When I'd finished all he said was, 'Good night, my darling. I'll buy you some white sliced in the morning.'

I made a point of taking the whisky back downstairs with

me. There was something about the speed with which Jack had got to the bottle, the way our hands had touched on the neck, the expression on his face . . . It reminded me *so* much of Lenny. Jack had never been much of a drinker, not that I remembered. Well, he drank, but only like most people did, not to excess. Perhaps I'd imagined it.

What the hell, I thought, and poured one for myself. I took it out into the yard and leant against the kitchen wall, listening to Eustace nosing about under the hedge and trying to work out how I felt. Confused? Yes. Worried? Yes. But not actually frightened. Not like I'd been before. More sort of . . . distanced.

Perhaps that was the Scotch, I thought, taking another sip. I wasn't used to it. I'd got the newspaper cutting on, when? Monday. And Jack turns up, out of the blue, on Thursday. It might be a coincidence, but after six years . . . He might have sent it himself. But why, if he was planning on seeing me? Why not just bring it with him?

I wasn't sure how I felt about Jack. A mixture of things. Seeing him in my kitchen like that had brought Lenny back so sharply that I'd felt as if he might walk through the door at any moment, as if he wasn't dead at all but had just nipped down to the pub or something. It wasn't rational, but, just . . . What? Jack's aliveness, his force, his . . . Oh God. What am I doing?

I hadn't seen Jack since Lenny's funeral. Too painful. He'd probably felt the same about me. All the same, I felt as if I'd been in a coma for six years and just woken up. Steady, Alice, I thought. Being with Jack – going to bed with Jack – wasn't going to bring Lenny back. And the way he'd behaved, in the kitchen, his voice had sounded almost as if he'd wanted to hurt me. And he had hurt me. Not much, but enough. I hadn't imagined *that*.

But I was *still* excited by him. I'd always fancied him. No point pretending. I'd slept with him, hadn't I? Back whenever it was. He'd started it, but I could have said I didn't want to. I *had* wanted to, and that made it my fault as much as his. He'd been consoling me after a colossal row with Lenny, when he'd bought me a mink coat for my birthday and I'd refused to wear it. That was the first time I'd seen Lenny get really smashed, and it frightened me. He'd rounded on me, called me an ungrateful bitch and told me to get out, and his eyes had looked so cold when he said it.

Jack was at the flat, they'd been working on something, and he said he'd take me home.

We went back to my flat and I was still pretty upset, so he got me some brandy, put his arm round me, and one thing led to another. Jack had sworn blind he'd never told Lenny what happened, and Lenny'd never asked me about it. But I'd often wondered if he suspected and if that was one of the reasons they'd quarrelled.

I had a sudden image of Jack holding my wrists behind my head, pinning me down on my back. He'd felt so powerful. I'd liked it, and he knew that I did. But that had been the only time. I hadn't let it happen again. I didn't want to think about it. I wasn't *going* to think about it. I drained the glass, called Eustace inside, turned the lights off, went upstairs to bed and fell asleep with the dog curled up behind my knees.

I was woken by a low, menacing growl. I sat up, turned on the bedside light and saw Jack standing at the foot of my bed. Naked and blinking with his mouth open and his face slack and bewildered, as if he wasn't properly awake. Eustace was facing him, rumbling like a volcano. How long had he been there? I hadn't heard him come in, but then I hadn't thought to close the bedroom door. He walked round to my side of the bed. Eustace, vibrating

61

with indignation, clambered over my legs to mark him. 'What's the matter, Jack?'

Jack took a step towards me. Eustace braced his front legs, thrust his chin forward and started to bark, ignoring my attempts to shush him. Jack, punctuated by Eustace, mumbled, 'Can't sleep . . . missed you . . . please . . .'

'Stop it, Eustace!'

Eustace carried on.

'. . . said you'd missed me . . .'

'I said I'd *thought about you*, Jack,' I yelled, 'it's not quite the same.'

'You've never been out of my mind. Please, Alice – bloody dog – let me . . .'

I shouted, 'What do you want?' above the din.

'. . . be with you . . . can't bear . . . please let me . . .'

'Just go back to bed, Jack, for God's sake. He isn't going to stop.' Jack took a step backwards, still mumbling.

I heard 'I need . . .' but the barks were elongating into howls, and the rest was lost.

'Jack. Why don't you go back to bed and try to get some sleep, and we can sort it out in the morning?'

He turned away. From the back, his shoulders looked defeated, pathetic. I'd seen Lenny like that a few times, but never Jack. I almost – but not quite – got out of bed to go after him. Eustace followed him as far as the doorway and lay down straight across it like a draught excluder. After the racket, the silence felt heavy, like a blanket.

His vulnerability had frightened me. That wasn't the Jack I knew. The business in the kitchen, that was . . . I don't know. I could handle that better, somehow. That was more like the old Jack . . . But this one was different. Defenceless. I'd never seen him like that. He'd always been unshakeable. Nerves of steel. And totally reliable as a performer. No matter what was happening, he'd always turn up on time, make sure the audience got their money's worth, and send them home laughing. Utterly professional. Everyone said that about him.

When he and Lenny were at the Fortune doing *Gnus Before Butter*, and Lenny was pissed out of his wits, Jack would go on stage night after night and cover up for him. Once, he'd done almost an hour of old-fashioned stand-up while Lenny was in the dressing room throwing up because of the Antabuse. Or rather, because he'd been taking Antabuse and drinking at the same time. I used to go and watch. I'd changed my shift to the afternoon because Lenny wanted me at the theatre – I'd be standing there thinking, what's going to happen this time, and literally shaking, but Jack never turned a hair . . .

But now, something was wrong. Something was really, badly wrong. The blankness in his face in the kitchen, as if there was a switch inside him that had just turned off, and now this. Perhaps I was right, he *was* drinking. Or maybe something else. Drugs?

From what I'd been able to see, he was still in pretty good shape. I wondered if he was still taking the diet pills. He used to pinch them out of girls' bathroom cabinets the same way he'd nicked bars of chocolate from Don Findlater's secretary's desk. That's what started it. Don's secretary was called Araminta. Minty. Though anyone less minty you can't imagine – she was more like an old lemon. But she always kept one drawer full of chocolate, because both she and Don had a sweet tooth. Minty was on to Jack, but she got tired of having to be on guard every time he came in, so she typed 'Fatso' on a sheet of paper and stuck that in the drawer instead.

Lenny thought it was hilarious, but it really got to Jack. Gave him a complex. Amphetamines stop you sleeping, don't they? And with the whisky as well . . . But even that . . . I couldn't put my finger on it, but there was definitely something else.

He's in a mess, I thought. I can't just kick him out. Besides . . . I turned off the light. It was easier to face up to things in the dark. If Eustace hadn't been there . . . Jack needed me. Needed someone, at any rate. And, no point in being dishonest about it – not to myself, anyway – so did I. Jack was right when he said I'd been on my own for too long. As for Val, Jack just *is* chronically unfaithful. Some men are. Their wives either accept it or leave, and Val had stayed put. If it wasn't me, I thought, it would be somebody else. Doesn't make it right, but . . .

None of this is right, I thought. Lenny dying wasn't *right*. Getting anonymous newspaper cuttings in the post isn't right, either. What's going on?

In the morning. I'll talk to Jack then. When he's got rid of the hangover.

The room was stifling. I got out of bed and padded over to open the windows. In the doorway, Eustace raised his head for a moment, and then shifted position onto his side. I crouched next to him and rubbed his tummy. The house was silent. After a few minutes Eustace began to snore gently, and I went back to bed.

CHAPTER EIGHT

Another beautiful morning. Boiling hot sun, birds singing, blue sky, brown grass. I tiptoed across the landing. The door to Jack's room was ajar so I poked my head round. Out for the count. Getting bathed and dressed and feeding the animals, it almost felt like an ordinary morning, except that I kept thinking, maybe he won't remember, maybe he will remember and won't come down, maybe he'll just phone for a taxi and leave.

I took Pablo for a ride to give Jack the chance to clear off without seeing me if he wanted to, but when I got back he was sitting on a chair outside the kitchen door, drinking coffee and watching the chickens behind his sunglasses.

'You left me alone with that monster,' he said, jerking his thumb at Eustace, who was sunning himself on the cobble-stones.

'I thought it was going to attack me. It kept backing into the furniture and barking.'

'He likes the sound of his own voice, that's all.'

'Well I don't. I've got a headache. That thing clomping about doesn't help, either.'

Pablo tossed his head up and down and Jack retreated to the kitchen doorway.

'What's wrong with it?'

'Nothing, he's just hot.' I slid off. Pablo took himself over to the trough.

'You're not going to let it wander about like that, are you?'

'Course not. He's going in the field with the other one.'

Jack watched while I untacked Pablo and sponged the sweaty bits, then followed us to the gate where my old grey horse was dozing in the sun with his back sagging like a hammock, and his chin resting on his favourite fence post.

'What's that one called?'

'Nelson. He's blind in one eye.'

'He's got all four legs, though. Unless one of them's wooden.'

'He laughs when you kiss him. Watch this.' I leant forward and brushed Nelson's pink, whiskery nose with my lips. Immediately, he lifted his head and curled his lip, showing his teeth.

'That's laughing?'

'Yes.'

'Perhaps I should start telling jokes to horses. Humans don't seem to find me funny any more.'

We leant side by side on the fence and looked across the field. 'How did you find me, Jack?'

'Looked in the phone book. I was quite surprised you were there.'

'From before. When I thought I was going to live here. But if you found my number, why didn't you just ring?'

'I thought you'd tell me to get lost.'

I didn't say anything.

'Would you have?'

'I don't know. No, I wouldn't.'

'Why did you marry that cunt?'

'Jeff? He isn't.'

'Isn't what?'

'What you said he was.'

'Say it.'

'No.'

'Don't be such a prude.' Jack nudged me hard in the ribs. 'Say it!'

'Stop being childish.'

'He gave you a hard time, didn't he?'

'He's got nothing on you, Jack, believe me.'

'*Touché.* But you can tell me. If you want to, that is.'

'Oh, just . . .'

The bizarre thing was, I almost did want to tell him. I've never really talked to anyone about what happened with Jeff, not even girlfriends. When I married him, two years after Lenny died, I thought I wanted to settle down. Security, children, all that stuff. A normal life. But somehow the impetus to have all those things just wasn't there for either of us. When I told Jeff I'd found out about his girlfriends, he said, 'I'm surprised it took you so long to guess,' as if we'd been playing some sort of game.

I think he was angry about being found out, more than anything. Certainly not apologetic: I remember him leaning against the draining board in our kitchen and saying, 'Come on, Alice, you know the score.' Which I evidently hadn't. But I'd thought, you know, we were *married* and everything, so I hadn't slept with anyone else. Hadn't wanted to.

Actually, I think that was part of the problem. I'd gone off the whole thing, really. I don't mean only sex, although that was pretty much going through the motions. I'm fairly sure Jeff never noticed, he wasn't that kind of guy, but I think he knew that my heart wasn't in the relationship, and that must have hurt. Yes, he'd behaved badly, but I should never have married him in the first place. Jeff wasn't Lenny, and I shouldn't have tried to pretend that he was.

Don't, said a little voice inside my head. Don't tell Jack anything.

'It didn't work out, that's all,' I said. 'We didn't have much in common.'

'Touched a nerve, didn't I? I didn't mean to.'

'Yes you did.'

'Don't say that, sweetheart. Some people just aren't meant to be together. Val and I, we've never had a lot in common, either, except the children. Do you know what she did, once?' Jack grinned. 'She made me a cake, for my birthday. I came back late from the theatre and she'd had to take the girls somewhere, so she'd left a meal on the dining room table with this thing in the middle, on a stand. I didn't really look at it until I'd eaten the other stuff, and then I thought I'd better have a bit because it looked great, icing and little flowers and all the rest of it. But what she'd written, across the top, not *Happy Birthday* or *Many Happy Returns* or anything like that, she'd put *You Selfish Bastard.* Pink icing, it was. Very well done. She told me afterwards she'd been taking classes. Cake Decoration. That's Val. Never does anything by halves.'

'What did you do?'

'Ate it, of course.'

'What, all of it?'

'No, just the *Bastard* bit, so the girls wouldn't see. Very nice it was, too.'

'When was this?'

'Oh, years ago. When Val still had a sense of humour. Mind you, I'm not sure she's ever found me very funny. She's always preferred Max Bygraves.'

'You'll be telling me she doesn't understand you next.'

'She doesn't.'

'Well, I don't understand you, either. Why did you really come here?'

'Haven't you missed me at all, Alice?'

'I told you . . .' I shook my head, confused.

68

Jack nodded in the direction of Pablo and Nelson. 'Your horses are queer.'

'What?'

'Look, it's nibbling the other one's neck.'

'Lots of horses do that. They're just friends.'

'Honestly, Officer.'

'Talking of sex, last time I was in London I saw your name on the poster for a blue film. Candy Knight. What was that all about?'

'Hardly a blue film, it was one of those mucky comedies she does. They're practically the only British films making money at the moment. To be honest, I didn't really know what I was getting into. I thought it was going to be like a *Carry On*.'

'Didn't you read it first?'

'Never saw a whole script. I didn't have a clue what was going on and they kept asking me to spank all these girls in frilly drawers. Not me, them. But it was pretty tame. Alfie Bass was in it, for God's sake. And Irene Handl. And Queenie Watts. Not amongst the spankees, obviously.

'The whole thing was done on a shoestring. They'd print it even if you cocked up your lines because they couldn't afford to redo anything.' He chuckled. 'I don't know why you're being so prim about it, darling. You've done stuff for men's magazines before now.'

'How did you know that? No, don't tell me. Lenny.'

Jack grinned.

'That was only once. God, it was weird. But that was different, that was just a body. You've got talent.'

'You're about the only one who thinks so. And this isn't *just* a body.' We walked back to the kitchen.

'Reminded me of when we used to do the shows at the Windmill, donkey's years ago. Can't imagine anyone paying to see that now, lot of birds standing around in the buff.'

Jack shook his head. 'Half the time the punters didn't know we were there, all they wanted was the girls. Everyone worked there, though: Jimmy Edwards, Hancock, Peter Sellers, even Morecambe and Wise, except they were called something else in those days. Anyway, what about breakfast? I couldn't find any bacon.'

'That's because there isn't any. I'm vegetarian.'

'Well, I'm not. And I can't learn lines on rabbit food.' Jack plonked himself down at the table and sighed. 'Haven't you got *anything* decent to eat?'

'We usually have toast.'

'That stuff you make, you'd never fit it inside the toaster.'

'Under the grill.'

'Well, if that's all there is, you'd better get on with it.'

I started the toast and went back out to pick up the milk before it went off. It was unsettling to realise quite how much seeing Jack brought it all back. And how much I still fancied him, in spite of everything telling me I shouldn't, shouldn't, *shouldn't*. I'd thought it might be different in the daylight, but it wasn't. I took a couple of deep breaths, trying to clear my head.

There was a yelp and a crash behind me. I dashed back into the kitchen. Jack was standing at the open door of the cooker, flailing at the smoke with a smouldering oven glove.

'It's *burnt*. This is fucking ridiculous. We might as well be living in a fucking *cave*.'

'I'll do some more.'

'We've got to get proper bread. I'm out of cigarettes, as well. You must have a village shop, for God's sake.'

I nodded. 'After breakfast. Eustace could do with a walk.'

'How far is it?'

'Half a mile each way. Do you good. Why didn't you come by car, anyway?'

'Lost my licence.'

'Oh.'

My heart sank. I *hadn't* imagined it.

'The village shop doesn't sell booze.'

'For Christ's sake, Alice, it was just bad luck, that's all. Could have happened to anyone. You're starting to sound like Val.'

'So you *did* have an argument.'

'Not really. She had a bit of a go at me, but . . .' He shrugged. 'I've been away for a couple of weeks. Working. Val's not bothered. She knows I'll be in touch.'

'So what was all that about your daughter's project?'

'Nothing but truth. You couldn't make it up, could you? Now, if you've finished interrogating me, why don't you have another go at the toast? I want to fetch something.'

I got cracking with the breadknife. After a couple of minutes, Jack returned and plonked a cookery book down on the draining board. 'I bought this for you. One of Val's. It's OK,' he added, seeing my face, 'she doesn't use it any more. I remembered you weren't much good, but it's all right, I can supervise.'

'Charming. How long are you planning on staying, anyway?'

I looked at Jack, then at the dog, who was slumped at my feet. They were wearing the same abject expression. I wanted to laugh.

'All right,' I said to Jack. 'Find something you like and I'll have a go at it this evening, but remember we've only got a village shop, not Fortnum and Mason.'

Halfway through breakfast, a thought struck me.

'*Hang on . . .* How come you've got that book with you, anyway? You said you haven't been home for two weeks. Were you planning on coming here all the time?'

Jack looked nonplussed, then said, 'Oh, I see what you

71

mean. I nipped back for a few things, that's all. Val was out.' He looked irritated. 'I left her a note, for Christ's sake.'

'That was sweet of you. Saying what?'

'Saying I was sick of not being able to turn round without some bloody woman bombarding me with questions!'

'Keep your hair on. I only asked.'

'Yeah, well . . .' Jack sighed and went back to the recipe book. Eustace, having demolished his breakfast, was looking hopefully at the table. I fed him Jack's toast crusts. 'Did the postman come?'

'Mmm?'

'While I was out.'

Jack looked up and shook his head. 'Didn't see him.'

'You'd know. Eustace goes mad.'

'How about *coq au vin*?'

'I suppose so. At least I've got the veg.' I didn't fancy cooking meat, but Jack obviously felt he couldn't exist without it. I left him making a shopping list and went upstairs to change out of my jeans.

I was hunting for a pair of shorts when I noticed something odd about my room. I've got this big wooden box where I keep hand cream and stuff, and it's usually on the floor by the bed, but for some reason, it was on top of the chest of drawers. My first thought was that I must have put it there this morning, but then I thought, I can't remember doing it – I mean, I *really* can't remember, so that was a bit odd. My bedroom isn't the tidiest place in the universe, but I was pretty sure I wouldn't have left the box up there because it looked so *strange*. You know how some things just don't go together? Well, it was like that. Weird. I mean, Eustace attacks it, sometimes, when it's on the floor, but I'd know if it was him because he pulls out the cotton wool and rips it up so it looks like there's been a snowstorm. In any case, there's no way he could get the box up there, even if he wanted to. When I went to put it back, I saw that everything inside was jumbled up. It hasn't got a lid, and there were all these manky things on the top like gooey old lipsticks where I scraped the last bits out with a hairpin years ago but never got round to throwing them away. The box looked like somebody'd dropped it and just tipped everything back inside any-old-how. *But it wasn't me.*

Jack's been in here, I thought. When I was out on Pablo. Going through my things. Looking for what, though? There was nothing to find. I looked round. Now the box was back in its usual place, the room looked right again. Opening drawers didn't tell me anything. I'm not much of a clothes-folder at the best of times, I just lob it all in together, so if Jack had been ferreting through my knickers I'm not sure I'd have even noticed.

Him saying he missed me and wanted to see me was all very nice, but I didn't believe he'd just come up with it out of the blue. Or that he'd spent the last two weeks working away from home. Perhaps Val had finally chucked him out. In which case, why not go and stay with his latest girlfriend? I'd never known Jack not to have a bit on the side. Several bits, sometimes. But if he was planning on staying for a while, why was he winding me up by going through my bedroom? What the hell is he playing at? I thought. I can't deal with this.

I pulled on a pair of shorts and went downstairs.

CHAPTER NINE

Walking down the lane towards the village, I said, 'You've been in my room, haven't you?'

'What?'

'While I was out on Pablo. You were in there.'

'No I wasn't.'

I looked at him. His eyes were hidden behind sunglasses, and the rest of his face wasn't giving anything away. 'Weren't you? My things were all jumbled up.'

'Must have been him.' Jack nodded down at Eustace, who was trotting along beside me.

'No.'

'You, then. Admit it, sweetheart, you're hardly the world's best housekeeper.'

'It wasn't me.'

'You're being paranoid. You've been on your own for too long.'

'All right, it wasn't you. But . . . Look, did you send me something in the post? A newspaper cutting?'

'Nope.' Jack shook his head. 'That wasn't me either.'

'I got one a couple of days ago. About finding a skeleton in a lake. Inside a car.'

'Oh?'

'In Wiltshire. It reminded me of that party.' I paused, but Jack didn't say anything. 'I thought perhaps it was you. It was weird, that's all.'

'Which party was that?'

'Ages ago. At Ivar Park.'

'I shouldn't worry about it. Some of the things I've had through the post, you'd be amazed. There's a lot of strange people out there.'

'This strange person knows where I live.'

'Well, it's hardly a secret, is it? You're in the book. Stop looking so worried. I'm here, aren't I?'

'Yes, but . . .'

'But what?'

'I don't know. It's just peculiar. I mean, if they – whoever sent it – thought I had something to do with it, or . . .'

'But you didn't, did you?'

'Course not! I wouldn't kill anyone. And even if I wanted to, I'd hardly be likely to drown them in the middle of—'

'Is that what it said? She'd drowned?'

'No, just that they'd found a skeleton. I don't suppose they can tell. It didn't say it was a *she*, either.'

'Didn't it?'

'You *do* remember, don't you? The girl who went missing. Kitty. Lenny knew her.'

'Did he?'

'Yes! That's why I left him, remember?'

'Vaguely. There was a lot going on. Lenny was choked, I remember that. Who sent you this thing, anyway?'

'I don't know, do I? That's why I asked you.'

'Keep your hair on. Anyone would think you had a persecution complex.'

'I didn't *imagine* it, Jack. The newspaper cutting or the mess in my bedroom.'

'Well, it's not worth worrying about. I wouldn't give it another thought if I were you. Did Lenny ever tell you about the time he fell down a lift shaft?'

'What's that got to do with it?'

'Did he? It's a great story.'

'Mmmm . . . don't think so.'

'Well, we'd gone to the East End to see this drag act – Dockyard Doris, been going for years – and we'd finished up in an Indian restaurant in Brick Lane. We were upstairs, and they'd got this dumb waiter for the food to come up, only it was broken, so they'd got this kid standing on a chair in the kitchen, and we kept seeing this little brown hand with a plate of curry rising out of this hole like Excalibur. Lenny went to have a look and of course he'd had a few . . . The next thing we saw was his bum in the air. He'd gone right over the edge. Nearly killed the poor little fucker underneath. We found him spread-eagled on the floor, bits of chair everywhere, and all the waiters muttering incantations and sprinkling him with rose-water . . . Jesus, it was funny.'

It just didn't ring true. I was sure Jack had been through my room, and sure, too, that he remembered more about Kitty than he was letting on. Seven years is a long time, but he was too vague, too dismissive. He hadn't really wanted to talk about Lenny, he'd just used the funny story to change the subject. Lenny used to do the same – it was a way of keeping people at arm's length. Jack told another story about Lenny, then another. I listened and nodded and smiled and thought, I don't believe you.

When we got to the shop I waited outside with Eustace while Jack went in. I picked the *Mirror* off the stand for something to do, and flicked through it: PRAYING FOR RAIN, DENNIS LEADS DROUGHT BATTLE, SCORPION BY POST TERROR FOR WIFE . . . But I couldn't see anything about bodies in lakes.

Jack stuck his head out of the door. 'Why are you reading that comic?' He twitched the paper away and shoved it back on the rack. 'Have you got any mushrooms?'

'No.'

'I'll get some.'

He went back into the shop. I waited a second before taking the paper down again. RAPIST IN NEW BEAUTY QUEEN SEX SHOCKER, THE FOUR LETTER WORD EVERY WOMAN DREADS BY MARJE PROOPS, SAVE A FIVER AT FINE FARE. Nothing at all.

Jack emerged with a plastic carrier.

'That was quick.'

He snatched the paper out of my hand.

'Do you mind? I was reading that.'

'Well you shouldn't. It'll rot your brain and then you'll die and then where will you be?' It was meant to be a nanny impression but it sounded wrong, forced, and his hands shook when he tried to fold the paper. After a moment, he bundled it up and threw it into the bin. I made out the words BODY FOUND IN PORNO FLAT across the top.

'Now look what you've done.' I gave him Eustace's lead.

'What are you doing?'

'Going to pay for the paper.'

Inside the shop, Mrs Bowers said, 'I'm sure I recognise him. Wasn't he on the telly, your fellow? He looks ever so familiar.'

'Jack Flowers.'

'That's it! I knew I'd seen him somewhere before. He used to be with that other one, didn't he?'

'Lenny Maxted.'

'That's right, Lenny Maxted. Too clever for me, all that talk. I like a bit of singing and dancing.' She leant across the counter. 'He can't bear to let you out of his sight for a moment, can he?'

'Sorry?'

'Well, it was the way he kept going over to the window. I couldn't think what he was doing. Pardon me, dear, but I thought maybe he was a bit, you know, not quite right in the head. Then I saw you out there.' She smiled and said conspiratorially, 'Must be nice for you, dear. It's not right being on your own, is it? Not at your age.'

I couldn't think of anything to say that wouldn't lead to lots of questions, so I just nodded and hoped she'd think I was being shy about it.

I came out to find Jack still standing beside the bin, staring down at the contents. He must have rearranged them while I was in the shop because the porno corpse headline had been replaced by TWENTY NEW KING SIZE PICCADILLY 45p. He looked agitated.

'Jack? There isn't anything about you in there, is there?'

'No. For Christ's sake, take the dog and let's go.'

He strode off so fast that I was practically running to keep up. My mind was whirling. What was all that business with the paper? He'd tried to make a joke of it, but he hadn't wanted me to see what was in it. Was that because I'd told him about the cutting? Either way, it didn't make sense: how did he know what was in the paper? It was today's, and I don't get one delivered, so he couldn't have seen it. Unless he already knew about the Kitty business, if that's what it was, and he was afraid I'd see something else.

Jack stopped at the bend to light a cigarette and flicked the match into the hedge. I dived after it. 'Don't do that, you'll set the whole world on fire!'

'Sorry.' He smiled at me. It reminded me of Lenny in the haystack, that first time. He looked at me for a moment and said, 'Penny for them.'

'Can I ask you something?'

'Go on.'

'When . . . you and I . . . You didn't tell Lenny, did you?'

'No, darling.'

'Not when you were in America, or . . .'

'I'm not *that* much of a shit, Alice,' Jack said, gently.

Before I could say anything else there was a rat-a-tat of hooves and a black Shetland pony, mane and stirrups flying, came careering round the corner. When he saw us, paralysed in the middle of the road, he stopped so suddenly that he almost sat down on his haunches. I grabbed hold of the trailing reins and the pony jerked his head up and backed away, eyes rolling wildly.

'It's all right.' I stroked his nose. He tried to take a lump out of my arm.

'Where did *that* come from?'

'Must be the Boyles'.'

'Boils?'

'B-O-Y-L-E-S. My neighbours. They've got a couple of ponies like this. They'll probably be here in a minute.'

Right on cue, I heard shouts and the clatter of hooves, and three more shaggy ponies, with children on board this time, hurtled into view.

'Christ,' said Jack, flattening himself against the hedge, 'it's the cavalry.'

'Ta, Alice.' Trudy, the eldest Boyle, was fourteen with bright red hair – and bright red acne to go with it, unfortunately. The choice of an orange T-shirt and a chestnut pony didn't help – she looked as if she was about to burst into flames. 'Lee fell off.'

'Is this one Ronnie or Reggie?' I asked her. 'I can't tell them apart.'

'Did he bite you?'

'He had a go.'

'Then it's Ronnie. We was going to come and see you, Alice. Dad says to tell you we've got the farrier coming Monday afternoon and he'll do yours if you bring them over.'

'Great. Tell him I'll be there.'

A small and very dusty-looking kid trailed into view, whacking the grass verge with his riding crop. 'Here he is,' said Trudy. 'Come on Lee, you stupid little prat.'

'She keeps taking the mickey,' Lee complained, taking Ronnie's reins from me. The pony nipped his arm. 'Ow! 'Kin 'ell!'

I frowned at him.

'Sorry, Alice. Can you hang on to him?'

I gave Ronnie a shove to stop him treading on my foot. 'Get up, quick.'

We said goodbye and watched them trot away down the lane. Jack said, 'My God, it's Norman Thelwell's worst nightmare. Plimsolls, no riding hats, naming ponies after the Kray twins . . .'

'That's their dad. Fred Boyle. He used to work for them. *He says.* Or it might have been the other lot, the Richardsons. Before he came down here, anyway.'

Bodies in cars in lakes, I thought, and added, hastily, 'It's probably all rubbish.'

Jack raised his eyebrows, then said, 'I'm glad you haven't got too horsey, Alice.'

'What do you mean?'

'You know. Hard of face. Large of rump. Like all those showjumpers.'

'Most of them are men.'

'Yes, well. They've got big arses, too,' said Jack, sidling towards me and putting a hand on my bottom. 'Not you, though.'

Eustace, following his nose, tugged me over to the other side of the lane, leaving Jack behind. 'Fred Boyle suffers from wandering hand trouble, too,' I said, over my shoulder.

'Does he now?' Just as Jack caught up, Eustace, nose down and oblivious, went zigzagging away on an invisible trail. 'Bloody dog. He's doing it on purpose.'

'He doesn't even know we're here.'

'What was all that about last night, then?'

'So you *do* remember. I wasn't sure.'

'I remember that thing carrying on like the Hound of the Baskervilles. You shouldn't let him sleep on your bed. It's not hygienic.'

'Nice, though.'

'Not as nice as me.'

'Says who?'

'We were great together, Alice.' Jack looked hurt. 'Don't you remember?'

'Mmm . . .' I pretended to be racking my brains. 'It's no good. You'll have to remind me.'

'What, here?' Jack caught up and put an arm round me. 'There's nothing I'd like more, but don't you think we'd better wait till we get home? Just in case the Pony Club reappear?'

'The Boyles wouldn't be allowed within a mile of the Pony Club,' I said.

Eustace set off again, jerking me forward and throwing Jack off balance.

'I've never been very keen on horses,' he said. 'Great big hairy things. Funny when you think my dad was a bookie.'

'I didn't know that.'

'No reason why you should. Sid Flowers, his name was. All on course, no shop or anything. I've always enjoyed gambling. That's why I joined the club – it had the best casino. And the sexiest girls, of course.'

'Do you still go?'

Jack shook his head. 'Full of Arabs. Whole of London's full of them. Bloody rag heads.'

Eustace made a lunge for the chicken in the carrier bag and Jack smacked him on the nose. He lay down in the middle of the road and sulked. 'Oh God, now he won't move.'

'Good.' Jack started kissing me. 'It's this hot weather,' he mumbled into my hair, 'When I saw you last night . . .' I disengaged myself, reached up and twitched away his sunglasses, then stepped back to look at him.

His eyes didn't look blank anymore, or bewildered, just amorous. Same old Jack. I can't hurt Lenny now, I thought. I didn't feel frightened, or paranoid, or anything, really, except . . . Well, I wanted him. Simple as that.

'What?' he said.

Something in the back of my mind told me it wasn't a good sort of excitement, but I felt excited all the same.

'What is it, Alice?'

I hesitated, then thought, what the hell, and kissed him back. 'Nothing.'

It was the effect they'd always had on me. Lenny and Jack. Jack and Lenny. I couldn't help it.

'You are lovely. What on earth made you marry that photographer?'

'Can't remember. Oh *yes*. He was offering Green Shield stamps.'

He laughed and ruffled my hair. 'You daft bint.'

'Come on,' I said, 'before we get sunstroke.'

CHAPTER TEN

We lay side by side on the bed in Jack's room, heads on pillows, staring at the ceiling.

'It happens.'

Jack said, 'Not to me, it doesn't.'

'Oh, *love*, it doesn't matter.'

'Of course it bloody matters.'

'It's probably just too hot, that's all.'

'I don't know what's wrong with me.' It was like when he'd come into my bedroom; the same bewildered tone.

I rolled onto my side and laid my head on his chest. 'When I said I couldn't remember, I mean about us, before, I was only teasing. You know that, don't you?'

'You don't have to be kind about it.'

'I'm not. It's true. It was great. It'll come back.'

I felt his chin brush against my hair as he shook his head. 'I'm falling apart, Alice.'

'What's up?'

Jack gave a bark of laughter.

'Sorry. I meant, what's the matter?'

He sighed. 'That film you asked me about, *Teacher's Pet*, I knew perfectly well what it was. I took it because it was the only thing going. It was the only work I was offered last year, that and another one like it.'

'What was the other one?'

'You don't want to know.'

'Yes I do.'

'*About the Size of It.* That was the title. It was about a flower and produce show. All these randy village women are competing to see who can grow the biggest marrow and they've got this young stud who helps them with the gardening. It was the usual tired old rubbish with them chasing him round the carrot patch and shots of his bum going up and down between the raspberry canes. Like I said, you don't want to know.'

'Well, what about now? You said you were doing a play.'

'*Charley's Aunt.*' He reached over, picked up a book from the bedside table, and put it under my nose. 'Help yourself. Starts rehearsing next week, then we go on tour, Windsor, Brighton and a few other places, then it comes into Richmond. Then the West End, if it's any good, which I doubt.'

I rolled over onto my stomach and started flicking through the pages. 'Which one are you?'

'Charley's Aunt. Lord Fancourt Babberley.'

'You'll have to wear a frock.'

'That's about all I'm fit for nowadays.'

'Oh, come on . . .' I turned the book over and read the bit on the back. 'It sounds quite fun.'

Jack was silent for a moment, and then he said, quietly, 'I don't think I can do it.'

I sat up and looked at him. 'What do you mean?'

'The play. Even thinking about it frightens the life out of me. I can't go through with it.'

'Why not? It's a good play, isn't it?'

'It's very good. It's ten times better than most of the shit that comes into the West End. That's one thing Findlater's right about.' Jack sighed. 'He keeps telling me I need a comeback, as if I didn't know, and bending my ear about *new directions*. What he means, of course, is that it's a chance to prove I can do something without Lenny. Cunt's

84

been dead six years and people still think we're joined at the hip. I might as well be dragging a corpse about. God knows I did it often enough when he was alive.'

'Jack, don't.'

'Alice, I'd been carrying him for years.'

'That's not fair.'

'Two years. More. Do you know what he did, Alice, when we were in the States? He'd disappear in the middle of the night and they'd find him staggering around on the free-way, drunk out of his mind. There'd be fucking great Mack trucks coming straight at him and he could barely keep himself upright. This was three, four nights a week.

'I used to go after him. Try and talk him round – Christ knows why I thought he'd listen. I'd be on the road dodging cars like a bullfighter, trying to reach him, shouting my head off, and when I got there he'd push me away. I mean, literally *push me*, he didn't give a fuck about the traffic. He'd got to the point where he didn't care about anything. The only thing he was interested in, apart from drinking everything he could get his hands on, was the script. He'd get obsessed about different lines, keep showing them to people on the set and saying, "Is this funny? Do you think this is funny?" It would be some electrician or make-up girl or something. What were they supposed to say? I could have told him, it isn't funny after you get through with it, it's fucking *tragic*.

'He didn't know what he was doing half the time, couldn't even see the camera. The night before they fired him, I'd managed to track him down after Christ knows how long, and I was standing beside this road watching him weaving about all over the place, and I thought, I can't do this, step into this traffic, I've got a family . . .'

Jack stopped and closed his eyes as if he was trying to stop tears coming, then said, thickly, 'I just shouted at him.

I said, "Go ahead and kill yourself, I couldn't give a fuck." They replaced him with a comic named Bugsy Duffit, an American. Old fashioned. He wasn't W.C. Fields, but he was all right. Don't know what happened to him after. Not much, I shouldn't think.

'They reshot all Lenny's scenes, but they must have known the film was a lost cause because it was never released in America, let alone anywhere else. I was on autopilot. I'd got to the point where I didn't know what I was saying anymore.'

I knew I'd start to cry if I talked about Lenny, so I said, 'But if this is a good play, funny, then why don't you—'

'Jesus, Alice! I. Can't. Have. Another. Failure. Got it?'

'But why should it be a failure?'

'You don't know what it's like. Night after fucking night, going through the motions. I don't think I can, that's all.'

Jack leant forward with his arms on his knees so I couldn't see his face, and said, 'Those kids we met, they didn't have a clue who I was. Five years ago, they'd have recognised me straightaway. This . . .' he flapped a hand at *Charley's Aunt*, 'it's my last chance. I know that.'

'Well, perhaps if you had a go at learning the lines you might feel better about it. I can help. I mean, if that'll make it easier.'

Jack put his arm round me. 'You are sweet.'

It made me realise quite how much I'd missed it. Being in bed with somebody, being cuddled, touched. I suddenly had a picture of myself lying next to Lenny, both of us saying the silliest sounding words that came into our heads, laughing and laughing. And then the other images crowded in before I could stop them: Lenny crashing upstairs in the early hours and falling into bed in a haze of boozy breath and pawing, not listening, assuming I wanted to as much as he did, and then not being able to – how it happened less

86

and less and finally stopped and I missed it, not because I'd liked it but because it was contact, and – *and because I did love him very, very much, and I tried really hard not to blame him, and, thinking back, I probably did everything wrong, but I didn't know what else to do . . . and when he died, I thought it was my fault.* I shut my eyes tight, trying not to cry.

'Alice? Are you all right?'

'What? Sorry, I was miles away.'

'Be a good girl and fetch my cigarettes, would you? They're in the kitchen.'

'OK.' I was so glad to have an excuse to leave the room that I jumped out of bed and ran downstairs without stopping to put anything on. There was no one to see except Eustace, who was conked out in the hall. He opened one eye to check who it was, then shut it again.

A trail of discarded clothes led from the kitchen door to the foot of the stairs. Jack's shoes, his trousers, my flip-flops, my shorts, his shirt, my top. Like a little story about what had happened. Or rather, hadn't happened. There was a bulky brown paper bag on the table, right in a patch of sun: Jack's chicken and bacon. Hoping they hadn't already gone off, I took them over to put in the fridge.

Jack's trousers were in a heap in front of the door so I picked them up and felt in the pockets for his lighter. It wasn't there. Instead, I found an envelope. Opened. I pulled it out – nosy – and glanced at it. It was addressed to me.

CHAPTER ELEVEN

Jack had lied. When I'd asked, he'd told me there hadn't been any post. The handwriting looked vaguely familiar, but I didn't recognise it. I turned it over, but there was nothing on the back. Then I heard a noise on the stairs. Jack was coming down.

I was still holding the letter. There's nowhere to hide anything when you're naked and I couldn't shove it back in Jack's trousers in case he wanted to put them on, so I dropped them and shot across the room to get my shorts. There wasn't time to get dressed so I stuffed the letter into one of the side pockets. I just managed it before Jack came in.

I heard him behind me and jerked round. He'd said something, but I didn't catch it. 'Wh . . . oh, right, the cigarettes. No. I haven't. Found them. I was just putting the meat in the fridge. We left it on the table. In the sun. I didn't want you to get food poisoning.' I made a face.

Jack gave me an odd look. I scooped up my T-shirt and bundled it together with the shorts, muttered something about nipping upstairs to get dressed and ran out of the room before he had a chance to say anything.

'Back in a sec!' I took the stairs three at a time and bolted myself into the upstairs loo.

My hands were trembling as I pulled the torn flaps of the envelope apart. A newspaper cutting fluttered to the floor. I picked it up and saw the headline: **COMIC'S CAR**

IN DEATH PLUNGE RIDDLE. Beside it was a photograph of Lenny. I read the bit underneath – **WAS SUICIDE FUNNYMAN A KILLER?** – and sat down on the wooden loo seat with a bump.

A car containing human remains belonged to dead comedian Lenny Maxted, say police. A record drop in water levels led to the gruesome discovery in a lake on the 100-acre Ivar Park estate in Wiltshire last week. The blue Aston Martin DB6 was spotted by a film crew working at Ivar Park House. Former owner Viscount Deveraux, who became Earl of Ivar on the death of his father in 1966, spent his fortune on drugs and celebrity parties at the stately home. Lenny Maxted and his partner Jack Flowers were frequent guests.

In 1970, Lenny Maxted's body was discovered in a cottage on the Ivar Park estate after a three-day orgy of drugs and booze. He had hanged himself. Aged just 40 at the time of his death, he had shocked viewers of the TV show *Close Up* a few months before by confessing that he was an alcoholic. Tragic Lenny told pals he'd sold the sports car – but it was still registered in his name.

Police are still trying to identify the remains, which are thought to be female. But was her death the result of a drunken, drug-fuelled accident – or was it murder? Did guilt drive Maxted to end his own life so close to the scene of the tragedy?

Police are seeking to interview Maxted's former partner, Jack Flowers, in connection with the discovery.

Ivar Park House, which featured in a series of horror films, has stood empty since Marcus Deveraux's death in 1973. He died of a heroin overdose – aged just 34.

I read the cutting a second time, then a third. Well, I say 'read', my eyes were moving over the words, but I could barely take in what they said. Judging by the type, it came from a tabloid, but there wasn't a name or date. I turned the scrap of paper over and stared stupidly at **NEW STIMULA, THE CONTRACEPTIVE SHEATH THAT LIVES UP TO ITS PROMISE**. Lenny couldn't have killed anyone. He just couldn't.

I turned the cutting over and looked at it again. *Accident. Murder. Thought to be female.* It had to be Kitty. They'd gone to that party together, after I'd walked out on him, I knew that. I'd been to Granddad's funeral the week before. I was only away a few days, but when I came back I'd found some of Kitty's clothes, stuff I recognised, on our bed. We were living in a pretty little house in Chelsea at the time, and Lenny wasn't in so I took Kitty's things onto the balcony and threw them – shoes, underwear, the lot – into the street so they landed all over the trees and cars, then I packed a suitcase and legged it. I didn't leave a note.

James Clarke-Dibley took me to the party. I didn't want to go, but he persuaded me and I spent the whole time dancing with him to show Lenny I didn't care, but all I could think about was him and Kitty together, and I felt so miserable.

I looked at the paper again. *Tragic Lenny told pals he'd sold the sports car.* That's what he'd told me, afterwards, when we'd made up. He'd said he was bored with it. What *pals*, anyway? Who had the journalist talked to? Not me. I could have told him Lenny wouldn't have hurt a fly. He used to get angry sometimes, lash out, but everyone gets angry.

The paper made it sound all connected: the body in the car, the drinking, killing himself – but I'd have *known*. They could have been writing about someone I'd never even met, let alone lived with. I mean, there were different Lennys, I knew that: Lenny the brilliant comedian; Lenny the drunkard, angry and bitter; Lenny the lecher who went out on the town with Jack. For six years I'd been holding onto *my* Lenny, the kind, funny man I'd fallen in love with, and trying not to remember the others.

I suddenly felt as if I might be sick so I knelt down on the floor and flipped up the seat. I stared into the bowl and waited for it to pass. Surely Lenny couldn't have *murdered* anyone? That bit, at least, had to be a mistake, and whoever sent me the cutting . . . My gaze fell on the scrap of newspaper on the floor beside the pedestal. *Police are seeking to interview Maxted's former partner, Jack Flowers.* If Jack was running away from the police, or from journalists, why come here?

And why bring that cookbook? What had he said? That he'd been away working and gone back to fetch things. Working on what? The rehearsals for his play hadn't started yet, he'd said so. And that other film, with the vegetables and things, he'd said that was last year. He'd been angry when I'd asked about the book. He'd tried to stop me reading the newspaper outside the shop. And he'd hidden the letter, hidden it *before* I'd told him about the other newspaper cutting. He must have recognised the writing. Perhaps he'd been getting cuttings in the post, too. If he did have something to do with Kitty's death, that would make more sense. But I didn't, so . . . And he *had* been looking in my room, and he *was* drinking. I shook my head. None of it made sense.

I got off the floor and washed my hands. Just keep calm, I told myself. I looked again at the envelope. It had a London postmark, same as the first one. I looked at the handwritten address and wondered what I'd done with the first envelope. Thrown it away? I couldn't remember.

Whimpering and snuffling noises were coming from outside the door. I opened it cautiously, but it was only Eustace, looking up at me and wagging his tail, one front paw planted firmly on my knickers. He didn't object when I retrieved them, just padded off to the top of the stairs and lowered himself to the floor with a sigh like a tyre deflating. 'Yes, I know, I'm very boring,' I said to him. 'At least let me get some clothes on, and I'll come down.'

Jack was sitting in a deck-chair under a tree in the garden, *Charley's Aunt* on the grass beside him. Eustace rushed ahead of me to sniff his trouser legs.

'He's getting used to you.'

'Yeah. I found my cigarettes.' He pulled a packet of Dunhill and a lighter out of his trouser pocket. 'Want one?'

'No thanks.' I put my hand in the pocket of my shorts and touched the envelope.

'Things to do,' I said, 'I'll leave you in peace.'

It was cool inside the barn, and my three guinea-pigs were happy to see me. The chorus of squeaks and whistles didn't stop until I'd put them outside in their pen. I watched them nibbling their way across the grass for a few minutes and envied them. It must be nice to be a guinea-pig. Uncomplicated. Provided you've got a good home, of course.

Jack hadn't mentioned the envelope, but he must have noticed it had gone. Unless he'd forgotten what he'd done with it, which was quite possible, given his state of mind. But surely somebody would phone me? Any halfway decent journalist would have been onto me already, I thought. To be honest, and I'm not sure why, because the last thing I wanted to do was speak to a journalist, I felt slightly pissed off.

Reading that thing in the paper, you'd think I'd never existed, and I'd certainly been a damn sight more important to Lenny than bloody *Kitty*.

Of course, they might have rung while I was out on Pablo and Jack hadn't answered, or he'd told them it was a wrong number or something. I went back to the barn and concentrated very hard on cleaning out the hutch. I had a quick flick through the top newspaper on the pile before I put it down and sprinkled fresh sawdust over it, but there was no mention of skeletons found in cars. I looked at the date.

Tuesday 10 August. Too early, probably. I couldn't remember the date of the first cutting. A quick poke in the dustbin ought to find it, I thought, teasing out fresh hay.

I don't know if it was something I'd seen in the paper, or just the connection with animals generally, but I suddenly remembered about the camels. You know when something comes back to you and it's so vivid that it stops you in your tracks? Well, this was like that.

Lenny had a few friends he used to drink with: John Forbes who was in their show was one of them, *he* only lasted till 1972, poor man, and there were a few other regulars as well. One evening I came back from the club and it was obvious he'd only just given them their marching orders because the place was a tip. Even the bedroom, the drawers were pulled out and my clothes were all over the floor. Things like that don't usually bother me too much, but that time I really lost it. I mean, I'd been on my feet for eight hours, and the last thing I wanted was to run around doing housework. Anyway, I had a real go at Lenny. I was shouting at him, 'What happened?' and saying the place looked like a slum and why didn't he clear up and all the rest of it, and this crafty look came across his face and he said, very slowly, to see how I'd take it, 'Well, some camels got into the flat . . .'

'Camels?'

'From the zoo, they'd come out on a spree. They broke into the bedroom.'

'Why didn't you stop them?'

'No, they were boisterous, they couldn't be stopped. They took out all your clothes and tried them on, then they went down to the shops and people said, "Oh dear, look at Alice, she's let herself go, she's gone all lumpy."'

'How do you know that's what they said?'

'I followed them. I needed to get to the off-licence.'

93

I'd sighed. 'Why doesn't that surprise me?' But I'd laughed and cleared up the mess.

John Forbes rang me a couple of days later, saying he'd been really worried about Lenny that night because he'd managed to convince himself that I was having an affair with God knows who, and the reason my clothes were strewn all over the place was because he was about to chuck them off the balcony, the way I'd done with Kitty's, and they'd had a real job persuading him not to.

That was when I started to think Jack must have told him. It was just before they went to the States. They were still just about on speaking terms, but when they came back – *forget it*. Don Findlater tried to get them together in a restaurant to sort things out, because Lenny wouldn't even talk to Jack on the phone by that stage.

I had no idea Jack was going to be there. I thought it was meant to be just Lenny and Findlater. That was the reason he'd insisted I come along, I remember because he'd said to me, 'You've got to come, I'm not spending another evening having my hand patted and drowning in waves of homo-sexual despair.'

It was at *Biagi*, and Lenny got halfway across the room, spotted Jack, bellowed, 'I'm not sitting at the same table as that cunt!' and charged out again. Everyone heard him. I just stood there, frozen, in the middle of all these tables, with everyone gawping at me as if I'd been the one who shouted it. I didn't know whether to stay or go but when I saw Jack coming towards me I thought I ought to say hello, at least.

Before either of us could get a word out this guy came bustling up to Jack and started on about how the language was disgusting, and in front of his wife and daughter and all the rest of it. I felt I ought to apologise for Lenny because the man was right, it *was* disgusting, but he totally ignored

94

me. He just kept on at Jack, getting more and more pompous, and then he said, 'Do you know who I am?'

And Jack – actually I suppose this would have been quite funny if the whole thing hadn't been so horrible – but he said, in this terribly polite voice, 'No, I'm frightfully sorry, I haven't the faintest idea who you are. Perhaps one of these charming people . . .' and he started going round the tables, tapping people on the shoulder, saying, 'Excuse me, I wonder if you could help us out. There's a man here who's forgotten who he is. You wouldn't happen to know, would you?'

It went on and on, with this bloke standing there *steaming* and looking as if he was going to land one on Jack at any moment, and all the other diners trying to pretend it wasn't happening.

That was the night Lenny threw his cigarette case at me. He was absolutely convinced I'd had a hand in setting up the meeting. I kept telling him it was all Findlater and that I'd been just as surprised to see Jack as he was, but he wouldn't believe me.

It was one of those silver ones, with sharp edges. I've still got the scar on my cheek. I told the Casualty doctor it was an accident, which it was, in a way, but he didn't believe me. Lenny blamed that on the camels, too. I tried to talk to him about it. I even tried to make a joke of it, pointed out that camels don't have the right sort of feet for chucking cigarette cases about, but Lenny just couldn't face up to anything. Every time he got drunk or upset someone or did something wrong, it was these bloody camels.

Except at the end. At the end, he'd blamed himself.

CHAPTER TWELVE

I went back to the house, tailed by Eustace, and straight upstairs to my bedroom, where I knelt down on the rug, lifted the bedspread and pulled out the shoebox. Lenny's last note to me was right at the bottom, underneath the postcards he'd sent me from the States. He'd always sent the most boring pictures he could find: motorway service stations, or whatever they call them in America, and ones from restaurants called things like McCrud's Diner showing lurid meals on plastic trays.

I unfolded the note. It's written on funny paper, grey and slightly shiny, like the sort they use for wrapping fish and chips. There are a couple of places where Lenny pressed down so hard with the biro that it's made a little tear.

> *My darling Alice,*
>   *Please forgive me for making you unhappy. It is no good any more I know I can't get back there and the despair and all of it is too much. I love you.*
>   *Lenny*
>   *Don't blame the camels. I have tried . . .*

The handwriting's so bad it's barely readable, and it turns into scrawl. There are five or six words at the end that are completely illegible. The police who'd questioned me had kept insisting I'd misread the word camels, and I tried to explain to them what it meant but they wouldn't believe me and we had this ludicrous conversation, round and round in circles. I was so freaked out that I didn't realise until afterwards that they must have decided it was a codeword for heroin or something, and they'd been doing their best to trip me up. If that had been true it would probably have taken them about five seconds, because I was far too out of it to start inventing things, and there was no solicitor or anything. They gave up in the end. I think they must have decided that I was as barmy as Lenny.

Don't blame the camels. Perhaps he'd meant more than I'd thought. The stuff at the end I couldn't read – did it mean he'd tried to blame them, denied causing Kitty's death, or killing her, or *what*?

The despair and all of it . . . No. I'd loved Lenny. I'd loved him so much. He couldn't have murdered anybody. It just wasn't possible. And why Kitty, anyway? If it *was* Kitty. It might be somebody else in Lenny's car. It isn't, said a voice in my head. You know it isn't.

Perhaps they'd had a row and she'd driven off in his car and had an accident, and nobody knew anything about it. An accident. I could accept that. *Except that Lenny'd told me he'd sold the car.* Why would he lie? I knew he'd taken Kitty to the party, he hadn't made a secret of it, so why . . . ? Perhaps he'd been confused, mixed up. I hadn't seen much of him after his grand entrance with Kitty but he wouldn't have been sober.

That must have been why he'd chosen to go back to Ivar. He'd told me he wanted to go somewhere quiet and think things over. About his career, he said. After America, he was adamant he didn't want to carry on with Jack, but the problem was, he'd never worked on his own. Neither of them had. Lenny kept telling me he'd be better off without Jack but the truth was, he was terrified. And lonely. Jack was his closest friend, they'd done everything together, and he missed him even though he was the one driving him away. I kept telling Lenny he'd be fine on his own, but what did I know? He wanted to think he could go solo but I don't think he really believed it, not right inside.

Don Findlater was dead against them separating. He'd invited Lenny out to lunch to talk things over. *Biagi* again – I was amazed they let us in after Lenny'd sworn like that, but Don must have squared it because no one said anything. Lenny'd insisted on dragging me along and when Findlater saw us come through the door, his face! Lenny was in a horrible mood that day and Findlater kept glaring at me like he wanted to stick his fork in my throat. It was *awful*.

They had this ridiculous conversation with Lenny insisting he'd got an idea for a series on his own and he was going to write it himself, and Findlater going on about how he should carry on with Jack, and he'd get them a tour and a TV special and all the rest of it. I was sitting there thinking it was all rubbish, because if Lenny had had an idea for a series, then he hadn't told me about it, and I didn't think the TV people would touch him after he'd gone on the box and told everyone he was an alcoholic.

Then Findlater started giving Lenny the business about being greater than the sum of their parts, and Lenny said, 'If you added up the sum of *your* parts, Don, you'd get the wrong answer, so why don't you just fuck off?' And that was pretty much it, really, except that Findlater started being spiteful and saying that Lenny'd be lucky to get panto in Rhyl if he was on his own. He flounced out after that, leaving us with the bill, and Lenny just sat there ordering more and more vodka. Every time I asked if we could go he shouted at me, so in the end I left him to it. One of the waiters had to bring him home in a taxi.

Lenny said he couldn't face touring again. I tried to tell

him it wouldn't be grotty boarding houses and all the rest of it, but he didn't want to know. And to be honest, the last thing I wanted was for him to go traipsing all over Britain, because even then I was still holding onto my stupid little dream about our life in the countryside.

It was just after that that Lenny asked Marcus Deveraux if he could have the cottage so he could do some writing for this TV thing he'd talked about. To this day I don't know whether he really did have an idea for a series – I didn't find anything that looked like notes when I went through his stuff – or whether he'd just said it to Findlater on the spur of the moment, and then thought he'd better come up with something. Whatever it was, he phoned me two days later from the local pub sounding incredibly drunk, saying he couldn't stand it and begging me to come immediately, so I did.

I thought the cottage was lovely until I got inside and saw what a pigsty it was. Clothes, empty bottles, ashtrays, you name it. You couldn't even *see* the floor. How Lenny'd managed to get it like that in forty-eight hours I don't know. He'd sort of anchored me to the sofa from the moment I arrived, wouldn't even let me unpack my bags. I kept saying I wanted to tidy the place because the mess was driving me mad, but Lenny'd got his arms round me and every time I tried to get up he'd say 'I want to hold you, I don't want you out of my sight,' and pull me back down again.

He was mumbling away in my ear, stuff about America, mostly, how the studio'd tried to turn them into Laurel and Hardy. Most of it didn't make sense, to be honest, and every so often he'd stop and doze off, but as soon as I tried to loosen his grip he'd wake up and start talking again. It was like looking after a giant baby. In the end he agreed we could go to bed. I was exhausted, but every time I dropped off he shook me awake and carried on talking. I wish I could remember what it was about, but most of it was incoherent and I didn't have much of a clue, even at the time. I must have gone to sleep in the end, because when I woke up the next morning the first thing I saw were these wide open eyes staring at me, and then I heard his voice and I remember thinking, my God, he hasn't stopped all night.

When he saw I was awake, he said, 'You left me. You fell asleep.' It sounded accusing, but I thought, he's got to be joking, so I said, 'That's what beds are for, remember?'

'No, I can't fucking remember. I haven't had a decent night's sleep in six months. I asked you to come down here and look after me and all you can do is pass out.'

'Lenny, I was shattered. Why don't I make some tea and we can find your pills and . . .'

He grabbed my hair. 'You're not leaving me!'

'Please don't do that, you're hurting me . . . I'm not leaving you, I just want to make some tea, that's all. Darling, please let go, it'll only take a moment.'

'I'm coming with you.'

Lenny trailed me round the kitchen while I put the kettle on and tried to find things. That's what it was like for the next two days. By the end of it I was like a sleepwalker, trying to tidy up with Lenny always a couple of paces behind me, bumping into furniture and knocking things off the surfaces, spilling his drink and clutching at my clothes, my hair, my legs.

We were both exhausted, and I had no idea what to do. The cottage didn't have a phone, and there was no way that Lenny was going to let me out of his sight for long enough to go and find one. I kept thinking he'd have to go to sleep at some time, but he just *didn't*. I'd say to him, 'Why don't you go and lie down?' and he'd accuse me of wanting him out of the way so I could sneak back to London to be with some boyfriend who only existed inside his head.

The final straw was when he suddenly did a sort of rugby tackle on me from behind, round my waist. We both lost our balance and I hit my head against the bedroom door-frame. I'd never really understood what it meant before, seeing stars, but I did then, I can tell you. He wouldn't let go. I tried to prise his fingers off, but he was squashing me, and all the time he was talking into my ear, things that didn't make sense, 'You can't leave me, you don't know what'll happen. You're bad luck, Alice, ever since I've known you . . . you're no good to me, you make me helpless . . .'

'You drink too much, that's why.'

'You've always wanted Jack more than me.'

'That isn't true, Lenny. Please let me go, I can't breathe.'

'I love you, Alice. You shouldn't be near me, but I love you.'

'I love you too, Lenny, but I can't . . .'

'Liar!'

He let go of me with one hand and I tried to turn round to face him but he was too quick. It's odd what you remember: there was a light switch on the wall in front of me, chest height, and I must have been looking down at it because the next moment it blurred out of shape and my head was jerked up and back as Lenny grabbed a hank of my hair, then I felt his palm smack down on the top of my head and turned my face just in time to stop my nose being smashed into the wall.

I felt an explosion of pain as my ear caught the side of the doorframe. I was sure I was going to vomit. I got my hand up over my mouth and I must have made a gagging noise because his grip loosened. There was a second's space between us and I lunged forward into the bedroom, slammed the door behind me and – to this day I don't know how – managed to lock it.

I barely had time to turn the key before Lenny threw all his weight against the door. Thank God for old houses, because if it had been plywood he'd have been through it in a second. Then I fell onto my hands and knees and retched and retched while he pounded on the door with his fist and shouted, 'What have you done to me?' over and over again.

I must have been in that room nine or ten hours, and I remember every detail: the painted wooden ceiling shaped like an upturned rowing boat, with beams running across like seats – Lenny'd used one of them to loop the belt round, later – the green carpet that had started to pong of old dog the minute I'd hoovered it; the big brass bedstead; the famous Chinese lady on the wall. There was a pretty window, three panes, too narrow for me to get through, so I pulled the curtains, blundered back in the half-light and curled up against one side of the wardrobe, shaking and shaking. My scalp felt as if Lenny'd pulled half my hair out, but my face wasn't hurting much. It wasn't till I was back in London that I saw the bruises, but I suppose they'd had time to develop by then. There was only one thought in my mind: *if I leave this room, he'll kill me.*

'Alice, I'm sorry. Please open the door. I'm not going to hurt you, darling, I promise I won't hurt you.'

'Not till you go away.'

There was a thud and a clank. He must have sat down on the floor, because his voice came from lower down.

'You said you loved me. I know I don't deserve it, I know.'

'I do love you, Lenny.'

'If you loved me you'd open the door.'

'No, Lenny, I can't, I just *can't . . .*'

'Don't cry, darling. No more crying. Come out and talk to me. You're so pretty, such a pretty bunny.'

'No, Lenny.'

He thumped the door. 'For God's sake, stop being so bloody childish. Oh, shit!'

There was a slopping noise. 'Mind the fixtures. Five shillings extra. Used to see notices in the boarding houses, on the doors of the rooms, *wet bed or mattress, five shillings extra*. We asked, did they get many aphib . . . amphi . . . those hopping fuckers . . . but the stupid cow didn't get the joke. You're laughing now, aren't you? At least I made you laugh. Open the door, darling, I won't hurt you.'

'*No*, Lenny.'

He bashed the door again. 'Come *out!*'

'Just leave me alone, Lenny.'

'This was your fault in the first place, all of it.'

'I don't know what you're talking about. Go away, Lenny, *please*.'

'I'll tell you what you are, Alice, you're a conniving bitch, and it was your fault. I'm going to count to three, and if you don't open the door, you're going to regret it. One . . .'

'I'm not talking to you any more, Lenny.'

'Two . . .'

'I'm not . . .'

'Three!'

He started battering the door. It was strong all right, but the whole wall seemed to quiver with each bang. I curled up in a ball on the floor and put my hands over my ears.

'Alice, come out of there!' He went on and on and on – sometimes cajoling me, sometimes shouting. Every so often he'd go off and get another drink, and then carry on . . . I kept telling myself he'd have to go to sleep at some point, that he couldn't keep it up for ever, but it took a long time.

I pulled a blanket off the bed and wrapped it round

myself, and then I must have dozed off for a bit because I woke up feeling horrible, clammy and sweaty. *But,* everything was quiet. Even so, I waited the best part of an hour before I dared to stick my head out of the door. Lenny was slumped beside it with his back against the wall. His feet were stuck out in front, his head was down on his chest, and he looked really out of it.

I'd thought he was in a deep sleep, but he must have been taking something, quite a few things, because I'd got my bag and everything together, and I was just on the point of leaving when I turned round in the doorway for a last look at him, and he was staring straight back at me. I nearly jumped out of my skin, but I needn't have worried. His eyes were open, but they were glazed and empty, and his face had this dull look. No light in it. I don't think he even knew it was me.

That was the last time I saw him alive.

CHAPTER THIRTEEN

I'd meant to phone his doctor the minute I got somewhere safe, but in the event, I didn't. Partly because I wasn't thinking straight, but also, well, I knew Lenny wouldn't thank me if he ended up in a clinic. He'd been before and nearly gone off his head, and it wouldn't have worked because it's a decision you have to make yourself, having the treatment. It's no good if you're doing it because someone else says so. But to be honest, the main thing I was thinking was, just get away from him as fast as possible. I got a milk train back to London. It took for ever, but with every little station we passed, I thought, at least it's a few more miles between us.

Four days later, I got engaged. Without knowing it. I'd answered the phone first thing, half asleep, and it was one of my girlfriends singing that Cliff Richard song, 'Congrat-u-lations and celebrations, when I tell everyone that you're in love with me . . .'

'Penny?'

'Mrs Maxted, I presume?'

'Penny, what's going on?'

'You finally bagged him!'

'*What?*'

'Earth to Alice? Anybody there? You. Bagged. Him. Lenny Maxted. Your fiancé, remember?'

'What are you talking about?'

'I've just seen the paper, darling. You clever old thing. All right for some. I bet you've got a *gor-or-or-or-jus* ring, haven't you?'

That was how I found out. Lenny'd telephoned the papers, or he'd rung Findlater and *he'd* telephoned the papers, or *something*, but anyway, there it was in the news, and I was horrified. A month before, a week even, it would have seemed like a dream come true, but I just stood there and thought, how the hell did I get into this?

Then Jack phoned.

'Lenny didn't tell me.'

'Me neither.'

'What do you mean? You're marrying him, aren't you?'

'He hasn't asked me. One of my friends rang and said she'd seen it in the paper.'

There was a long silence before Jack said, 'What's he playing at?'

'I haven't a clue.'

'Have you seen him?'

'Yes.'

'Is he all right?'

'Not really.'

'I see. Look, I don't know why I'm even bothering to say this, but ask him to get in touch.'

'It's a bit difficult. He hasn't got a phone down there.'

'He can go to a call box, can't he?' Jack sighed. 'Never mind. Anyway, congratulations and all that.'

'Thanks.'

'Well . . . I've given up expecting him to phone. If he doesn't want to talk to me, he doesn't. It's fucking ridiculous. Oh, forget it. Bye, Alice.' He hung up. After that I tried to phone Marcus Deveraux at Ivar, but no one answered.

I sat by the phone for two days waiting for Lenny to call, but all that happened was friends kept ringing up saying, 'Congratulations, when's the wedding? Are you having a big do?' I had no idea what to tell them. There were journalists as well, ringing up and wanting details. The phone was on a little stand with a mirror above it, and I kept hearing myself say how happy I was, and then catching sight of my bruises and thinking, this is *mad*.

On the third day I gave up trying to get hold of Marcus and got the train back to Wiltshire. I'd slapped on half a ton of make-up, a floppy hat and the largest sunglasses I could find, but even that didn't hide the mess. All the way people were staring at me, and by the time I got off the train, I was ready to boil over. I don't think I've ever been so angry in my life as I was then.

I got a taxi from the station but when we got to the cottage all the curtains were drawn – this was lunchtime – and Lenny didn't answer the door. I asked the driver to take me to the nearest pub to look for him. Full of locals, and the minute I walked in – *silence*. It was all men except for this old battleaxe of a barmaid, and when I asked her about Lenny, she said, 'Oh yes, we know him all right,' and looked me up and down as if I was on the game or something. Then one of them called out, 'Don't worry darling, I'll take you home,' and they all started laughing and whistling. I couldn't get out of there fast enough.

The taxi-driver told me there was another pub up the road, so we went there – same story – and then he took me to another one, about a mile away. He must have realised I was upset because when I started to get out he said, 'You'd best stay here, dear. I'll go. What's his name?'

'Lenny Maxted. He's tall, and . . .'

'Oh, off the telly. I thought it must be.'

'Why?'

'I had another one from London the other day, after him.'

'Another woman?'

107

'Man. Day before yesterday, it was. Told me to wait. He was only in there ten minutes before I took him back to the station. I didn't see Mr Maxted open the door, the bloke told me. "Who do you think's in there, then?" He was all like that, very cocky. I said, "I don't know," because it could have been anyone, so I said that, then he said, "It's only Lenny Maxted, what do you think of that?" Very full of himself. I said, "What are you visiting him for, then?" just making conversation, but he said, "Oh no, I can't talk about that." I don't know what he wanted to tell me for in the first place.'

The driver hesitated for a moment and then he said, 'I don't like to say this to you, dear, but I thought it might have something to do with drugs. He had that look to him. Cockney accent. Not that that's . . . Well, I'm not being funny, but he was a bit, you know, bit of a *spiv*, that's the word I'm looking for. Don't hear that much nowadays, do you? Not that you'd remember, of course. I'll just be a minute . . .'

He went into the pub and came out shaking his head. 'Never seen him. Mind you, this one's a bit of a walk from the cottage, especially if you've had a few.'

'Never mind. Thanks. Can you take me back to Ivar, to the big house?'

'Right-oh. Don't look so worried, love – we'll find him.'

But we didn't. Marcus wasn't there, either. This young guy – smart suit, but rough-looking – answered the door and the first thing he said to me, before I could get a word out, was, 'Marcus with you?'

'No, I was hoping—'

'Then where the fuck is he?'

'I've no idea. Do you know where Lenny is?'

'Lenny?'

'Maxted. He's staying at the cottage.'

'Not you as well. I'm not the fucking butler, darling. I've been pissed about from arsehole till Sunday, so why don't you just fuck off?'

He slammed the door.

I got back in the taxi. 'Nothing doing. Can you take me back to the cottage, please?'

'Going to wait for him, are you?'

'I don't know.'

People often say they have a premonition about suicides, but I didn't. I thought I'd find Lenny passed out on the floor and I was angry with him, and that's why I did what I did, because I wanted him to bloody well pull himself together and sort things out with Jack.

The front door of the cottage was locked. I went round the back, but that door was locked as well. The driver came after me.

'Any luck?'

I shook my head. 'I'm sure he's in there. There's a window in the kitchen I can get through, but I'll have to break it.' I think he was about to argue but something in my face must have stopped him because he said, 'Well, love, it's your decision, but they're not going to be very pleased . . .'

I picked up a brick or something, and he said, 'Here, let me. You'll hurt yourself.' I remember he took off his cardigan – it had leather patches on the elbows – and wrapped it carefully round the stone before he did it, and then he bashed out all the bits of jagged glass round the edge so I'd be able to climb in without cutting myself. I paid him, and he said, 'I hope you know what you're doing,' and held the curtain out of the way while I scrambled through – not easy in high-heeled boots – and jumped down into the kitchen.

Even in mid-afternoon it was pretty gloomy because all the curtains were closed. The door to the sitting room was open, but it was dark in there, too. I suddenly felt frightened to go in. 'Are you all right in there, love?'

'Fine. Just trying to find a light switch.'

'I'll be off, then.'

I stepped forward and bumped my hip against something big, with edges – kitchen table – then back and straight into a row of empty bottles that rolled across the lino like skittles. 'Lenny?'

Silence. The sitting room door was open. The darkness was dense, almost menacing, and I couldn't bring myself to walk into the middle of it, in case . . . what? I don't know, really. Perhaps it *was* a premonition, but I was almost too frightened to move. I reached inside and patted the walls beside the door for a light switch, and then I remembered it was by the bedroom door. I'd been nose-to-nose with it. 'Lenny?'

I slid round the door and began inching my way along the walls. I was going slowly, trying to avoid chairs and things, but I must have missed the switch because the next thing I knew, I put out my hand and there was nothing there. The bedroom door was open – it took me by surprise and I lost my balance, and then my face and neck hit something soft, bulky. Cloth, but solid underneath, cold – *body* – and then I looked up and saw his eyes. Gobstoppers, with a dull gleam like something congealed.

That's when I must have started screaming because I remember the taxi-driver – he'd waited to make sure I was all right – pulling me back through the window and taking me down to the police station. I don't remember much of what happened next: being wrapped in a blanket, seeing the blood on my knees, being given sugary tea and a policewoman with nice eyes telling me to keep still while she dabbed my hands with TCP, and then the interview, round and round in circles, not being able to take it in . . .

CHAPTER FOURTEEN

I got to my feet and blew my nose. Lenny had died at Ivar Park. So had Kitty. His car was in the lake. *Don't blame the camels.* Jack knew. More than he was willing to admit, anyway. And he was hiding.

I'd run away from Lenny. I'd been young, but all the same, I'd failed, hadn't I? Perhaps if I'd stayed with him . . . *Jack needed my help.*

Perhaps he'd received that cutting, too, and that was why he'd recognised the handwriting. But if he did want me to help him, why not ask? Why the pretending? Perhaps he couldn't. He's almost like two different people, I thought. There's the old Jack, but then all that business about *Charley's Aunt* and not being able to do it, almost as if he'd given up. Reckless, that was it. He'd come to the end of the road and he didn't *care* what happened. 'I don't understand,' I said to Eustace's rump, which was sticking out from under the valance. 'I don't think I *want* to understand.'

I felt so confused. Why couldn't Lenny just have waited? I thought, angrily. I know that's not how it works, people commit suicide when they're so desperate that waiting isn't an option, but . . . Eustace wriggled out from under the bed and sat down beside me. 'You've got fluff on your ears,' I told him. 'You can't go downstairs like that.'

I knew that if I started to cry I wouldn't be able to stop, so I bent down and hugged Eustace instead. He struggled in my arms, indignant at being squashed, then squirmed away from me and sat, eyes narrowed, scratching his ear with a hind foot.

I pushed the box well under the bed and went back to the barn. By the time we got there I was still shaky, but pretty certain I wasn't going to cry again. Jack was squatting beside the pen, staring at the guinea-pigs.

'Lenny must have told you about that film we were working on in the States.'

'Not really. He never talked about it.'

'Well, you know it was called *White Rabbits*, don't you? One of the jokes was that these two magicians had a couple of rabbits in their apartment, part of the act, but they kept breeding, so each time there was an interior shot there'd be a few more and by the end they were all over the carpet and the furniture and everywhere. Probably the funniest thing about it, but they were all over the set, shitting on every-thing. I nearly sat on one once. Christ, it was a nightmare, the whole thing. Some bright spark at the studio had the idea they were going to bring back slapstick. Never thought to ask if either of us could actually do it. I don't think they'd even seen the act. We knew it was a disaster, right from the beginning.' Jack shook his head.

'You can feed them if you like.'

I fetched the carrot bucket. The guinea-pigs heard the rattle and rushed to the wire netting, squeaking.

'They won't bite, will they?'

'Jack, they're guinea-pigs, not lions.'

He lowered the carrots gingerly into the pen. The noise stopped immediately.

'All these animals, they're substitute children, aren't they, really?'

'Are your children substitute pets?' I shot back.

Jack said nothing. I couldn't see his face. He was still for a moment, then stood up without looking at me and began walking back to the house. Irritated, I almost shouted, 'Don't dish it out if you can't take it!' but there was something about his shoulders that stopped me. It was the same as last night, that weary, defeated slope, and again, it reminded me of Lenny.

All the same, I felt angry. Stupid, Christmas-cracker psychology. There was some truth in it, though. I'd messed things up where people were concerned, so I'd made myself a family of animals, instead. Like my mother.

It hurt. Sod it, I thought. I'm not going after him. He can stew in it. I stayed outside for a couple of hours. There was lots of stuff that needed doing, but I couldn't keep my mind on it. At half-past six I fed the horses, then headed back to the kitchen with a fistful of bay leaves and sprigs of thyme, and a plastic carrier bulging with wadded damp newspaper, sawdust and guinea-pig droppings.

I stopped beside the dustbins, took the lid off one and started rummaging around for the envelope that had held the first newspaper cutting. 'Lost something?' I turned to see Jack leaning against the side of the house. He'd washed and changed and looked much happier.

'No, just tidying up. Here . . .' I handed him the herbs, plonked the smelly carrier on top of the other stuff, squashed it down a bit and clapped the lid on top. Bang go my chances of finding anything now, I thought.

'I'm going to have a bath, OK? Then I'll start cooking. I'll only be about half an hour.'

'Fine.'

I caught a whiff of Jack's breath as I went past. He'd had a drink. Or two.

'Now what?' he said, irritably, catching my eye.

I didn't answer. 'I've told you, Alice,' he shouted after me, 'I'm not like Lenny.'

Sitting in the bath, I thought, Oh yes you are.

Afterwards, I pulled a long dress out of the wardrobe on the landing. Halston. I hadn't worn it for ages. I paused in front of the long mirror in the door. Jack was moving about downstairs. I could hear him talking. Not the words themselves, but a steady rhythm of speech. It sounded as if he was reciting lines. I took my shoes off, then turned and pushed open the door of his room.

CHAPTER FIFTEEN

I walked round to the end of the bed and looked down at Jack's suitcase. The shirt he'd been wearing was crumpled on the floor next to it. I sat down on the end of the bed and nudged it aside with my foot. Underneath were a hairbrush and a brown glass bottle of pills. I didn't recognise the name.

I opened the case. There was an empty chest of drawers in the room, but he hadn't unpacked. Carefully, I lifted one corner of a pile of folded clothes. Another pill bottle. Two more in the side pocket. I didn't recognise any of those names, either, but I'd have bet on uppers, downers or sleepers. Or maybe all three. At least that explained the behaviour, I thought: up one minute, down the next. And with the booze as well . . . It was more than that, though. Something else. Kitty? If it was an accident, why not just go to the police? There was definitely something more. Something worse. But what?

I rummaged on the other side of the case, under Jack's toilet bag, and found a rectangular box. Brown cardboard. Too narrow for shoes. In any case, there was a lumpy drawstring shoe-bag sticking out from under the bed. Drab green. I caught a glimpse of a Cash's name tag sewn into the top. Must have been one of his daughters', for school.

I opened the box. Inside, surrounded by tissue paper, was a grey canister. It looked as if it was made of metal. It had a screw top and a flat base and reminded me of the plastic jars of loose sweets in the village shop, only smaller.

I listened for a moment – Jack's voice sounded louder now, more confident – then closed the lid and slowly eased the box out of the suitcase. It wasn't heavy. There was a white label stuck on one end: ENFIELD CREMATORIUM. It was an urn.

For a split second, I thought, *Lenny?* and almost dropped the box, but I knew it couldn't be, because we'd scattered Lenny's ashes round his parents' stone. I read the rest of the label:

Crem No. 25489
Date: 15/05/76
The late: Susannah Meredith Flowers
Cremated Remains: Removed by Funeral Director

Susannah is Jack's eldest daughter. Or was.

And I'd just asked him if his children were substitute pets. Oh, *great*. I put the box back in its place and went back to my own room.

Why hadn't he *said* anything? I tried to remember the conversation we'd had when he arrived. He'd talked about Rosalie. And Val, although that was only because I'd mentioned her. I hadn't asked about Susannah. To be honest, I hadn't remembered her name until I saw . . . God, how thoughtless. But I'd been so taken aback when he arrived, and what with – *everything*— How old must she have been? Twenty-four? Twenty-five? Illness, car crash, drugs . . . ? She was the reason they'd got married. Lenny'd told me. As soon as Jack had finished his national service, there was Val's dad. 'My daughter's got a bun in the oven. You marry her, or else.' So he had.

I barely knew Val, but I'd always felt rather sorry for her. She had the big house and all the mod cons, but she was stuck out in Hertfordshire and most of Jack's life was in

London, which suited him down to the ground, but she must have felt pretty left out. I'd met his daughters just once. We'd been for a picnic on Hampstead Heath, Lenny and me, Jack and the girls. No Val. I think he was looking after them for the weekend because she was in hospital or something.

He had a Bentley at the time, a huge blue thing that Lenny teased him about, and they'd arrived in that with a massive hamper of food from Harrods or somewhere. They were teenagers. Susannah must have been about sixteen, but they seemed younger. Very quiet, and beautifully dressed in checked gingham, one in blue, the other in pink; little hostesses handing round the food and putting everything away afterwards. That's about all I remember.

They didn't seem to know Jack very well. It was like they weren't familiar with him, if that's the right word. I got the impression he didn't spend much time with them. It was all quite solemn, because Lenny wasn't jokey with them, either.

When I first met Lenny and he'd told me that story about being at Jack and Val's when the neighbour threw the burning dildo over the fence, I'd assumed he'd spent quite a lot of time there, but I don't think he and Val really got on. He never said anything negative about her, but they obviously didn't like each other much. I don't think Jack was too bothered. He never talked about his family. When he'd talked about Rosalie and her art project, it was the most I'd ever heard him say. Keeping the two halves of his life separate, I suppose.

Lenny told me that Jack liked being married because it gave him the perfect excuse not to get serious with anyone. He said Jack's way of looking at it was that the worst had already happened – he'd been caught. So as long as he stayed married and *in the net*, so to speak, it couldn't happen again. If one of his girlfriends wanted more, if she was pregnant or something, then Jack would say she'd have to get rid of the baby because Val wouldn't give him a divorce, so – nothing doing.

I went over to the mirror. Now who's going in for amateur psychology, I thought. He'll tell me if he wants to. In the meantime, *cooking*. Just about the last thing I wanted to do, but . . . I put on some lipstick. And blusher. Mascara, even. I felt stunned. What a terrible thing to happen. Poor Susannah. No wonder Jack was in such a state. Children aren't supposed to die before their parents, it's the wrong way round. Perhaps he felt he couldn't talk to Val about it. Things like that drive people apart, don't they? Poor Jack. No wonder he needed to escape.

I went downstairs. *Charley's Aunt* was on the kitchen table. Eustace was sprawled on his back on the rug, and Jack, drink in hand, was leaning down from the sofa to rub his tummy.

'OK, *coq au vin* coming up.'

The chicken was a big, dead lump in my hands. As soon as I took it out of the fridge, Eustace rolled over and trotted across the kitchen to sit beside me, drooling and shuffling on his rump. His concentration on the meat was total, adoring. Mine wasn't. I shouldn't have agreed to this, I thought. I'm going to mess it up. I struggled with the knife and dug my fingers into the flesh, trying to tear pieces away from the carcass. The thought of somebody actually putting any of it in their mouth and chewing and swallowing made me feel queasy.

Under the thick white skin the meat was pink and glistening, breast, thighs, legs. I had a sudden image of drowned Bunny Kitty in the car, her bosom sitting snugly in the costume like two plump pillows, the pink, healthy cleavage turning first blue-white then putrid green as she sat there dead and strapped behind the wheel. Was she? Behind the wheel? Had I read that, or just imagined she'd been in the driver's seat? Could they even *know* where she'd been sitting?

I glanced down at the chicken's disjointed carcass. Wouldn't the bones separate, anyway? It's only flesh – tissue – that holds us together, and if it had rotted away, wouldn't they just float apart? I pictured the leg bones like a heap of sticks in the footwell, the ribcage lolling on the seat beside the skull . . .

I dropped the knife and rushed to the sink, hands over my mouth.

'*Alice!*'

I turned my head and saw Jack coming towards me. He looked unsteady.

'Are you going to throw up?'

I shook my head. 'It's passed. I'll be all right now.'

He rubbed the back of my neck. I could smell whisky. 'Too much sun, you silly girl. You'd better sit down.'

'Honestly, I'm fine.'

'Come here.' He put a hand behind my head and pulled me towards him, his fingers caught up in my hair. I shook him off and ducked under his arm.

'I want to know if you've learnt your lines, first.'

'For Christ's—' Jack began, then stopped abruptly. 'You can hear me if you like. While you peel the onions. As long as I get a reward.'

'OK.' I took the bowl of vegetables over to the table and sat down, propping the play open against a pair of candlesticks. 'What page?'

'Seventeen.'

'It says here, *he never attempts to act the woman. No effeminate female impersonation business.* I told you it wasn't like real drag.'

'Oh, you're an expert now, are you?' Jack yanked a chair into place opposite me, sat down and banged a bottle of Glenfiddich down on the table. Almost a third of it was already gone. 'I have read the fucking thing, you know.'

'I know you have. Where did you get that?'

Jack's eyes glittered. 'At the back of your corner cupboard. You were hiding it from me, weren't you, Bunny Alice? And all its friends and relations.' He looked triumphant.

The cold, hollow feeling in my stomach was horribly familiar. I willed myself to keep calm.

'Quite honestly, Jack, I'd forgotten what was in there. Didn't you see them last night?'

'No, because last night I got palmed off with Johnnie Fucking Walker.'

'Which you took out of the cupboard yourself, remember? I had nothing to do with it. Listen, if you want this meal before midnight, you'd better let me get on with it.' I picked up an onion and leant forward to look at *Charley's Aunt*.

Jack poured himself what looked like a quadruple measure of whisky and waved the glass at me. 'Go on.'

'Right. Lord Whatsit appears at the window carrying a large Gladstone bag, and he climbs in. Now you.'

Jack started reeling off his lines in a monotone. *'Where the Dickens are you? I wanted to borrow some fizz. I wonder where they keep it . . .'*

I listened, peeled, chopped, and gave the cues. He was surprisingly fluent, given the amount he'd had to drink, and he'd learnt quite a lot of pages.

I got up to fry the chicken, taking *Charley's Aunt* with me. Jack followed. *'How do you do, Sir Francis?* Did you ever come across Danny Watts?'

'That's not in it.'

'I know, but do you remember a bloke called Danny Watts?'

'No. What's that got to do with anything? I've lost my place now. Oh, yes. *How do you do?*'

'*I'm Charley's Aunt from Brazil – where the nuts come from.*'

'Hey! You were looking over my shoulder!'

Jack backed away, looking sheepish.

'Have you been cheating all the time, reading it upside down?'

'I do know *some* of it,' he said, indignantly.

'How much?'

'I don't know, *some*. A few pages.' He finished his whisky. 'Can I do anything?'

'You can get some wine. There's a rack under the stairs with a few odds and ends, but you can't have any. It's all going in the pot.'

'We can't have dinner without something to drink, Alice.'

'Get two bottles, then.'

Jack went out, and came back a few minutes later with two bottles of red, looking pleased. 'These'll be fine.'

He opened them and took one back to the table, where he helped himself to another enormous measure of whisky. When he put the bottle back on the table, it was only half full. He followed my eyes and exploded. 'Don't be so bloody tight! What's the matter with you? Don't you normally offer people a drink when they come to your house? I'll bring my own next time.'

'What in? A Pickford's van?'

'Don't talk to me like that, you provincial bitch!'

The cookery book smacked against the wall above my head and plummeted straight down onto the stove, knocking my frying pan off the gas ring. A jet of blue flame shot up.

'It's on fire!' Before I could get to the oven gloves Jack lurched past me, grabbed the book with his fingertips, 'Aaaaaaaah, shit, *shit*, *SHIT!*' dashed over to the sink, and threw it in. There was a splash and a hissing noise, then silence. We looked at each other and started to laugh.

I had tears coming out of my eyes and Jack wasn't a lot better. We were lurching about in front of the oven, clutching each other, flailing and gasping. Jack was hunched over, squeezing his burnt hand under his armpit. 'Jesus, that hurts.'

'Stick it under the tap,' I said, weakly. 'I need to pee.'

The second I closed the kitchen door behind me, I stopped laughing. It *had* been funny, but I'd been there so many times with Lenny, giggling hysterically but being terrified that he could just *turn*, any minute . . . I thought of a conversation I'd had with one of Lenny's doctors, the last one. He'd told me that if Lenny didn't stop drinking he'd be dead within a year. The doctor was old – well, near retirement – and he said, 'My advice is, leave him. There's nothing you can do. You're young and pretty. Save yourself.'

Save yourself. I hadn't, had I?

I looked into the bathroom mirror. 'What about this time?' I asked. My reflection lowered her eyes and didn't reply.

The man's daughter's just died, I thought. I can't turn him out.

I sighed. 'I owe you, Lenny,' I said, out loud. 'I'll look after Jack. Just help me, that's all. Help me get through this.' As I turned away from the mirror I had a sudden impression of a flick of dark hair, a gleaming shoulder and the upturned corner of a sly smile, as if someone had been standing beside me and I'd glimpsed them for just a second out of the corner of my eye. Kitty. I took a deep breath, then dried my hands and returned to the kitchen.

CHAPTER SIXTEEN

Jack was back at the table, one outstretched hand holding *Charley's Aunt*, the other clasping the glass to his chest. He looked as if he was having trouble focusing. I fished the sodden cookery book out of the sink. 'Bin it,' said Jack. 'Just tear the page out.'

'How's your hand?'

'I'll live.' He let the book topple out of his hand onto the table. 'Let's pack it in, Alice.'

I shrugged. 'Fine. There's no point, anyway, if you're cheating.' I turned away to rescue the frying pan.

Jack sighed. 'People don't want to see me poncing about in a frock, Alice. They want serious stuff. Politics. David Hare, Howard Brenton. People saying "fuck" on stage. Something *daring*, so they can boast to their middle-class friends over the spag bol.'

'I've never even heard of Howard . . . Whatshisname. And anyway, you can't say everyone wants heavy stuff, I mean, look at *No Sex, Please – We're British*.'

'*No Sex, Please – We're British*?' His voice was high, mimicking. 'You haven't got a bloody clue, have you?'

'Not about theatre, no,' I said, as calmly as I could. 'I've hardly ever been.'

Jack glared at me. 'It's all right for you, you don't have to spend the next two months slogging up and down the country saying "I'm Charley's Aunt from Brazil *where the fucking nuts come from.*"' He banged his glass down on the table.

'No,' I agreed, 'but then I'm not an actor.'

'Neither am I, you stupid cow! I'm going to fucking *die* out there. You know, Alice – what we used to do in the theatre. Twice nightly. We could do *anything*, and now look at me. *Good evening, ladies and gentlemen, I'm Jack Flowers and I can't get it up once nightly, never mind twice.*'

He drained his glass. I ran to the whisky bottle but Jack was faster, scooping it off the table and cradling it in his arms, gazing down as if he was holding a baby. 'Come *on*.' I held out my hand for it. Jack raised his head and shook it slowly, triumph in his eyes. 'Oh no you don't, Bunny Alice.' He twisted in his chair, turning his back on me. I took the red wine instead – pointless, but I had to do something – and put it beside me on the worktop.

I finished the recipe in silence, left the whole lot to simmer and went to sit down opposite Jack. The whisky bottle stood on the floor by his chair. It was almost empty. I leant forward and held out my hand. Jack took it.

'Talk to me,' I said. He slumped to one side, his face on his outstretched arm, and looked up at me from under his eyebrows. Woeful, dark-rimmed bloodshot eyes. 'What's going on?'

Jack sighed. 'I haven't got a fucking clue. Never did have.'

'That's not true.'

'Yes it is.' He hesitated, and I thought he was going to tell me about his daughter, but he said, 'Do you remember, Alice, the first time we . . .' He lowered his eyes. 'Lenny'd bought you that fur coat and hit the roof because you wouldn't wear it, and you were crying.'

He was smiling at some memory. 'Lenny's mum. He'd told her what happened, she was in a home by then and a bit past it, and she said to him – *she said*—' Jack snorted, fighting laughter. 'She said, "Well, you should have got her one of those *stimulated* fur coats." '

He fixed his eyes on me again. 'But, what I said about us, the first time, it *was* good, wasn't it?' He sounded almost pleading. 'What you said, upstairs . . .' His thumb rubbed circles on my palm.

'Yes,' I said. 'I meant it.'

'I love you, Alice.'

'You're drunk, Jack.' I pulled my hand away.

'No, I know, but you weren't like the others. You were special. We both wanted . . . loved you.' He sat up and looked at me accusingly. 'He wouldn't share.'

'What do you mean, *he wouldn't share*? Jack, I'm a human being, not a . . . a . . . train set.'

'We always shared,' he said. Petulant, like a child.

'Really? Did you share Val?'

'*Val?*' Jack sat up. 'Val my wife?'

'Yes, *Val your wife*. How many other Vals do you know?'

'Of course not.' He looked disgusted.

'Oh, not Val. Just all the others. That's all right, then. I can't believe I'm sitting here listening to this. It obviously never even crossed your mind that *I* might have an opinion on the subject.'

'Well, you expressed it, didn't you?' He looked triumphant again. 'I didn't force you, did I?'

'No, but . . .' Confused, I looked down at the table. 'That wasn't what I . . .'

'You wanted to, Bunny Alice. Just as much as I did.' He leant back in his chair and tried to click his fingers at me. 'Come here.'

It was his expression that really got to me. Smugness, confidence, arrogance, all of that. And the way he obviously thought I'd still find him irresistible even when he was pissed as a newt. And because what he'd said was right. I *had* wanted to as much as he did, and he knew it.

'Oh, just – *belt up!* I've had enough. Either you can tell me what's going on, or you can just . . . *fuck off*, OK?'

Jack stared at me. 'I don't know why you're getting hysterical all of a sudden.'

'Look,' I said, as calmly as I could manage. 'I'm going to see to the food because if you don't eat something you'll fall off that chair and I'll have to pick you off the floor. I don't know why you're here. I don't even know if *you* know why you're here, or why you went through my room and hid my post, because I know damn well you did, and right now, I couldn't care less. We'll have dinner and you can leave first thing tomorrow and that's it.' I yanked open the nearest drawer and grabbed a handful of knives and forks.

Jack pulled himself to his feet and lurched towards me. The Scotch bottle was swinging from his hand. 'You started all this,' he said. His eyes were poisonous. 'It was your idea in the first place.'

I felt as if someone had punched me in the stomach.

'Lenny told me,' he said. 'It was your idea.'

I saw the glass blur in the air as he raised his arm. I'm not quite sure what happened after that. I know I flung the cutlery at him and put my hands over my face, and then there was a crash and the next thing I saw, through my fingers, was Jack staggering sideways and practically falling on top of Eustace, who shot backwards and collided with the dresser. It rocked back and forth, plates cascading down the front. Neither of us moved until everything was still again.

Jack mumbled something about wanting a cigarette, and I mumbled something back, I've no idea what. It was a real effort not to flinch as he leant past me to put the bottle on the worktop. He misjudged the distance and it shattered at our feet.

'Good job it was nearly empty,' I said. The words came out too bright, stupid.

'Lenny said it was your idea,' Jack insisted, as if I'd disagreed with him. 'He *told* me.'

'What do you mean, my idea? I don't know what the hell you're talking about. For God's sake, just go and sit down and let me clear up this mess.'

As I leant into the cupboard for the brush and pan I heard the clink of a bottle behind me. When I turned round, Jack was back sitting at the table, pouring himself a glass of red wine.

'Do you know how I found out he was dead, Alice? A headline, that's how.'

'But surely, Don Findlater . . .'

'We were on a yacht. He couldn't get hold of me.' Jack shook his head. 'A headline in a fucking newspaper.'

'Try and eat something.' I put a plate of *coq au vin* in front of him and fetched cutlery. He ate and drank sloppily for a few minutes, dark sauce spraying his shirt front and his unbuttoned cuff soaking up spilt wine from the table, then pushed away his plate.

'*You* aren't eating anything.'

'I'm not hungry, Jack.'

'Stop staring at me, then. I'm not a zoo animal.'

'I can move if you like.' I got up and went over to sit on the sofa with Eustace. Jack ate a bit more and then pushed away his plate. 'I'm sorry,' he said. 'I didn't mean to – you know. I was upset, that's all. Got a bit carried away. Anyway, I feel much better now. Let's go for a walk.'

I looked at my watch, eleven fifteen. The pub was shut. If we were out of the house, at least he'd be away from the source of booze for a bit. To be honest – history or no history – I'd got to the point where I didn't much care what happened as long as I could get rid of him in the morning.

Jack picked up the wine bottle and looked at me expectantly. 'Glasses?'

'You've got one.'

'You'll need something to drink out of, won't you?'

'OK.' I took a clean one off the dresser.

Eustace watched me from under his eyebrows as I closed the back door, but made no move to follow. I set off towards the middle of the village, Jack beside me. Given how drunk he was, I thought, he was amazingly steady on his feet.

It was fairly warm out, and bright because it was almost full moon and there weren't any clouds. Apart from the odd rustle, it was silent, and neither of us said anything until the church came into view behind the trees. Jack laughed. 'What's this, confession time? Bit late for that, isn't it?'

'I don't know, Jack. Is it?'

'I didn't . . . Oh, never mind.' He launched into a breathy imitation of a school choir. 'Oh Go-dour-helpinage-espas-tourhope-for-yearsto-come-Mour-shel-ter-fromthe-stor-myblas-TAND-OURET-ER-NAL-HOME!'

I tugged at his sleeve and tried to shush him, worried that he'd wake the people in the cottages, but he stopped of his own accord. 'What's that?' he hissed. 'At the end of the road, *what is it?*' He pointed to where the lane gives onto the big road. A girl was standing there. We could see her in the orange glow from the street lamp on the corner. Young and slim, long hair hanging down her back, hands shoved into the pockets of her denim jacket.

'Is it a ghost?' he whispered.

I was surprised to see real fear in his eyes. 'She's probably waiting to thumb a lift. It's all right.'

'Alice, *you don't know*. It's all much closer than you realise. For Christ's sake, let's get away from her.' Jack turned away from me and started fumbling with the latch on the churchyard gate. 'It's bad luck. An omen. I don't want to look.'

We walked along the path between the headstones. 'Let's have a drink.' There's a wooden bench built round the base of one of the big oak trees by the church porch. We sat down on it. I let him pour me some wine, more in order to empty the bottle than because I wanted it, and facing in slightly different directions made it easier to pretend to drink and then tip it on the ground.

'You're not usually superstitious,' I said.

'I heard a story once. A girl hitch-hiker, young, like that one, she was killed, and now her ghost stands on the spot where she got the lift and if anyone picks her up, they crash. The drivers always die.'

'How was she killed?'

Jack didn't answer.

'Sounds like a bad horror film.'

'How do you know? It could be true.'

'Yes, it could.' I stared very hard at the side of the Selwood family's mausoleum and said, 'She could have ended up in a car at the bottom of a lake, couldn't she?'

Only the trees moved. Jack mumbled something.

'I didn't hear you.'

He leant forward. I thought he was about to be sick, but he just buried his face in his hands. 'My daughter, Susie. She's dead.'

'I'm sorry, Jack.'

'She wouldn't eat anything. Val tried and tried, things she liked . . . She just wouldn't . . . She was in hospital twice, this place where they make them eat. They don't let them out until they've put on weight. We thought it was working, but she had this way of standing on the scales so it looked like more.'

He looked up. 'We didn't know, Alice. And when she came back home and Val told me she'd started to eat, not much, but I thought it was back to normal because girls are always dieting, aren't they? Leaving half their food. All girls. *Women*. You do it. You've done it ever since I've known you.'

I thought of the Bunny Mother's big scales, what you'd use to weigh a sack of spuds, and blowing myself out at costume fittings so the seamstress wouldn't nip it in too tight, because if you put on a couple of pounds you knew about it, even if it was just the time of the month. 'We used pills. You know we did, you used to nick them.'

Jack looked shocked. 'I never took them home. What Susie had wasn't anything to do with that. It's a disease. *Anorexia nervosa*.'

'I think I might have read about it, but . . . I'm very sorry, Jack.'

'Val found a bucket in Susie's wardrobe. She'd been throwing up afterwards, so she never . . . And it got worse and worse.'

'Didn't you notice she wasn't gaining weight?'

'Couldn't tell. She was always wearing jumpers and things. And I was away a lot. Working.'

'But you said the only work—'

'I wasn't living there. Don't look at me like that. Val was all right. The house is paid for. I needed some time on my own.'

'So, when did you move out?'

'Mmm . . . Seventy-two.'

'*Four years* ago?'

'Don't give me the big eyes, Alice. I've had enough grief from Val without you joining in. It's not as if I never went to see them. And I went back afterwards, got rid of the flat. It was what Val wanted. She'd had a rough time. Susie was four stone when she died.' He sighed. 'Val blamed Rosalie at first, said she put ideas into Susie's head, going on about diets. Then she said it was my fault. Said Susie was trying to

131

get my attention. Could have picked up the phone. Knew . . . knew where I was. What Val said . . . feels guilty herself. For Chrissake she's her mother, not me . . . ought to have done something. Rosalie won't even talk to me. Nothing. Why I gave her the money. The art thing . . .'

'Jack?' His head lolled back, touching the tree trunk. I put a hand on his cheek and turned his face towards mine. He looked utterly lost. I wasn't sure if he even knew I was there. I stroked his hair. 'Come on. Time to go home.'

'No!' His hand shot up and grabbed mine. 'Not till she's gone.'

'Who's gone?'

'The girl. *Out there.*'

'Shall I go and look?'

'No. Don't leave me.'

'It'll only take a second.' I couldn't loosen his grip. 'Jack, I can't, *please* . . .'

'No! I don't want you to.'

We sat in silence for a couple of minutes. Jack's head drooped onto my shoulder, but he still didn't let go. 'It's meaning . . . meaningless. What Lenny used to say . . . if there's a . . . you know, up there somewhere . . . must be just like, like . . . a force. Electricity. No reason . . . why things happen. 'S random. *No . . . fucking . . . point.*'

My wrist felt as if it was trapped in a vice. 'Where's the wine, Jack? Why don't you have some more?' The bottle was on the ground, and Jack dropped my hand to reach for it. I stood up. 'Wait there.'

I heard him mumble something that sounded like 'bitch' but he didn't try and stop me. When I came back he was lying on the bench with his knees drawn up, the empty bottle in his fist. 'It's all right, she's gone.'

'In the lane . . . waiting . . .'

'She isn't. I checked. Let's go home, shall we?' I said, trying to pull him upright.

He leered. 'Ooh, you're so strong . . .'

'Lugging bran sacks,' I said, tugging. 'Come *on*.'

'Be gentle with me.'

'Oh, shut up, Jack. Move!'

'You won't respect me in the morning . . .'

'I don't respect you *now*. Get *up*.'

'Wait.' He tottered behind the tree, threw up and came back wiping his mouth with his sleeve. 'Better.'

'Good.'

In the lane, Jack was subdued. I'd been wondering how on earth I was going to get him up the stairs, but when we got back he let me pull off his shoes and trousers and put him to bed on the kitchen sofa. I found a damask tablecloth – the only thing big enough – covered him with it, and was about to go upstairs when he mumbled, 'Stay with me.'

'No.'

'Please, Alice. I don't want to be alone.'

'No. Absolutely not.'

Jack put out his hand. 'I'm not going to hurt you. Just want to tell you something.'

'All right,' I sat down beside him. 'But make it quick, I'm tired.'

'About my dad. When I was a kid. He'd carved a chess set for me out of an old broom handle. Took him weeks. He liked to do things with his hands, keep busy, but sometimes he'd get these black moods where he wouldn't talk to anyone, just sit and stare into the fire for hours.

'You could never tell when it was going to happen, it would just come on him, and it was like Mum and I weren't there any more. You couldn't be in the room with him so we'd go off into the kitchen, but this one night, we had a look round the door and he's chucking things in the fire, one by one, and watching them burn. My mum whispered to me to go and see what he was doing, 'cause he could be a bit unpredictable when he was like that, and it made her nervous in case he decided to take it out on her, you know. I've tiptoed up to his chair, and he's got the whole chess set on his lap, lobbing it into the flames. Pawns first, then the castles and bishops, then the knights, then the kings and queens . . . Didn't stop till he'd burnt the lot. It was the only thing he'd ever made for me, but he never said why he'd done it.' Jack's eyes closed. 'I haven't thought about that for years. Alice, you listening?'

'Yeah.'

'I know I haven't been much good to Val, or the girls, but I never . . . oh, I don't know. Don't know why I told you that, really. Just . . . Stay with me, darling.'

I let go of his hand and stood up. 'I'm sorry, but I'm going to bed. On my own. That's final.'

'OK,' he said, meekly. 'I'm sorry, too. See you in the morning.'

'God knows what *that* was about,' I said to Eustace, who was waiting in the hall. He gave me a baleful look, huffed his way up the stairs and barged past me into the bedroom. I wedged a chair under the door handle before I undressed and pulled the curtains, then climbed into bed. After a second, I climbed out again and took a nightdress out of the chest of drawers. One of those billowy Victorian things with lace and *broderie anglais*. It felt a bit safer, somehow, having it on.

I lay down. After a few minutes, there was a thud as Eustace landed beside me. I felt a heavy paw on my stomach, followed by his chin. His eyes gleamed in the darkness. I stroked his head. 'Am I forgiven, then?' He yawned.

Jack had never been depressed, at least, not so far as I knew, but he'd always had a short fuse. I'd used to think people exaggerated about his temper until I heard him go completely berserk once, in a studio. He'd threatened to ram a microphone up the producer's arse if he didn't sort out some technical hitch, and we were all sure he meant it, too.

When was that? They'd been recording an album – sketches – and Lenny'd been withdrawn, sitting in a corner and not talking to anyone. I'd thought it was normal – hangover – but . . . It was their last one, *Jack and Lenny in Aspic*. 1969, that must have been. Easter? Before that party at Ivar. Jack and Lenny were getting on all right then, not like when they'd come back from the States. I tried to remember when it had started to go wrong. Lenny's drinking was part of it, but he'd been doing that for a while.

Even though I'd worried about what Jack might have said to Lenny about us, I'd never really understood the cause of the row between them, because it couldn't have been that on its own, or Lenny would have said something about it. I'd assumed it was to do with work and getting on each other's nerves – any relationship can go through a bad patch – but I hadn't talked to Lenny about it. He'd never seemed to want to, and anyway, it wasn't as if I could've given him any advice. I mean, it wasn't my world, just like the club wasn't his. *Police are seeking to interview Maxted's former partner, Jack Flowers* . . .

I closed my eyes and Kitty's face rippled in front of me, greenish flesh and tendrils of floating hair like waterweed, watching me with that knowing smile. *Oh God, why is this happening?*

I curled up and stared dully at the edge of the pillow for a while before I realised where I'd heard the name Danny Watts before. It hadn't rung a bell when Jack had asked me if I'd ever come across him, but that was because I hadn't. I'd *seen* his name, though. Pinned up by the fridge. On one of Lenny's lists. *People Who Deserve To Be Shot*. Big, unsteady capital letters on lined paper torn out of a diary. Who was he? Not a relative. Not a friend as far as I knew. A critic? The name didn't sound right, somehow. A critic's name would be . . . well, posher. Actor? Director? Not another comedian – I'd remember.

I sat up. *Danny Watts. DannyWattsDannyWattsDanny-Watts.* Lenny's address book was somewhere. A box in the loft. It wouldn't say who Danny Watts *was*, though. Perhaps he'd sold pills. I could pretend I was after Black Bombers or something, and—

'*GOD ALMIGHTY!*'

A crash so loud it jolted me forward. Eustace flew off the bed as if he'd been kicked and rushed to the door, growling. I hugged my knees to stop myself shaking, shut my eyes tight and began to count to ten – *one, two, thr*— Another crash. A crack and then a tangled noise, as if something had hit the wall and landed on the floor. Splintering. Not glass. Plastic? *The phone oh Jesus not the phone.* Then silence. All I could hear was my heart.

CHAPTER SEVENTEEN

I don't know how long it took before I moved – thinking back, probably only half a minute but it felt like much longer. Then I got out of bed, eased the chair from under the door handle and edged round Eustace, who'd started whining and pawing the wood, frantic to get downstairs. I opened the door a fraction and wriggled through so he couldn't follow. 'Stay here,' I whispered. '*Please.* Just. Stay. I'll be back in a minute.'

The light was on in the kitchen. Jack was underneath it, dark-faced and tottering like a punch-drunk boxer, the receiver in his fist and the rest of the phone trashed at his feet. He'd ripped it out of the wall.

I hesitated for a second, then made a dash for the back door. Saw Jack take a step towards me. Saw blood on his forehead. Twisted past him as he tried to grab me and missed. Wrenched at the latch *not locked thank God* and belted across the yard and down the lane.

Phone box. On the green. Past the church, rectory, cottages, farm gate. Stones. Feet hurting – got to – get to – phone box. I yanked open the door *let it not be vandalised.* OK. Jack – not following – calm – keep calm – money. Oh, God no money. Police, call them free – but police would say – domestic – Jack hadn't hit me – or – I'd asked for it— Phone who? Wait. Breath back first. Think, *think* . . . Returned coins . . . I put my fingers in the slot, and . . . 2p. Thank you, God. I stared at the coin in my hand. The

137

sleeve of my nightdress was torn. I couldn't remember it happening.

Who could I call? Mum's never been on the phone. Jeff? The concrete floor felt like sandpaper on the soles of my feet. I started to shiver. Yes, Jeff. Right. 0-1-4-3-5-4-8-6-1. Come on come on come *on*. Jeff was always a late-night person – if he was in. But then he'd most likely have someone with him so he wouldn't answer anyway. *Please, Jeff, it's me* . . . There was a click and then a voice, and for a moment I thought it was Jeff answering and I started to speak, but it carried on talking and I realised that it must be some sort of machine. I was going to put the phone down, but then I heard it say something about recording a message.

'Jeff, it's Alice. I'm sorry, but—' There was a beeping noise, then more silence. 'Are you still there? Sorry, I know you're not actually *there*. I don't know if you'll hear this, but if you do, it's Alice. I know I said that already, but it's just . . . look, I'm sorry, but I'm in a bit of trouble and I didn't know who to ring. Just . . . it's Jack – Flowers – Lenny's partner, he came down here and he's . . . I think he's going mad. I got some anonymous stuff in the post, newspaper cuttings. I'm in a call box, my phone's broken – well, Jack broke it – so you can't call back, if you wanted to, I mean . . . I don't know what I'm saying, really, just . . . I'm a bit freaked out, and . . . Look, I have to go back now because . . . the animals and everything, but—'

Long beep. I couldn't ring him back – no more money. Now he'll think I finally have gone round the twist. He was always telling me I was mad.

I put the receiver back and slid down to sit on the floor of the box. Now what?

Val. She doesn't even know where Jack is. I should have phoned her before. She must be frantic with worry if she's seen in the paper about the police wanting to talk to . . .

No. I couldn't do that to him. Or to Val, for that matter. Jack was in enough trouble already. And besides, his career – what was left of it, and . . . *And Lenny.* I didn't want him, well, either of them really, to be remembered for something horrible. It was bad enough, after Lenny died. People he'd barely known carrying on like they'd been his best friend for years, and saying things to the papers about booze and drugs and how he'd thrown his talent away. I wanted him to be remembered for making people laugh, because that was what mattered. The rest of it was none of their business. And the woman in the car – Kitty, or whoever she was – well, she was dead, wasn't she? Surely the police would be able to identify her, and then her parents would know and she could be buried, and . . . well, that was the main thing. They didn't need Jack for that.

I stood up and dialled the operator, praying she'd put me through to get the number – which she did – and that Jack and Val weren't ex-directory – which they weren't. 0-7-0-7-8-7-9-2-6-4. Right. Reverse the charges.

I dialled the operator again, repeating Jack and Val's number in my head. 'My name's Rosalie,' I told the woman, praying that Rosalie wasn't at home with Val. 'I'm her daughter.' I hung on, crossing my fingers, while the operator did her stuff, and then—

'Go ahead, caller.'

'Thanks. Hello?'

I remembered Val's voice, soft and slightly lispy. 'Hello? Rosie, for heaven's sa—'

'No . . . No, it's not. It's . . . Look, I'm sorry about that, and I'm sorry to disturb you so late—'

'Who is this?'

'I don't know if you remember, but my name's Alice, Alice Jones. I'm afraid I didn't have any money on me, and it's a bit—'

139

'What makes you think I've got anything to say to you?'

'It's not . . . I mean, I don't think you have, but it's Jack, he's—'

'I don't want to know. You've got a nerve, ringing me up.'

'Please, Val. Jack's in a terrible state, he—'

'Well, *Mrs* Jones, you've made your bed, haven't you? Now you can go and lie in it.'

'I'm not—'

She hung up.

I stepped out of the phone box, tore the trailing lace off my cuff and took it over to the litter-bin. I'd only met Val a few times at dinners and things, but she knew I'd been Lenny's girlfriend. One of them, at any rate. Black curly hair, grey eyes, sharp nose, graceful. She'd reminded me of a drawing of a gypsy in a book I'd had as a kid.

The last time I'd seen her was at Lenny's funeral – six years ago, but when I phoned she'd known who I was immediately, even though I'd used my married name. She hadn't been surprised, either. When I'd mentioned Jack she'd said she didn't want to know, which was odd. Unless she already did. Know he was here, I mean. Not that I'd actually said he was. Or had I? I couldn't remember. But in any case, why would he tell her? He'd always been obsessive about keeping the two sides of his life separate. They say wives are always the last to know, but she had to have some idea. And she obviously did know, or she'd assumed, that I'd slept with him. She must feel the same way about me as I do about Kitty, I thought. I couldn't blame her for that. If I was married to Jack, I'd be suspicious not just of me, but of every woman on the planet. Poor Val. Mind you, if Kitty'd ever said that to me, 'Poor Alice', I'd have called her a hypocrite, and I'd have been right.

I shook my head and looked down at myself. The front of

my nightie was dusty and bedraggled, and the white cotton looked grey in the moonlight. Like a shroud – how they must look when you've been in the earth for a bit. Probably how I looked, too. My feet were turning blue.

I picked my way back to the farm and stopped at the gate. What the hell am I doing? I thought. Save yourself, that's what the doctor had said. He meant from Lenny, but it came to the same thing. Jack could hurt me, really hurt me. He'd said he wouldn't, but in the kitchen, when I'd dashed past him, I'd seen the look on his face, and I *knew*. When he was like that, anyway. Like when he'd come towards me with the Scotch bottle swinging in his fist and his face had looked so *evil*, then the next minute he'd been contrite, saying sorry. He won't even remember any of it in the morning, I thought. Lenny never had, and he could get pretty vicious when he'd been at the brandy. We'd have blazing rows, and then when I reminded him of the things he'd said he'd be horrified and swear he'd make it up to me, and beg me not to leave.

Save yourself. I looked over at my car. The keys were in my bag, in the kitchen. So was Jack. I heard a snort from the field. Pablo. And Eustace was waiting for me in the bed-room. I couldn't leave them. Hobson's choice. Wasn't that something to do with horses? *This is my home. There's nowhere else to go.*

The place was in darkness. Can't risk waking him up, I thought, and walked round the side of the house. The sitting room window was slightly open. I hitched up my nightdress and climbed through, padded across the room, inched the door open and slithered into the hall, where I stood, straining my ears for any sound from the kitchen. Silence. I tiptoed up the stairs. If you tread right on the edges they don't creak. I shut the door, wedged the chair back under the handle and climbed into bed, dirt and all, trying not to think about what might happen if Jack decided to join me. At least there's Eustace, I thought, as the dog clambered on top of me and buffeted my face with his nose.

After a couple of minutes, he curled up and began to snore. Val's words came back to me: *You've made your bed, now you can go and lie in it.* Well I was, wasn't I? Lying in it, I mean. I suddenly remembered what Jack had said – *It was all your idea in the first place.* He couldn't have meant us sleeping together, because that wasn't my idea. I mean, yes, I'd done it, but he'd come on to me, not the other way round.

You started all this. Lenny'd said it, too. At the cottage at Ivar. He'd shouted it through the door. *This was your fault in the first place, all of it.* Was that what he'd meant? Had Jack told him I'd seduced him? No, it had to be something else. But what? I turned onto my back and stared at the ceiling. What had I started? What had I done?

CHAPTER EIGHTEEN

I was exhausted, but I couldn't sleep, not with Jack downstairs in the kitchen. It was weird, though, because it was Lenny I kept thinking about, not him. I think it was because – well, that last time I *did* run away and perhaps if I'd had the guts to stay put, things might have turned out different. But I was frightened. I mean, really *scared*. I honestly did think Lenny was going to kill me.

Sometimes I look back – I mean, even still – and think, how could all that have happened? It's easy to sit here now and say, if only I'd done this or that, but at the time, the way he just . . . *deteriorated*. I should have been paying more attention, but I was so excited about buying the house, and I thought it was all going to happen. We'd redecorate and sort out the garden, get a dog and maybe even start a family. Honestly, the way I imagined it was like one of those corny bread adverts, not real life. I was living in a dream, really. In my mind, everything was going to be wonderful and the problems would just disappear into thin air.

I'd felt so optimistic, it stopped me seeing how bad things really were. Lenny would go on for hours about the Americans and what bastards they were for sacking him, and how it wasn't the right film and blame Jack for getting them involved in the first place. I didn't know what to say to that because Lenny'd been just as excited about it before they went, saying it was their big chance, you know, to be international, not just British. But I thought I could smooth it over, that if I did all the stuff with the house and everything I could make things go right, and I didn't realise – well of course, I didn't *realise*, I didn't know the half of it . . .

And there were other things, too: Lenny was drinking more and more, he'd seen all these doctors and taken the pills, but none of it worked and he always ended up back at square one. I used to say to him, 'Don't you want to stop?' He'd say he did and I'd believe him – I couldn't *not* believe him – but I don't think it was true. It was almost as if he accepted he was on a sort of collision course with the booze, and nothing, certainly nothing that I was offering, could alter it. Fatalism. That's the word.

I thought it was my fault because I wasn't . . . *enough* for him to stop drinking. But if he felt guilty about what happened at that party, if the dead girl was Kitty . . . *Don't blame the camels.* Saying it was his fault. There'd been something about that in the paper. I got out of bed and felt on the floor for my shorts. The cutting was still in the pocket. I switched on the lamp. *Did guilt drive Maxted to end his own life so close to the scene of the tragedy?*

The world seemed to have stopped. Getting back into bed was like moving through wet cement. *Tragic Lenny told pals he'd sold the sports car . . . Police are seeking to interview Maxted's former partner . . .*

I lay down on my back. My body felt dense and heavy enough to fall right through the bed. I've had enough, I thought. Please, God, just let me go to sleep. I don't want to think about this.

I must have dropped off after that, because about an hour later something woke me up. The house creaks sometimes, but I'm used to that. This was more like a movement, but not close. Couldn't tell if it was upstairs or downstairs.

Like scratching, scraping. Big mice with big feet, I thought, stupidly. Something bumping along the ground.

Jack? I sat up in bed, listening. Nothing more. The house was quiet again, and Eustace was still dead to the world. Maybe it *was* mice. Jack must be flat out by now. He hadn't woken when I'd climbed in through the window, and with the amount he'd put away . . . My mind drifted off to the taxi-driver at Ivar talking about the cocky bloke he'd driven to the cottage. Drugs, that's what he'd said. Was that Danny Watts? He'd definitely been on Lenny's list, and Jack had asked me if I remembered him.

I knew I wasn't going to get back to sleep. Lenny's address book was somewhere in the attic. Might as well go and have a look. Anything would be better than lying here worrying.

I got up and took the chair away from the door. Eustace sat up and looked at me with his head on one side, as if he was asking a question. 'You stay here,' I said, 'I won't be long.'

I took a torch and started tiptoeing across the landing. To get to the attic I had to go down the main stairs, across the hall, through the dining room and up the other stair-case, which is a lot of creaky boards to cross without making a noise. I felt like a burglar in my own house, but I didn't know what Jack was up to. If he had gone back to sleep, I didn't want to wake him.

The attic's full of trunks and cartons, Lenny's stuff, mostly, a lot of lumps and bumps under dust-sheets. The single light bulb is weak and dusty and doesn't shine into the corners, so it's eerie enough even without the stand hung with Lenny's hats and coats that looks like a huddle of empty men. I kept glancing over my shoulder at it as I went through the boxes. I thought I knew which one the address book was in, but of course it wasn't and I ended up going through about six before I found it.

By the time I'd finished, my fingertips were grey with dust, my feet were filthy and the front of my nightdress looked like a floorcloth. I picked up the address book and took a last look round.

Granddad's armchair stood alone in the far corner. Blue brocade, with the piping falling off and the seat sagging and the stuffing falling out of the bottom. Unusable, but I'd kept it because it was his favourite. The dust-sheet must have slipped, or . . . *wait a minute.* There'd been other things there, more boxes, and . . . where had they gone? I didn't just make it up, I thought. Jack *was* looking for something. He'd been up here, too.

I couldn't remember seeing the strip of light under the sitting room door on my way down the main staircase, but it was definitely there when I crossed the hall to go back up it. Heart thumping, I stood in the dark, wondering what to do. I couldn't hear anything. I put my foot on the first step – an inch too far over – and it creaked.

'Alice?'

I froze.

'I know you're out there.'

I didn't reply.

'Come and talk to me, darling. I'm lonely.'

'I just wanted a glass of water,' I gabbled.

'No you didn't. Come *on.*'

'I'm tired, Jack. We can talk in the morning.'

'There's something I want you to see.'

'I've seen it before,' I said, hoping he'd laugh.

He didn't. 'Just get yourself in here.'

'Can't it wait?'

'No. Don't make me come and get you.'

I tiptoed across to the linen chest, opened the lid just a fraction so I could slip Lenny's address book inside without disturbing the flowers on the top, and shut it as gently as I could, holding my breath. Then I went over to the sitting room, walking normally, and opened the door.

The first thing I saw, on the wall opposite, was a rectangle of moving black and white shapes. The film was grainy and scratched and the picture was broken up by two of the vertical timber beams. It was hard to tell what was going on at first, but I could see a crawling tangle of pale shapes. How many? More than two. Male and female. Spots and glitches winked as thighs, calves, buttocks and stomachs squirmed against each other.

There was no sound except the whirr of the projector. The room was dim and hazy with smoke. Jack's armchair stood a few feet away from me, and I could see the top of his head and one hand dangling down at the side, holding a cigarette. I craned my neck round the door and saw the projector. Lenny's. From the attic. Sitting on top of the sideboard.

'Come in and sit down.' Jack sounded completely sober.

'You want me to watch a *porn film*?'

'Why not? It's yours.'

'No it isn't. I don't watch this sort of rubbish.'

Jack twisted round to look at me. 'I know you don't, darling, but this is important.'

'*Important*? Jack, it's half-past three in the morning and this is a blue film and not a very good one, either, by the look of it.'

'Please, Alice.'

I suppose I might as well humour him, I thought, because he's bloody well going in the morning.

I squeezed behind his chair and went over to sit on the rug in front of the fireplace, as far away from him as possible. He hadn't managed, or bothered, to get his trousers back on, and the damask tablecloth I'd used to cover him was wrapped round his waist like a sarong.

I could sense that he was watching me, so I tried to look in the direction of the film without actually seeing it, which was easy enough because it was just a big, soft-edged jigsaw of shunting flesh and you couldn't really work out what was whose. 'How anyone finds this stuff a turn-on is beyond me,' I said. 'I'd rather watch pai—' I stopped, because there was a jerk, and the camera, which had obviously just been plonked at the foot of the bed, suddenly focused on the back, and bum, of a man humping away at a woman who was on all fours in front of him, his hands clamped round her hips for more purchase. For some reason it made me think of the pushme-pullyou in *Doctor Dolittle* and I started to giggle, but then the man bent right over and there, kneeling up, the woman's face in his crotch and a hand on each side of her nodding head, was— 'Oh, *God!*' I scrambled to my feet. 'Jack, stop it! Turn it off! Please, just turn it off!'

He didn't move. He looked hypnotized, staring at the film – at himself.

'It's Lenny, isn't it? The other man . . . it's Lenny.'

'Yes.'

'You *bastard*. I don't know why you're trying to humiliate me, but you've succeeded. I hope you're happy.' I made for the door.

He jumped up to stop me. I tried to hit him, scratch him, anything, but he grabbed my wrists.

'Let me go,' I spat at him. 'I hate you.'

'Alice, wait. I know how it looks, but it's not—'

'No, you don't, you don't know anything.' We struggled in silence while the projector carried on whirring. In desperation, I put my head down and tried to bite his knuckles.

'Pack it in! All right, I don't know anything, but you've got to stay and watch the end.'

'Why? So you can really rub my nose in it? Listen, I know Lenny wasn't exactly faithful to me, but you don't have—'

'Alice, stop it. Calm down.'

'Why should I?'

'Because if you don't, I'm going to slap you.'

'Oh, please, be my guest! You nearly knocked my head off with that bottle last night, once more won't make any difference. Let – me – go!' I shook my arms from side to side, trying to break free of him, but he hung on.

'Alice, I'm warning you, if you don't behave yourself, I *will* slap you, and it'll hurt.'

I glared at him.

'Come on, listen to me for a minute. I'm sorry I upset you. I didn't mean to. It was crass, I know that, and I've said I'm sorry, but you've got to see to the end. After that you can hit me or call me a cunt or do anything you like, OK?'

'OK.'

'Again. Look at me this time.'

'I said *OK*, OK?'

'If I let go of you, will you stay put?'

'Yes.'

'Promise?'

'*Yes.*'

'Fair enough.'

He dropped my wrists and readjusted the tablecloth round his waist. 'Now, *watch.*'

More close-ups. Splotches and starbursts flashed over a wriggling knot of legs, hips, torsos – fingers with coarse black hair – Jack's – flattened against a breast, a wrist with a watch – Lenny's – came to rest on the woman's stomach, long fingers with painted nails stroked his arm.

'Who is she, Jack?'

I needn't have asked. A second later, the bodies dis-engaged themselves and the screen was suddenly filled by

149

the back of the woman's neck, dark hair draped across the nape, and then her hand came up and swept it backwards in a glossy slither as she turned her head – and there she was. I should have guessed. Bunny Kitty, looking straight into the camera with smudged lips and a glistening, triumphant smile.

CHAPTER NINETEEN

Then she was gone. The film ran out and the loose end slapped and flapped against the projector as the take-up spool carried on turning. Jack walked over, turned it off, and looked back at me. There was silence except for the noise of the fan.

'Can I go now?'

'Alice?' He started towards me. 'Come here.' He opened his arms as if he wanted to hug me, and the tablecloth slipped from his waist and fell in a sort of moat round his ankles.

I stared at him for a moment, then said, 'I'm going to have a bath.'

'Alice, wait—'

'Leave me alone. And put some trousers on. You look ridiculous.'

He didn't follow me. I ran a bath and soaped myself mechanically and washed my hair – half a dozen times? I don't remember. The water was grey and disgusting, but I didn't want to get out. That look on Kitty's face. I could almost see it in front of me, a disembodied head hovering above the taps, smirking. Like that cat in *Alice in Wonderland*, disappearing and leaving its grin behind. So pleased with herself.

I'd never been naïve about Lenny. I mean, he was handsome and funny and there were lots of opportunities. I didn't expect him to be a saint. I always forgave him, though. In a weird way I quite liked that, making up, because he was always really sweet and there'd be flowers and presents and I used to think, if he ever *stops* telling me, that'll be the time to worry.

Seems like another life. Sometimes I look back and think, was that really me? But if you love somebody, it makes you act differently. I mean, I put up with so much from Lenny, but with my husband, Jeff, when I found out he'd been unfaithful to me almost from the word go, I just shrugged my shoulders, *oh well, that's it, then*. I knew it wasn't worth fighting for.

I had been furious about Kitty, though. Coming back to the flat after Granddad's funeral and finding her things all over the place, that was *horrible*, and the thought that they'd been in our bed made me feel really sick. We were apart for, what? two months? after that, and I made him buy a new one, sheets and everything, before I agreed to move back in. That was after he'd been on that TV show with Jack. He rang me up and asked me if I'd seen it and would I come out to dinner. He was on his best behaviour all evening. Even pretended to be drinking tomato juice, although I knew it wasn't, and things went on from there, really. But that was hard to forgive. Also because I was upset about Granddad, and Lenny didn't tell me, I just found these knickers under the pillow and make-up and stuff in the bathroom. And because it was *Kitty*. When I saw her afterwards, in the changing room at the club, she'd had the same smile on her face, so self-satisfied. I couldn't help imagining them together, and it made my skin crawl. I didn't know if he was still seeing her. He'd denied it afterwards, and I'd believed him, but *now* . . . He could have been lying.

When did they make that film? And *where*? You couldn't see much of the room. I thought back. Worn lino on the floor, grubby-looking bed, and I'd caught a glimpse of a buttoned headboard and a few streamers of plastic – one end of a fly strip – in the doorway. Probably rented by the hour. I imagined Jack and Lenny striking a deal with a seedy little man, with Kitty, all curves and legs in her minidress, hovering behind them as they handed over notes, Lenny staring at her bum as she swayed ahead of him up a dingy Soho staircase, Jack fondling her on the landing, impatient, while the seedy man unlocked the door, pushing her against the wall . . . Scuffed paper, chipped paint, his hand up her skirt, and then . . .

Thinking about it was unbearable, almost painful. Actual physical pain. Instead I reached for the pumice stone and rubbed my shins viciously, 'God, I hope – it's you, Kitty – in that car – I really, really hope – it's you – I really, really – do—' until my legs were raw and it hurt too much to carry on. Then I threw the pumice stone across the bathroom and burst into tears. The memory of it, how unhappy I'd been, how devastated, going to work at the club after I'd left Lenny, seeing that smug look on Kitty's face when we stood side by side in front of the changing-room mirror, our eyes meeting and sliding away again as we put on our make-up and pinned our ears in place. That *look*, even with a hairgrip between her teeth, Kitty the cat who got the cream . . . I wasn't eating, I wasn't sleeping, and having to see *her* every time I went in to work. 'I hope it *was* you, Kitty, you bloody deserved it.'

I wiped my eyes with the flannel. Of course Lenny was going to swear he hadn't seen her again in the time we were apart, except when he'd taken her to the party. He'd have said anything, because he wanted me back, didn't he? He'd been all over me for a while, and of course I was over the moon about it. Not that I'd let him know it. I'd thought I was being so clever, Miss Sophisticated, playing it cool –

being in control, for once. Those first few weeks when we were back together, I even thought – *un*believable – that I could get him to stop drinking. God, I was stupid.

But one thing's for sure, that film – it couldn't have been made after we'd got back together, because Kitty'd gone by then, hadn't she? Even though we never actually worked together at the club – she was usually in one of the gift shops – I was going to change my shift so I didn't have to see her, but then I thought, why the hell should I rearrange my life because of *you*? To be honest, I probably *would* have changed it, because there was a real atmosphere, but it was only about two weeks, and then one day she didn't show up and that was that.

I used to literally *pray* that she wouldn't come back. I wasn't the only one, either. There were a lot of people she hadn't got on with, so they weren't going to lose any sleep over it. But it was great for me, because it meant I could enjoy my job again. I mean, OK, so I've done a few things I'm not particularly proud of, but not on film, for God's sake. Well, not so far as I know. And she knew, all right. It was probably her idea in the first place. Pretty stupid, because what's the point of filming it, anyway? I mean, it's not exactly one to show the grandchildren, is it?

At least Lenny hadn't kissed her, not in the bit I'd seen. That really would have been unbearable. I wrapped my arms round my legs and put my head down on my knees. This cannot be real, I told myself, it's too horrible.

Jack must have a copy of that film, I thought. He'd obviously seen it before or he wouldn't have known what it was. It might have been his idea, and he could have persuaded Lenny to set up his cine-camera. Perhaps it wasn't the first time they'd done it.

I felt really sick. Why had Jack shown it to me? What was he thinking – that it would *turn me on*? The idea was so vile it made my stomach turn over. I couldn't stand the thought of being in the same house as him, never mind the same room.

Then I remembered. The day before, his eyes looking down into mine, and then me slithering down the bed, and him saying, 'No, Alice, it's no good, I can't.' On the film, him pushing Kitty's head down and grinning . . . how I'd touched him, *consoled* him, even . . . that busy jumble of bodies . . . Oh, God. Stop it, *stop thinking*. I never wanted to see Jack again, ever. It was as if he'd crossed a line, somehow. That is *it*, I thought. The last straw. *And here I am, all over again.* So tired I barely exist. Not that there was much there in the first place, if you took away the ears and the tail.

Love, I thought. There was always love.

And look where it's got me. I felt as if I'd been awake for a hundred years. It was almost light. Six-fifteen. I hauled myself out of the bath, wrapped myself in a towel and went upstairs to pull on some clothes. The house was still quiet when I came back down. The kitchen door was shut, and the dining room, but the sitting room door was slightly ajar. I had no idea which one, if any, Jack might be behind. I hadn't heard him go upstairs, but if I'd been running the bath, I'd have missed it anyway. I tiptoed back and forth across the carpet, stopping to listen. No sound from any of them. In the end, I stopped outside the sitting room door, took a deep breath, and gave it a little push with my fingertips.

Jack wasn't there. I turned on the light – the curtains were still drawn – and saw the projector, still on the sideboard. The film wasn't in it, but there was a round, flat tin lying on the carpet, with *Eastman Kodak* embossed on the lid and a strip of what looked like Elastoplast stuck across it. When I picked it up, I saw a date, written in felt-tip: *19/8/69*. 19 August, 1969. Lenny'd sworn he hadn't seen Kitty while we were apart, and we'd been apart then. Must have been just before that party. He *had* lied to me. No wonder Kitty'd looked so pleased with herself. What a *bitch*.

I prised it open. The black tin spool of film was inside. I couldn't bring myself to touch it. I'd tried so hard to hang on to all the good memories, the great times we'd had together, but right at that moment I couldn't think of a single one. It was as if I was seeing it all from a different angle and everything seemed dirty and sordid and cheap, and I'd meant nothing to him and . . . 'Why did you do it, Lenny?'

I shut the door and went over to kneel in front of the fireplace. There wasn't much kindling or paper in the basket, but it would do. I was just leaning over to grab the matches off the coffee table when I heard the sound of the latch being raised.

'Go away!' I bellowed. 'I mean it, Jack ! Get away from me!'

There was a pause, and then the latch clicked back into place. Shaking, I lit match after match and tossed them into the fire, then I up-ended the tin and the spool of film fell into the middle of the blaze. I sat and watched it flare up and crinkle down to nothing. It didn't take long.

As I got up, I caught sight of my face in the mirror over the mantelpiece. It didn't look like me. Lopsided. One eyebrow seemed much higher than the other. The skin under my eyes looked raw and stretched. I hadn't remembered to wash my face and last night's make-up was collected like seams of coal in lines I hadn't known were there. I lifted the hem of my T-shirt and scrubbed at them. Better, but the hard stare was frightening. I tried a smile. That was worse, if anything.

'Scotch,' I said to the woman in the mirror. 'Scotch, Canadian, Bourbon, Rye . . .' She started to cry. 'Irish, Gin, Vodka, Rum, Brandy . . .' I turned away and carried on, stumbling over the words, 'Liqueurs, Mixed, Blended, Creamed, Beer, Wine, One for the money . . .' repeating the call-in sequence over and over again while I went outside and fed the hens and fetched hay for the horses and checked the water trough and did all the other things I usually do. I was probably only muttering, but the words were loud and strong in my mind, almost as if I was building a wall to keep the image of the three of them together out of my head.

By quarter-past eight I'd run out of things to do. Eustace bustled ahead of me into the kitchen, wagging his tail and hoping for breakfast. *Charley's Aunt* lay on the table and the remains of the phone were strewn across the floor, but no Jack. He'd been there, though. The door to the hall was open.

As I bent to pick up the shattered phone, I caught sight of the corner of the linen chest and remembered Lenny's address book. I tipped the pieces into the bin, nipped across the hall, retrieved it, and fled back into the kitchen. Watts, Watts, Watts . . . nothing under *W*. D for Danny? *Diane* . . . *Debby* . . . *Denise* . . . None of them had surnames, apparently. I flicked over the page. *Daisy* . . . *Donna* . . . Bingo! *Danny W*. An address in Ledbury Road, Notting Hill Gate, London W11.

A sharp crack somewhere above my head made me jump. Floorboards. I shoved the address book in one of the dresser drawers and started deboning the remains of the *coq au vin* for Eustace's breakfast. Another crack, further over. I held my breath and shut my eyes tight. *Don't. Come. Down. Just. Don't. Come. Down.*

Stop the world, I thought, I want to get off. I'll leave a

note on the kitchen table telling him to get lost and then I'll go back to bed.

I was searching for a pencil when I heard the postman. Eustace galloped out to bark at him, and Ted gave him a biscuit, which he spat out.

'Charming! There you go, just the one today.' He handed me an envelope.

'Thanks. Ted . . .' I stopped, not sure what I'd been going to say.

He looked at me expectantly. 'Did you want to ask me something?'

'No, just . . . No, it's OK. Nothing, really.'

'Wait . . . You all right?'

'Yeah, just tired.' I smiled at him.

'You sure?'

'I'm fine, honestly.'

'OK. See you, then.'

'Yeah. Bye.'

I stood in the doorway and watched him go. I wondered about running after him, but couldn't think what to say. I mean, I hardly know the man, beyond saying good morning, and it wouldn't be fair to involve him. It was just . . . wanting to talk to somebody, but then I thought, *where would I start?* It's all so freaky, he'd probably think I was . . . I don't know. Mad or something. Making it up. Hitting on him, even, and I could definitely do without that. Anyway, he had his job to do. I can always go into the village later, I thought. Have to, anyway, to sort out the phone. There's probably a waiting list. *Oh, God.* Can't deal with that now. Sleep. Sleep, sleep, sleep.

I was about to take the letter upstairs when I remembered that Jack was up there, so I went back to the sitting room instead. The fire had burnt itself out, and all that remained was the blackened spool in the middle of a pile of ash. I glanced at the writing – familiar – then hooked a finger under the flap and ripped open the envelope. Newspaper. Big black headline. BODY FOUND IN PORNO FLAT. Half a page with a grainy photograph of a tall terraced house.

BODY FOUND IN PORNO FLAT . . . Yesterday morning. Crumpled newsprint in the bin outside the village shop. Of course. The paper Jack hadn't wanted me to see. I'd gone in to pay for it, and when I'd come out, that headline hadn't been on top any more.

'What's that?'

CHAPTER TWENTY

I nearly jumped out of my skin. Jack was standing in the doorway. He'd changed his clothes. A mauve shirt, buttoned in the wrong holes, hung, untucked, below a crumpled linen suit.

'Just a bill.' I stuffed the envelope and cutting into the pocket of my jeans. 'I'd like you to go now,' I said. 'You can walk into the village and call a taxi from there.'

'You've burnt the film, haven't you?' He nodded towards the fireplace.

'Yes. Jack, listen to me. I want you to go.'

'That's what Val did.'

'*What?* You showed it to *Val*? You actually showed *that* to your wife? How could you?'

He opened his mouth, looked at me, and then shut it again.

'How low can you go, Jack? Are you going to tell me she *enjoyed* it? I can't believe this. You're not even ashamed, are you? You bastard. You complete and utter *bastard*! You're selfish and vile and you don't give a toss about anyone else, not even your *wife*, just so long as you can get your kicks. I'm surprised she didn't kill you. I'd have bloody murdered you. How could you *do that*? You're just . . . you're . . . I can't even put it into words. You disgust me. Just get out of my house and out of my life and stay out, OK?'

'It was Lenny as well, remember?'

'Don't try and hide behind Lenny, Jack. At least he had

the decency not to make me watch that – that – *filth*! At least he was ashamed enough to—'

'So am I.'

'You've got a funny way of showing it.'

'You don't understand, Alice.'

'You can say that again! I don't understand how you can have a threesome with that whore and make a film of it and take it home and— What was it, Jack, a special treat for Her Indoors? Saturday night at the flicks? Did you buy her a box of chocolates as well? Too right I don't understand. But then I'm probably just too stupid to get it, because that beats me, all right, how you can—'

I stopped. The words I'd been about to say hung in the air between us.

'How I can live with myself?' Jack asked. He held out his handkerchief. I snatched it and blew my nose.

'Alice, you've got to believe me. It wasn't like that.'

'Oh really? What was it like? Did somebody put a gun to your head? God Almighty, Jack, you're something else, you really are. When Val said . . . no wonder she didn't want to know. I can't even bear to look at you.' I shook my head, lost for words.

'*What did you say?*'

'Nothing. Forget it. Just go.'

I started to turn away, but Jack caught hold of my upper arm and jerked me back towards him. 'No, what did you just say about Val? You've talked to her, haven't you?'

'Take your hands off me.'

'Have you talked to her?'

'Jack, I'm warning you, let *go*.' I tried to push him away, but he grabbed my other arm and shouted into my face. 'Tell me!'

I winced, couldn't help it, but I wanted to show him he didn't scare me, so I said, 'What if I have?'

'She doesn't know I'm here.'

'Oh yes she does,' I said, triumphantly. 'I told her. Last night. There's a phone on the village green. Now get *off*.' I tried to shove him away but he tightened his grip.

'You stupid, *stupid* bitch! Who else?'

'No one.'

'Who *else*?'

'Only Jeff. No one else.'

'Who? Oh, your ex-husband. Did you phone the police?'

'No.'

'Don't lie to me, Alice.'

'I'm not. I thought about phoning the police, but I didn't do it, OK?'

He looked at me intently, trying to work out if I was telling the truth.

'Come on, Jack. If I *had* phoned them, this was last night, remember? They'd be here by now.'

He said nothing.

'Wouldn't they?'

'Val. She'll tell them.'

'No she won't. I didn't, did I?'

'No, but—' The world, and my head, exploded. There was a knock on the back door, Eustace opened up like a machine gun, barking and thudding against the panels, and Jack slapped me across the face so hard that I lost my balance and tripped over the coffee table.

I tottered to the nearest armchair and sat down, clutching my cheek, barely aware of the racket. My face stung like hell. Even my eyeball felt boiling hot, as if it was about to pop out of its socket. I hunched over, stunned, then Eustace quietened down for a moment and I heard a girl's voice, '. . . not here,' and a boy saying something in reply.

I raised my head. Jack put a finger to his lips.

'Not the police,' I whispered. 'The Boyles.' He looked at me blankly. 'Trudy. The girl we met yesterday. In the lane.'

'What does she want?'

'How should I know?' I got to my feet like an old woman. My face was throbbing and my legs felt unattached, as if my thighs had melted. I started towards the door, but Jack pulled me back. 'Keep your voice down.'

'Why?' I wrenched my arm free and yelled, 'Be with you in a minute!' as loud as I could.

Trudy called back, 'No problem,' and then, 'OK if we give the ponies a drink? We left them in the lane.'

'Help yourself. I'll be out in a sec.'

'What are you playing at?' Jack hissed, grabbing hold of me again.

'Will – you – leave – me – alone?' I jabbed my elbow into his stomach and stumbled into the kitchen. Eustace trotted up to me, confused because there were people outside waiting to make a fuss of him and I wasn't letting them in. 'It's all right, I'm coming.' I followed him back to the door and was about to open it when I heard Jack's voice behind me, very quiet.

'Don't move.'

I ignored him and released the latch. 'I mean it, Alice. Don't open that door.'

'Oh, for God's sake . . .' I glanced round. He was standing in the doorway, something in his hand. I turned away – blinked – realised what I'd seen – then turned back to look again.

He was pointing a gun at me.

CHAPTER TWENTY-ONE

I almost laughed. It looked like a toy. He must have had it in his pocket, but the suit was in such bad shape that I hadn't noticed the bump.

'You're joking.'

He shook his head. 'You're going to do exactly what I say, Bunny Alice, because if you don't . . .'

He took a couple of steps towards me, and stopped. Everything seemed to have slowed right down to zero and my brain was a big, empty space. Somewhere in the middle of it, I heard an oily, metallic click. Saw his thumb press down, same as I'd seen in films. The hammer. He'd pulled the hammer back.

The gun, and Jack, came closer. Eustace bounced at my feet, desperate for me to open the door. I looked down at him, at the gun, at Jack's face. Saw, in a flash the idea I'd given him, and – too slow – made a dive for the dog. Jack was faster. He grabbed Eustace's collar and dragged him backwards. The dog's growls turned into choking noises as Jack twisted the leather to tighten his grip.

'No, Jack, please!'

'Shut up.'

Eustace scrabbled at the flagstones, trying to get away, as Jack dug the barrel into the back of his head. The dog's eyes, terrified and pleading, locked onto mine.

'It's all right, darling, it's all right,' I whispered. 'Jack, look at him. You can't. *Please*, he's all I've got.' I could hardly get the words out.

Jack looked up at me. 'It's real,' he said. 'If you don't—'

'Anything you want. Just don't hurt him.'

'Alice, you all right in there?'

Jack jerked his head at the door. 'Tell her you're coming.'

'Sorry, Trudy. I'll be right out . . .'

Jack said, 'Put your sunglasses on.'

I looked round the kitchen. 'I don't . . .'

'There. On the dresser. Go on. Right, just stick your head round the door and tell her you've got a headache – migraine – and you can't stand the light.'

'But what if—'

Eustace yelped as Jack jabbed him, hard, with the gun. 'Do it!'

'OK. OK, I'm doing it. Just don't . . .'

'Wait. Tell them you want a paper. There's 50p on the table. Give it to them. They can stick it through the letter-box and keep the change. Got that?'

I nodded.

'Get the money, then.' Eustace started choking again as Jack hauled him into position behind the door and squatted down beside him, one hand on his collar, the other pushing the gun against the back of his head. The dog flattened himself on the floor, quivering.

Jack looked at me critically. 'Right, pull yourself together. Blow your nose. Your face could do with a wipe, as well. That's better. Now, open the door like I told you, and don't even think about it, Alice, because I mean it. I'll kill him.'

I nodded. Eustace looked up at me with huge, forlorn eyes. 'It's going to be all right,' I said, as gently as I could, then turned away and opened the door.

Trudy and Lee Boyle stood side by side, flanked by two sweaty, irritable-looking ponies.

'Sorry about that. I'm not feeling very well.'

'What you been up to?' asked Trudy.

Lee looked knowing. ''Angover.'

'Something like that.'

'Did you spew up?'

'Lee-*ee* . . .' Trudy rolled her eyes. 'Leave it out. All it was, Dad said to tell you the farrier can't come Monday so it'll be Friday instead.'

'Your phone's not working,' said Lee. 'Dad tried to give you a bell.'

'Yeah, it's out of order. Thanks for letting me know.'

'No problem. You got any Coke?'

'Sorry, I haven't. Only water.'

'Nah . . .' Lee shook his head. ''S'all right. Come on, Trude.'

'Could you do me a favour? Get me a paper from the shop? I'll give you the money.'

I held out the 50p piece. 'Keep the change, if you want. Then you can buy some Coke.'

Lee pocketed it. 'Nice one, Alice. What do you want?'

'Mmm?'

'What paper?'

'Oh, yeah, sorry.' Jack hadn't said. 'The *Mirror*, if she's got any left. Or the *Express*. I don't mind.'

'All right,' said Trudy. 'You look like you should be in bed.'

'Yeah, well, thanks.'

I started to close the door, but Lee said, 'Ted told us, that bloke you was with yesterday, he used to be on the telly.'

'Yes, that's right.'

'My dad knows all them famous people. When we was in London he was always going round their 'ouses an' that.'

'That's nice,' I said, lamely. There was a frantic scrabbling behind the door, followed by choking noises.

'That your dog?' said Trudy. 'He sounds a bit funny.'

'Has he got a hangover, an' all?' asked Lee. 'Does he drink beer?'

'Who, Eustace?'

'Yeah, like that dog up the pub. That drinks beer. I seen it.'

'You never,' said Trudy. 'You never been in the pub.'

'Yeah I have. I seen it drink a whole pint.'

'Liar.'

'Look, I'd better make sure Eustace is OK. If you just stick the paper through the letter-box, that's fine.'

Trudy gave me a shrewd look. 'You sure you're all right, Alice?'

'Yes, honestly. A few hours' sleep and I'll be fine.' I smiled at her. 'It's my own fault. Shut the gate, though, won't you?'

'Don't worry. See you on Friday. Dad said three o'clock, all right?'

'Yeah. Great. Bye, then.' I closed the door, took off my sunglasses and put my hands up to my face. I saw Jack through my fingers, sitting with Eustace on the floor. The dog strained towards me, whining, but Jack didn't let go of his collar. 'When they've gone,' he said.

We listened to clopping noises in the yard, the click of the gate, Lee's voice, 'Cheers, Alice!', then hooves thudding on the parched ground, and fading away until we couldn't hear them any more.

'They've gone.'

'Clever girl.' Jack let go of the dog and stood up. Eustace rushed towards me and I sat down on the floor and hugged him. 'It's OK, baby, it's OK, I won't let him hurt you. Jack, please put the gun down. He's shaking.'

'He's not the only one.' Jack put the gun in his pocket. 'Can I have a drink?'

I looked across the room and then down at the dog, who had his chin on my knee. The cupboard seemed a long way away.

'I don't want . . . You won't . . .'

'He'll be fine.' Jack sat down at the table. 'I won't move from here. Go on, be a sweetheart and find me some decent booze.'

I picked myself off the floor and went across the room, Eustace at my heels. It felt like walking along a tightrope. I looked at the dusty remains of Lenny's drinks cabinet. *Scotch, Canadian, Bourbon, Rye* . . . How could I pour them down the sink without Jack noticing? *Irish, Gin, Vodka, Rum* . . . 'Brandy?' I held up the bottle.

'Good idea,' said Jack, as if I'd suggested it. 'Have one yourself,' he added. 'You look as if you could do with it.'

I poured for both of us and sat down on the sofa. After a moment, Eustace landed beside me with a flump. 'That's better, isn't it?' I said, stroking him. He curled up and watched Jack warily from under his eyebrows.

'Bottoms up!' Jack raised his glass. 'You did great, Alice. I'm surprised how well you lie.'

We drank in silence for a few minutes. The brandy hurt my throat. My fear was starting to turn to anger. How could he be so calm, so offhand about what he'd just done? I struggled to control my voice. 'Why are you doing this, Jack?'

'I don't know. I'm fucked up. I'm sorry, Alice. When you said you'd talked to Val, I just thought . . .'

'I said it wasn't the police. I *told you*.'

'I just . . . I panicked, that's all.'

'What are you doing with a gun?'

'Oh, it's just . . . you know.'

'No, Jack, I don't *know*. You don't just produce a lethal weapon and say it's nothing. You could have killed me, or any of us. It's dangerous, for Christ's sake.'

168

'I told you, I'm fucked up.' He picked up the bottle. 'Want some more?'

'No. You've got to go to the police, Jack.'

'I can't.' Jack poured more brandy into his glass, drained it, and shook his head. 'It's all gone too far.'

'What's gone too far? Look, none of this has anything to do with me, and I don't . . .'

'Oh yes it has, Bunny Alice. You're part of this, whether you like it or not.'

'No, it *hasn't*. This is your problem, and you need to sort it out. You can't blame me for any of it. I was fine, Jack, I was enjoying my life, and then you just come along. I didn't invite you, and then . . . all this . . . and . . .' I could feel my eyes filling up. I put my glass down and dug in my pockets for a tissue.

'Hey!' Jack stood up. Eustace shot off the sofa and into the hall.

'You frightened him.'

'He'll be all right. He's a *dog*, for Christ's sake.'

'I love him.' The tears stung my face. I scrubbed at them with the back of my hand.

'I know. What have you done with my handkerchief?'

'Oh, over there.' I flapped a wrist at the dresser. 'On the . . . thing.'

'Right.' He fetched it and sat down beside me. 'Here you are. Now, then. That's better, isn't it?'

'No,' I sobbed into the handkerchief. 'No, it bloody well isn't.'

'It's not that bad.' I felt Jack move his arm and leant forward to stop him putting it round my shoulders.

'It's us against the world, Alice.' He got up again, went to the window, drew the curtains and sat back down. 'Isn't this cosy?'

'*Cosy?*' I stared at him.

He smiled at me. 'I could live here. I might even get used to that old dog of yours, eventually.'

'What are you talking about, *live here*? You've just threatened me with a gun, remember?'

'Yes, but I wouldn't . . . You know that.'

'Wouldn't you?'

'Alice, you know me, I lose my temper, but . . .'

'You meant it. You meant it before, as well.'

'Hey, come on.' My shoulders tensed as he put his arm round them. My whole body felt raw. 'Kiss me.'

'Don't, Jack.'

'It's all *right*.' He didn't move. I didn't believe what he'd said about not using the gun, and I didn't want to upset him in case he took it out of his pocket again, so I didn't move, either.

'Were you really happy?' he asked.

'When?'

'What you said before. About enjoying your life.'

'Yes.'

'Are you sure?'

'Well, I was getting on with it, and that was . . .' I mopped my eyes.

Jack pulled me towards him so that my head was resting on his chest and tightened his grip on my shoulder to keep it there. My whole upper body was skewed uncomfortably, and his linen jacket scraped my bruised cheek. He put the fingers of his free hand under my chin and tilted my face up to his. 'Sorry I hit you. Does it hurt much?'

'I'll live.'

Bad choice of words. I glanced down at the bulge in his jacket pocket. Wrong side, unfortunately. If it had been the pocket next to me, perhaps. I suddenly wondered if the gun was still cocked. Could it just go off of its own accord, if he knocked it or something?

'I've made your jacket wet.' I edged away from him, but he didn't let go of my shoulder.

'A few tears won't hurt it. Come on, dry your eyes. We've got to think.'

'We? You need *help*, Jack.'

'You *can* help me, Alice.' He stroked my hair. 'You've got such a big heart. All these creatures you look after . . . surely there's room for me as well?'

'Jack . . .' I tried to pull away from him, but he hung on to me.

'No, it's all right, it's all right. Come on, tell me what you said to your – to Jeff.'

'He wasn't there.'

'Has he got one of those machines that record messages?'

'No,' I lied.

'OK. What about Val?'

'Just – you were upset, that's all.'

'How did she sound?'

'Angry. She didn't want to talk to me.'

'That's not surprising. She's always had a thing about you.'

'Why? She hardly knows me.'

I felt Jack shrug. 'Christ knows.'

I wondered if I could pick his pocket. Sitting down, there was no way to get to the gun without making it obvious, and I could hardly follow him round the kitchen if he got up. All the same, I'd have a better chance. And if he'd had a few he'd be less likely to notice. I knew it was dangerous, but I couldn't think what else to do.

His glass was empty. He won't stop me if I get up to give him a drink, I thought.

'More brandy?' I said, and wriggled out from under his arm.

'Aye thang yow. God, I *hate* Arthur Askey.'

I handed over the bottle and sat down at the table. Jack refilled his glass and patted the sofa. 'Come back.'

'In a minute.'

'Val did burn that tape, you know. In the incinerator.' He grinned. 'I told her she ought to set fire to it and chuck it over the fence. Revenge for that dildo old Tweed Tits lobbed at us. That's a great story, it really is.'

'I've heard it. Lenny told me.'

'Oh yes, so he did. Your first date, wasn't it? That's going back a bit.'

'How do you know?'

'Because he told me, Bunny Alice. He told me what fun it was and how much you'd laughed and how sweet you were for being so upset about his dad. That was another great story, of course.'

'It was *horrible*. That stuff killed him eventually.'

'Killed who?'

'His father. The phosphorus, or whatever it was.'

'Is that what he told you?'

I nodded. 'Industrial disease.'

'Lenny's dad died 'cause he was an al-co-hol-ic, darling,' said Jack. 'Like his son.'

'Then why . . . ?'

Jack rolled his eyes. 'Sympathy. Works every time.'

'I meant later on.'

Jack looked thoughtful. 'My guess is, he wanted the old boy to have a bit of dignity. Didn't want to remember him like that. And it was the *way* he died, as well. He was in the kitchen when he had the stroke, you see, and he fell with his head in the dog bowl, where it had its water. It was quite a big dog they had, and it was one of those plastic washing-up things. You know: three, four inches of water. He drowned. That was how they found him. Face down in the dog bowl. I mean, what a way to go.'

'He could have told me.'

'No.' Jack shrugged. 'It was all too close to home. I mean, what did you expect him to say? "When I grow up I'm going to pickle myself like Pater?" Where are my cigarettes?'

He got up and began wandering around the kitchen, singing, '*I don't know where he's going, but when he gets there I'll be glad. I'm following in Father's footsteps – Yes! – I'm following the dear – old – Dad.* God, this place is a tip. Where – are – my – bloody – *cigarettes?*'

'I don't know. Where you left them.'

'Upstairs.' He looked at me with loaded eyes and shook his head. 'Oh no you don't, Bunny Alice. Where I go, you go.' His hand went into his pocket. *That* pocket.

'Come on. You first.'

We went upstairs. His room was a mess. Dirty clothes were strewn over the floor, dotted with ashtrays, empty glasses and bottles of pills. The bedclothes were pulled back and the bottom sheet rucked and stale. Susie's urn was up by the pillows. I looked at Jack in his crumpled suit, and had an image of him lying on his side on the bed, fully clothed, cradling it in his arms. Unbearable. I turned away and my eye caught the green shoe-bag, empty and limp, hanging from a hook behind the door. Perhaps the gun had been inside it.

The cigarettes were on the chest of drawers. Jack picked them up and stuck them in his pocket – the other pocket – then looked down at the bed. 'Wait.' He grabbed hold of the top sheet, dragged it over the urn, and tucked it in, clumsily.

'Shall I do the other side?'

I thought he hadn't heard me, but after a moment he said, 'No, leave it. Go.'

We went back downstairs to the kitchen. I sat at the

kitchen table with my head in my hands, while Jack drank more brandy and walked about, lifting things up and putting them down again for no apparent reason. *Do something*, said a little voice in my mind. *You're on your own. No one's going to rescue you. Do something.* Like what? I felt exhausted.

Jack sat down opposite me and leant forward, arms on the table. 'Lenny raved about you, you know. Mind you, he usually did, the first time. Oh,' he said, stagily, 'I forgot. It wasn't the first time, was it? I believe your first coupling took place in a haystack. Very appropriate, I always thought.'

'Jack,' I said through gritted teeth, 'this isn't *fair*.'

'You can say that again, Bunny Alice. I know all your little secrets, you see.'

'Stop it.'

'It was all your idea, you know.'

'Rubbish.' I looked up. 'You keep saying it's all my fault and my idea and I haven't a clue what you're talking about.'

'Don't you remember? Your first date with Lenny – once you'd been introduced, I mean. You suggested it.'

'Suggested what?' As I was saying it, I heard Lenny's voice in my head: *Have you done that, then? Been in bed with two men at the same time?* And I'd said – oh, God – I'D SAID, *No, do you want to try it?* 'I don't know what you're talking about,' I repeated.

'You *do* remember, don't you?'

'No!' I'd just *said* it, that was all. I hadn't wanted to *do* it. It was just conversation. People say things all the time, don't they, and it doesn't mean . . .

'I'd just thought, you and Lenny, you know, how you shared your girlfriends, and I didn't know . . . I thought that was what he meant, but he was really shocked when I said it. But it wasn't as if I was suggesting anything, just . . .

Oh, for God's sake! If I'd have known it was going to be such a big deal I'd have kept my mouth shut.'

'Hoist with your own petard, darling. You gave us the idea.'

'You don't need me to put ideas into your head, Jack. And as for filming it, you dreamt that up all by yourself.'

'We didn't.'

'Oh, what, so you ended up in bed with two other people and a movie camera by accident? Pull the other one, it's got bells on.'

'We didn't know we were being filmed.'

'What did you think the camera was?' I asked. 'A hat-stand?'

Jack sighed. 'We couldn't see it.'

'I don't understand.'

'Two-way mirror. Oldest trick in the book.'

'So you weren't . . . so . . .' I had this huge sense of relief – until I remembered that bright, triumphant smile. 'Kitty knew, didn't she?'

Jack nodded emphatically, his eyes wide. 'Oh, *she* knew.'

CHAPTER TWENTY-TWO

I stared at him. 'Then you mean she . . . Oh, Jack. *No.*'

'Oh, *yes.* She really stitched us up.'

'Lenny never . . . not a word. I had no idea.'

'She threatened us. *News of the World, Sunday People* . . .'

'They wouldn't.'

'They bloody well would. We were on television then, remember? Prime time viewing.'

'So you gave her money?'

'No choice.'

'Did you tell Findlater?'

'No.'

'But he'd have understood, wouldn't he? I mean, that's always been a risk for *them*, hasn't it, someone finding out, and he was your agent. Surely he'd have known what to do, got a lawyer, an injunction or . . . I don't know, there must have been something he could have done.'

Jack cleared his throat. 'We did talk about it.'

'But you just said . . .'

'No, I mean Lenny and I. We talked about it. We were going to tell him.'

'So why didn't you? *Oh, God, Jack . . . No . . .*'

My stomach got there before my brain. I knew I was about to be sick.

I catapulted myself across the kitchen, one hand clapped over my mouth, leant over the sink and threw up. Brandy and bile. Revolting.

I bent over, heaving, aware that Jack was watching me.

'Still in one piece?' he asked, when I'd finished.

'Just about,' I said, shakily.

'Here.' Jack offered me his brandy glass. 'Rinse your mouth out.' I shook my head and stuck my face under the tap. When I stood up, he was beside me, holding a towel.

I let him lead me back to the table. He sat down opposite me again. I knew the answer, but I had to ask. I had to hear him say it.

'It is Kitty in that car, isn't it?'

'Alice . . .' Jack looked down at his hand as it inched along the table towards mine. He rubbed my arm with the backs of his fingers for a moment, then stopped.

'It is, isn't it?'

He went on staring at his hand. I jerked my arm away. 'Don't bother lying to me, Jack. I know it was Lenny's car. It was in the paper. The bit you tried to hide from me.'

There was a long silence.

'Tell me!'

'Yes.'

'Now tell me it was an accident.'

Jack's hand began to crawl towards my arm again. It looked like a hairy crab. I shut my eyes tight. 'Just, *please*, tell me it was an accident.'

After a moment, Jack said woodenly, 'It was an accident.'

'Thank you.' I got up. 'I'm going to make some tea.'

Jack hovered behind me as I filled the kettle, lit the gas and put some tea in the pot. I couldn't concentrate. Every time I turned round, he was there, blocking my way so I had to step round him.

And inside my head, well, chaos. It had to be an accident, I kept thinking. Lenny was drunk. Kitty'd asked for it, she'd done it, it was her, not him, HER, he couldn't help it, the car must have got out of control, and . . . Perhaps he wasn't

177

even in the car, perhaps she'd taken it, pinched it. That's it, wouldn't put anything past her. But then, Lenny'd taken her to the party, hadn't he? After she'd blackmailed them HE'D STILL TAKEN HER TO THE PARTY. Why? Why had he done that? It didn't make sense. None of it made sense. *Don't blame the camels.* He'd written it. Oh God. *It must have been an accident,* clamoured my brain. *It must have been because I WANT IT TO BE.*

Again, I had a sudden impression of Kitty's face, a come-hither look over her shoulder, enticing and mocking at the same time, and that *smile*—

'Shit!' A mug slipped through my fingers, plummeted to the floor and smashed.

'Let me do that,' said Jack. 'You sit down.'

I slumped on the chair beside the dresser.

'You're shivering.' He pulled the throw off the back of the sofa and draped it over my shoulders. After a moment, he put a mug into my hand. 'Three lumps,' he said. 'You're in shock. Drink it.'

I struggled to make my hand and mouth co-operate as tea slopped down my chin onto my T-shirt. After a few swallows, I gave up. Jack held out his cigarettes. 'Want one?'

'Why not?' He lit it for me and handed it over. After a while, I said, 'Val. Did she know?'

'Yes. I didn't want to show her the film. She made me. She kept saying she couldn't believe we'd been that stupid.'

'She's not the only one.'

'I know.' Jack stood looking at me, smoking and flicking the ash into the sink. I had no idea what he was thinking.

'If that's true,' I said, slowly, 'Val made you show her that film, then why did you have to show me? I mean, you came here to get Lenny's copy of the film, didn't you? That's why you went through my room, isn't it?'

Jack was silent.

'*Isn't it?*'

'Yes,' he said, quietly. 'Yes, it was.'

'After they'd found the car, you wanted to be sure. That's really why you came, isn't it? Never mind all this guff about wanting to see me again. But why didn't you just *ask* for it? You could have told me it was something else – old footage, anything. I'd have believed you.'

Jack turned away from me and stared out of the window. 'I don't know. It's all such a *mess*. When I was up in your attic looking for it, I never meant to watch the bloody thing. All I wanted to do was get rid of it, but I found myself with the projector, and again, I didn't intend . . . And even while I was setting it up, I didn't know *why* I was doing it, and then you came down . . .' Jack ran water over the stub of his cigarette, dropped it in the sink and turned round to face me. 'I was angry, Alice. I wanted to punish you.'

'Why?'

Jack looked at the floor, shaking his head. 'I was jealous. You and Lenny, it was so . . . I didn't have anything like that in my life, and it was the way, I don't know, he wanted to spend all his time with you, and if he wasn't with you, he was talking about you. I couldn't get him to concentrate on the stuff we were doing, and . . . Oh, I don't know. We'd always talked about girls a lot, but it was just part of it, it wasn't *everything*. I told you, it was the *way* he talked about you, that was different.'

'How do you mean?'

'Well, for one thing, he was always telling me things you'd *said*.'

'Like about the threesome, you mean?'

'Not just that. But that thing with Kitty . . .' Jack turned round to get himself another cigarette, and I almost missed the rest of what he said. 'I talked him into it. I thought it would be like old times.'

I stared at him, speechless.

'The funny thing was . . . afterwards, he blamed you for it, not me. He said if you hadn't left him—'

'I left him because I came home and found Kitty's knickers under my pillow and I couldn't take any more of it!'

'I don't mean that. You'd been spending a lot of time away . . .'

'My grandfather was *dying*, Jack. What was I supposed to do? Not see him?'

'No, of course not, but Lenny was lonely. He couldn't cope on his own, you know that. And I suppose . . . all right, I encouraged him. I was seeing a bit of Kitty – well, a lot of Kitty – and she liked Lenny. She'd met him before a few times, and . . . you know . . .' Jack shrugged. 'It was only to take his mind off things. It was nice to have things back how they were before,' he said, defensively, 'have a bit of fun.'

'Fun!' I spat. 'A bit of *fun*! Jesus, when I think – the dates – you must have been planning your . . . your . . . while my granddad . . . I can't take this in.'

Suddenly I was on my feet, screaming at him, 'Why'd you *do it*?' and before I knew what was happening, the mug had left my hand, hit him squarely in the chest and exploded on the flagstones. Jack stooped to pick up the pieces, a dark stain spreading across his shirt. I leant against the dresser and watched him in silence.

'We'll be drinking out of the horse trough at this rate.' He straightened up and tipped the pieces into the bin.

'I had to talk him round,' he said, inspecting his fingers for slivers of china, 'and then I phoned Kitty, and she was keen, so . . .'

'Why didn't you just do it at Lenny's?'

'He didn't want to, and obviously my place was out of

the question. Kitty said she wasn't sure about her flatmate, but she knew somewhere we could go—'

'I bet she did.'

'So we just left it up to her. She organised the whole thing. Christ, Alice, when we found out, you can't imagine . . .'

'No,' I said, 'I can't imagine being that stupid, for one thing.'

'You've got every right to be angry.'

'Thanks for giving me permission.'

'I'm just trying to explain what happened, that's all.'

'I don't understand why Lenny blamed *me*.'

'He felt you'd abandoned him.'

'I *told* you . . .'

'I know, I know. But Lenny didn't see it like that.'

I nodded, remembering the fights we'd had over me going on working at the club, when he'd wanted me to stop and I wouldn't. He could never understand why I needed it.

'He was in love with you, Alice. He needed you.'

'So did Granddad.' I stared at a splash of tea on the skirting board. Jack was right. What a bloody awful mess.

'It was like a nightmare. After. When we were in America.'

'You said.'

'When he told me he didn't want us to work together any more. Looking back, he'd been building up to it while we were in the States, but at the time it felt like, well, just out of the blue. Betrayal. He was my best friend, Alice, and I'd lost him. I couldn't believe it. Val kept on yapping about how it was all for the best, but she didn't understand. Apart from anything else, it was professional suicide. Findlater hated the idea.'

'I remember. Tell me, why did you tell Val and not him?'

'Had to, after the party.'

'Why?'

'Needed help. Kitty had a copy of the film. We had to get rid of it, but we could hardly go round to her flat – we'd have been recognised – so I asked Val. She got it.'

'How did she get in? Did you have a key to Kitty's flat?'

Jack hesitated. I watched him with a sinking heart, knowing what the answer was going to be. 'You didn't, did you?'

He shook his head.

'So how did you get it?'

'From her bag.'

'But wasn't that in the car? I mean, in the water?'

'It was in the house. The cloakroom. She'd got changed, remember? Into the Bunny costume. She left it there afterwards.'

'So she wasn't leaving. She hadn't taken the car.'

'Alice, it *was* an accident. We'd all had a lot to drink. You know how things happen. None of us were thinking clearly. But no one would have believed it, especially if they'd seen the film. That was why we had to get it.'

I looked at him and thought, I don't believe you, either. 'Why didn't you tell me all this last night?'

'I was going to, but you stormed out.'

'What did you expect me to do? Clap?'

'And then this morning, you were so angry. I had nightmares.' His face crumpled and he began to weep in great, heaving sobs. 'I dreamt you took Susie's ashes and tipped them out and trod on them. It was horrible.'

I stared at him. 'I'd never do anything like that. I'm not that sort of person. Come on, you know that.'

Jack buried his face in his hands. His words came out jerkily, through his fingers. 'It was – my fault – Susie got ill. The doctor, specialist bloke, he said – she thought if she was slim – get – *attention. She* thought she was ugly – if she was pretty, I'd want to see her, be at home more. We always told her she was, but she didn't believe – took after me, more – big, not like Val and Rosie, felt she was the odd one out – Val must have told the specialist guy that we rowed about me seeing other people – women. Can't blame her for that, but you don't know what kids pick up, what they hear. Susie thought – her fault . . .'

I put my arms round him. 'Come on . . . Those things, stuff in people's heads – ideas – they *happen*. It wasn't only because of you . . .'

'That girl last night, by the graveyard.'

'The hitch-hiker?'

'Yes. I thought for a moment . . . she had a look of Susie, the way she was standing there on her own in the dark, lost. We were filming near Susie's school once, and I went to see . . . hockey match. All the girls, playing, and she was standing in the goal on her own. The others must have given her their jumpers because she was wearing three or four, and one round her shoulders, like a shawl. She was all bundled up, but she looked so cold, unhappy – I wanted to go over, talk to her, but it was a lesson, and she didn't know I was there. I thought she'd be embarrassed, she wouldn't want me to be there, so I didn't. I just went away.'

'Oh Jack, that's so sad . . .' I rubbed his back.

He made no attempt to hold me, but we were standing very close and when he moved his arm to wipe his face I felt the gun thump against my hip. The thought *grab it* was so strong in my mind that for a second I thought I might have said it out loud, but Jack didn't move away. I carried on stroking his back and gradually – very gradually – started moving my right hand lower down, nearer his pocket.

'Val said I never talked to Susie. What made her tick, all that stuff. I told her I'm not a psychiatrist, but she said, show an interest. We didn't get the chance to talk on our own much, but I'd kept this picture she'd done when she was a kid, copied it out of a book or something, and I was giving her a lift somewhere so I thought I'd ask her about that. It was a horse, galloping along beside a train. I didn't know if she'd remember, because it was years later, but it was the only thing I could think of, and she did remember, and she told me . . .'

'What did she say?' I murmured, putting my head against his chest. I carried on stroking his back, trying not to break the rhythm, my right hand inching down a little bit further each time.

'She used to have this daydream, if she was on a train, she'd imagine she was galloping along the embankment on a big horse, and it could keep up and jump over all the bridges and things. She said when she got on the train she'd make a sort of . . . signal, in her mind, and the horse would come outside the window and she'd leave her body in the carriage and jump on its back. So I asked her if she did it in planes as well because we'd been on a few holidays to Spain and places, and she said, "No, Dad, don't be silly. Horses can't fly." That was it, really.'

'That was sweet,' I said, trailing my fingers round towards the front of his jacket, not daring to look down in case he guessed what I was up to.

'But I got it wrong. Susie was so excited when she was explaining it, like they used to look at Christmas, she and Rosie, when they were little. I'd asked the wrong question, and I could see she was thinking, he doesn't understand and she . . . just closed up again. I know it doesn't sound like much, but it was important to her, and I didn't . . . I couldn't . . .'

'Oh, darling . . .' I could feel the edge of the pocket. Now if I could just get my hand round the gun . . . 'Never mind . . .' Two fingers . . . *three* . . .

'I should have died, Alice. Not her. It should have been me. You don't know what it's like, just walking down the street, feeling sick, worthless. You look around, and you just think, what's the point? It wasn't Susie's fault, it was mine, everything was my fault, and it should have been me.'

'It's not like that, Jack. We all make mistakes, all of us.' Touching the metal . . . Just . . . get my fingers . . . underneath . . . Jack moved slightly and my hand slipped, I scrabbled for the gun, but—

'No!' He grabbed my wrist and tugged my hand clear of his pocket.

'Aaaah, Jack, don't!' I tried to pull away from him but he got behind me and twisted my arm behind my back.

'That *hurts*.'

'Good.' He hitched my arm higher. I jerked forwards and backwards, trying to break his grip, but my hips were right up against the worktop and he was pressing against my back, squashing me, and there was no room to move. I lashed at him with my free arm – useless – tried to kick out – yelled as my knee smacked into the cupboard door, tried again and connected, but not enough.

My foot glanced off Jack's shin and he staggered for a moment, righted himself, then put his other hand on the back of my neck and shoved my head forward, so that my hair was brushing the wooden draining board. The pain was almost unbearable, and struggling was making it worse. I screamed.

'You're breaking my arm!'

'Serve you right.'

'Stop,' I panted. 'Please. Let go.'

'Not' *jerk* 'bloody' *jerk* 'likely.'

I tried to make myself go limp, shut my eyes tight and ground my teeth, anything to control the pain, but my arm was agony, my shoulder was on fire. 'You're killing me, *please* . . .'

He started to push me towards the back door. He doesn't care, I thought, he *is* going to kill me, he doesn't care. God, help me, make him let go, *make it stop*. I heard the click of Eustace's nails on the lino and caught a glimpse of him through my ragged hair, standing like a statue in the hall doorway, confused, one front paw held slightly off the ground, head tilted to one side and eyes enquiring. '*Help me!*' I braced my legs and flailed at the draining board with my free hand, trying to grab something – anything – to use as a weapon, but there was nothing there. I couldn't twist round far enough, couldn't see, couldn't *think*.

Jack's knee thudded into the backs of my legs. I felt my own knees buckle and I couldn't straighten them, and for a moment my entire body weight was hanging from my shoulder and upper arm and it felt like they'd snap. I screamed again but he didn't let up, just pushed my head down, this time with more force because he was standing over me and the pain was even worse. I slumped against the door on my knees and begged him to stop. God knows what I said, it probably didn't make sense anyway, but he let go in the end.

'Don't try anything.'

I shook my head. I couldn't. My right arm was throbbing and useless.

'Get up.'

'Wait, my arm . . .'

'Now!' Something cold and hard jabbed the nape of my neck. The gun. I scrambled upright and stood facing him, cradling my right arm. He stared at me and I suddenly thought, he's got no idea what it's like to be me. He's not even seeing me as a human being. The gun was pointing at my chest. I forced myself to look at him, not it. His eyes were expressionless, like brown marbles.

'Jack, it's me. It's Alice.'

'I thought I could trust you. Because of Lenny. I thought you'd do it for Lenny.'

'I'm *on your side*, Jack. That's why I didn't phone . . .'

'But you weren't there for Lenny, either, were you? Not at the end. Not when it mattered. Oh, yeah, all that stuff about your granddad, but where were you when Lenny *really* needed you? Up in London. Up to fuck knows what with fuck knows who. Christ knows why I thought you'd help me, you weren't even listening! You just wanted to get hold of this,' he jerked the gun, 'so you could go running off to the police. Then I'd be gone and you could carry on playing at being Marie fucking Antoinette. I'll bet you've never thought about Lenny at all, never mind me. He even wanted to tell you. About Kitty. He wanted you to know. I told him we couldn't trust you, and I was right, wasn't I? You treacherous *bitch*!'

He jabbed my chest with the gun, pushing me backwards. His eyes were venomous.

'I . . .'

'Shut up. Open the door.'

My right shoulder was a fireball of cramp. It felt like I'd never be able to move my arm again. I turned away from Jack and fumbled at the latch with my left hand. The stifling heat hit me as I pulled back the door, and for a moment, the yard was silent. Then Eustace suddenly came to life and barged past us, barking and racing around as if he expected a game. Jack ignored him. 'Where's the key for your stables?'

I've got two loose boxes. One of them's padlocked. I use it to store hay in the summer because Pablo and Nelson live out.

'In my boot.' I pointed to a pair of wellies standing by the mat.

'Get it.'

I up-ended the boot with my left hand and picked the key off the floor.

'Out,' he said. 'Go on.' I walked ahead of him across the yard to the boxes with Eustace, still hopeful, bouncing in front of me. Jack's going to lock me in, I thought. Just lock me in, not kill me. Then he'll go. He'll take my car and he'll go. And OK, I'll be locked in, but I'll be able to escape somehow or someone will come and he'll be gone so it'll be all right and then . . .

'Undo it.'

It was a big padlock with a handle that went through the bolts on both halves of the door. I tried to hold it steady with my right hand, but my shoulder felt like molten lead and my fingers were numb.

'Hurry up.'

'I'm sorry. Can you hold it for me?'

Jack moved closer, so that our heads were almost touching. I could feel the gun just under my ribs. He picked up the padlock, waited while I opened it, then stepped back. 'The door.'

I swung the top half open: hay bales, floor to ceiling.

'What's in the other one?'

'Nothing. It's empty.'

'Open it.'

He stood behind me while I undid the bolts. Eustace crowded our legs, sniffing the ground. He pushed past me as I pulled back the doors, making me lose my balance. I collided with Jack, felt the gun hard against my spine and for a moment I thought that was it. *Let him kill me. Don't let me be paralysed. Anything but that.* A flash in my mind, my spine snapping in a starburst of knobs of bone and gobs of fluid, and then he pushed me forward into the loose box. I bounced off the wall and swung round. *Got to face him, if he's going to do it he's got to see my face, my eyes, got to see . . .*

He was standing on the threshold, his face blank. 'Get the dog out.' I got hold of Eustace and tried to haul him to the door. He anchored himself to the ground, groaning and trying to slip out of his collar as I pulled him across the floor. Jack bent forward in the doorway and our hands touched for a second on Eustace's fur. There was a snarl and a yelp as he grabbed a handful of the dog's skin and dragged him into the yard. I lifted my head and caught a blur of frantic brown and white and a last glimpse of the gun before Jack slammed the door and left me in darkness.

CHAPTER TWENTY-THREE

I heard Jack shoot the bolts into place and close the padlock, then retreating footsteps as he walked across the yard, to . . . where? The house, he'd have to go back to the house. Yes. I heard the back door creak, then shut. I stood in the dark, waiting for my eyes to adjust, straining my ears. Surely Jack would go now? Surely he'd take my car and leave? The keys were easy enough to find. All he'd have to do was look in my bag, and that was on the dresser, easy to spot.

Unless . . . what he'd said about Lenny, about me not being there for him, unless he had some warped idea that he was going to punish me for that. And where were *you*, Jack? I thought, angrily. Where were you when Lenny needed you? You were his best friend. Jack had done exactly the same over Susie, hadn't he? Blamed Val, blamed anyone but himself, and then . . . what he'd said about feeling guilty and worthless – he's trying to do the same to me, I thought, load me with his guilt over Lenny, when God knows I've got enough of my own to contend with.

I've got to get out of here, I thought. Get the police. I racked my brains. I hadn't shut the door of the other stable. Had Jack? *Think.* I'd heard three bolts being slid into place, and there were three on each stable, one on the top half-door and two on the bottom. That meant he hadn't. So that was a way out, but . . .

I looked around. The partition between the two stables

stopped a few feet below the roof, and the gap in between was divided into four by wooden uprights. At the moment, though, it wasn't a gap but a solid wall of hay bales. Denser than straw, heavier and harder to shift. Packed solid, too. Lengthwise, unfortunately, so I couldn't pull them through whole onto my side. But what if I broke them into sections? I'd never manage it with the baler twine holding them together – too tightly packed. I had nothing to cut it with. Even teeth were out, supposing that were possible, because I wouldn't be able to get my head to it. But if I could get my hand between the bales and get hold of the twine, I might be able to tug it off. One string at least, and then it would be easy. I'd need something to stand on, though. The water bucket in the corner. Empty it and turn it upside down. I measured the distances with my eye. It might, *just*, make me tall enough. If I went for the bale nearest the door, I could make a space big enough to crawl through, and then I could push the next bale into the yard and jump down after it. Yes. Good plan.

But – I needed both arms in working order. Concentrate, I told myself. I curled and uncurled the fingers of my right hand, trying to ignore the prickly bursts of pins and needles, then started to swing my arm backwards and forwards. Don't think about what happens if you can't get out, don't think about Jack, don't think about anything else *at all*. This is all there is. Nothing else in the whole world but this.

No noise from the yard. Jack must still be inside the house. Why doesn't he *go*? I thought. Packing, that's it, he's packing. I've got to believe that. Anything else is too . . . No. Don't think about it. Concentrate. How long have I been in here? Five minutes? Can't be more. Wish I'd got my watch on. Must have had it this morning when I was doing the animals. Then I remembered taking it off when I'd washed out Eustace's bowl for breakfast. That seemed like weeks ago, not hours.

The evening feed. Supposing I couldn't get out? The animals . . . I imagined them waiting as the dusk turned to darkness, hungry and bewildered: the horses standing patiently in the field, heads down, the guinea-pigs on their hind legs at the wire mesh, the hens wandering around the garden, not shut up. Foxes. *Eustace.* If Jack left without shutting the gate, if he wandered off . . . I pictured his body, lifeless and broken, in a ditch at the side of the road, his glossy brown and white fur matted with blood . . .

Stop it, I told myself. Just stop it. That isn't going to happen. Everything will be all right. You've got to believe that. Concentrate. Swing your arm. Back and forth. That's right. That's good. Getting better all the time. But what if Jack *doesn't* leave? What if he does decide to come back in here and . . . No, I thought. He'll calm down. He won't do that. But he hadn't *said* anything about leaving, I'd just assumed it. If he thought Val would tell the police where he was . . . I'd told him she wouldn't, because *I* hadn't, which didn't make a lot of sense. But if she'd known about what happened at that party, and she'd gone to Kitty's flat, didn't that mean they could charge her with something or other? Burglary, or being an accessory? Slow down. *Think.*

What would be the *point* of Jack shooting me? What could I tell the police? First off, that Kitty'd been blackmailing Jack and Lenny over that film, which I'd burnt, anyway . . . I could tell them that the body in the lake was Kitty, which they might know already, by now. But if the car, and she, had been underwater for seven years, how could there be any evidence? All right, they'd connected it with Lenny – his car – but how could they prove it *wasn't* an accident? As for going to the newspapers, same thing. And even if I had anything to tell them, I wouldn't. All that stuff they'd written about Lenny after he'd died. I wouldn't touch any of them with a bargepole. In any case, Jack and Lenny weren't exactly hot news any more, not front page stuff, at any rate. I suddenly remembered the cutting in this morning's post. Jack had come in before I could read it. What had I . . . *Of course.* Stuck it in my pocket. Where it must still be. I breathed in, rummaged for it with my right hand, prickly but working, thank God, and pulled it out of my jeans.

The stable was pretty dim, but there was a bit of light showing underneath the bottom half of the door. I took it over there, arranged myself very gingerly on all fours, and flattened it on the concrete floor. By keeping it close to the sliver of dusty daylight, I could just about make out the words.

BODY FOUND IN PORNO FLAT

The man found shot in a Notting Hill Gate bedsitter last week has been named as Daniel Francis Watts. Watts, 37, is known to have had connections with pornography and prostitution and worked as a camera operator on films such as *How's Your Father* and *In My Lady's Chamber*, starring Britain's self-styled Sex Queen, Candy Knight. Police have begun a murder investigation and the Obscene Publications Squad have been called in to investigate hardcore material found on the premises.

Danny Watts. Who was in Lenny's address book. And on his List of People Who Deserve To Be Shot. And who got shot. Last week.

Keep calm. I told myself. Be rational. *Think.* I read it a second time, then got off my knees and sat down with my back to the door. Those films Jack was in, *Teacher's Pet* and the other one, those had Candy Knight as well. If Danny

Watts had worked on her other films, apart from the ones in the paper, then Jack did know him. He'd asked me if I remembered him, so he must do. Must know *of* him, at any rate. And Danny Watts was a cameraman. And, of course, *of course* . . .

Kitty's accomplice. I tilted my head back against the wooden boards and stared up at the rafters. It all made sense. I hadn't thought before – too upset, too tired – but there was no way she could have set up that film by herself. You have to know what you're doing to work a movie camera, and she wasn't exactly the sharpest knife in the box – not that I can talk – but even if she'd done films like that before, it didn't mean she'd understand the technical stuff, whereas Danny Watts . . . that was his *job*.

Anyway, how would she have set the film running? If the camera was positioned behind the mirror, she'd have had to keep popping next door, wouldn't she? Unless there was some sort of remote control switch, and that didn't seem very likely. Jack said she'd organised the whole thing. With Danny Watts's help. I'd made a chance remark to Lenny about a threesome, and Lenny'd told Jack, and Jack wouldn't let it go, so Lenny'd agreed, and they'd walked right into it. Talk about lambs to the slaughter.

And they'd blamed *me*. What is it about men? I mean if Jack, if *either of them*, had just thought with his brain for half a second, instead of his dick . . . I shook my head in disbelief. How could two intelligent people be so *stupid*? The blackmail hadn't ended with Kitty's death, of course it hadn't. When she'd disappeared, that was even more reason . . . Even if Danny Watts hadn't been at that party, it wouldn't have taken long to find out that *she'd* been there, and that Lenny and Jack had been there, and that that was the last time anyone had seen her. It wouldn't take a genius to work out what had happened. I groaned. That was why Danny Watts, assuming it *was* him, had visited Lenny in Wiltshire two days before he died. Not to bring him pills, but to ask for more cash.

Lenny had never said anything to me about money problems. He'd never said anything to me about money, full stop. He wasn't mean, just vague. I wasn't doing badly at the club, but of course he earned way more than I did. And when we were living together he'd often given me money. I'd never asked, he'd just handed it over. Handfuls of notes, never counted it, never told me what to spend it on. Not that he had a clue about housekeeping, he used to open the fridge and say 'What's all this stuff doing in here?' Completely bewildered, as if he expected to find, I don't know . . . a hat or something. Occasionally he'd have a go at me for spending too much, but then he'd go out and buy a case of Chateau d'Yquem or an expensive present for someone, and he wouldn't bat an eyelid. We'd never talked about money. Thinking about it, there were a lot of things we'd never talked about. Too late now.

I made myself think back to that visit to the cottage at Ivar, when I'd found him. The journey, the taxi, asking for him in pubs, then up at the house, 'Not you as well.' That's what the man who'd answered the door had said. As well as who? Not Danny Watts. The taxi-driver hadn't said anything about taking him up to the house, just that he'd dropped him at the cottage, waited, then taken him back to the station afterwards. In any case, if Danny was blackmailing Lenny, he'd hardly want to advertise his visit, would he? But if *Jack* had gone to see Lenny as well . . .

He said he'd found out about Lenny's death from a newspaper when he was on holiday, but this would have been at least three days before, so . . . But Jack had been pissed off with Lenny for not telling him we were engaged, and surely Lenny would have said something, if . . . It didn't make sense. They weren't even speaking, so why would Jack go all the way down there? To try and patch it up? They might have argued, and Jack might have . . .

No. Impossible. Lenny'd left a note.

It still didn't make sense. And why had Lenny taken Kitty to the party?

Her death might have been an accident, but Danny Watts's wasn't. And Lenny, however much he may have wanted it, couldn't have had anything to do with that, because he was already dead.

Jack killed Danny Watts.

Jack has a gun.

Jack is still here.

CHAPTER TWENTY-FOUR

The world – *time* – stopped, and I was in the middle of that big, empty space again. The place where you realise truly terrible things and it's all silent and dead calm. I could feel blood pounding in my ears. Breath inside my nose. Air against my skin. I won't feel any of those things when I'm dead.

'No!' I knocked the back of my head hard against the stable door. Don't give way to it. Don't cry, don't panic, and whatever you do, don't scream, because if you start you'll never stop. Think of something, anything. *Scotch, Canadian, Bourbon, Rye . . . Our Father which art in heaven . . . Irish, Gin, Vodka, Rum . . . Hallowed be Thy Name . . .* Be calm. Be rational.

Why? Jack wasn't being rational, he was falling apart. Booze, pills, Kitty, Lenny, Danny Watts, his daughter. He had nothing to lose.

I have *got* to get out of here. I wiped my nose on the back of my hand and got to my feet. I took hold of the handle of the bucket, lifted it a couple of inches, gasped, and transferred it to my left hand. I was about to tip the water on the floor, then changed my mind, took it over to the manger and poured it in there instead. The manger's plastic, sealed. I might need the water later on. If I'm still alive.

WHICH I BLOODY WELL WILL BE BECAUSE I AM NOT GOING TO DIE. I took the bucket over to the partition, up-ended it and stood on it. On tiptoe, I could just hold on to the top. I'd got no idea how I was going to climb the wall. I was wearing monkey boots, which was good, more grip, but there were no footholds at all, and my arm was throbbing from just lifting it above my head. I certainly wouldn't be able to pull myself up with it. I turned and looked back at the manger. It's triangular, with a flat bottom, so if I took it out of its metal frame in the corner, up-ended it and put it on the floor underneath the bucket, then I could stand on both of them. It would mean I'd lose the water, but what the hell.

It felt pretty wobbly. The bucket only just fitted on top of the upturned manger, but it was OK, and when I stood on it my head and neck came above the partition. The bales were wedged together really tightly. I'd bribed the Boyles to help me stack them a few months ago. I glanced at my watchless wrist. Trudy and Lee should be back soon. The letter-box was at the front of the house, but everyone local came through the yard at the back. If I could get their attention somehow, they could get Fred to call the police, although knowing Fred, he'd probably be straight round here himself. But either way, I'd get help.

Or they might be in a hurry and just run up the path to the front door, in which case they could have been and gone already and I wouldn't have heard them. But there's always Ted in the morning, although anything could have happened by then. Except there isn't, because tomorrow's Sunday, so he won't come. Oh, God. But it's all right because I won't *be* in here tomorrow. By tomorrow I'll have got out and I'll be safe and all this'll seem like a bad dream. I pushed my arm between the bales and hooked my fingers under the twine, but the tough orange plastic cut into my skin and wouldn't budge, and I couldn't get enough purchase on it without falling off the bucket.

OK, start again. I reassembled my makeshift stool,

climbed back on and started to try to tug the hay away from the bale. *Jeff.* I'd left him a message. Perhaps he'd . . . No, he won't, I thought. He'll probably just think I've gone round the bend, and besides, he might not get it for a week. He could be on location, on holiday . . . anywhere. I groaned. Why had I tried to get the bloody gun? What on earth was I thinking? I must have been out of my mind. That sort of thing only ever works in films, not real life. In real life people end up *dead*, I thought, grimly. Or crippled. I was lucky he hadn't shot me on the spot. And I shouldn't have let him have the brandy. Just made it worse. Oh, yeah, and how were you going to stop him? jeered a voice in my head.

Too late now. Get on with it, get on with it. Hay was starting to come out now, first in wisps and then in handfuls. Soon I'd be able to demolish the whole bale. I climbed off my manger and bucket for a moment, repositioned them so it was easier to reach, and carried on. What about Val? Would she come? Not on my behalf. 'You've made your bed, now you can go and lie in it,' was what she'd said on the phone. But surely she'd come for Jack if he was in trouble? It hadn't sounded like that, but afterwards she might have changed her mind, and my address was in the phone book, and . . . *Address.* I froze.

Jack had recognised the handwriting. But not because he'd been sent cuttings. He'd recognised it *because it belonged to his wife.*

Jack said Val knew about Kitty. If she'd sent the cuttings, then she knew about Danny Watts, too. I racked my brain. What else had she actually said on the phone? That I'd got a nerve to ring her up, and she had nothing to say to me. But she'd known who I was, and she hadn't been surprised, even when I'd mentioned Jack. But why send the cuttings to *me*? Not because I'd slept with him – hundreds of women had done that. No. It had to be something to do with Lenny . . . that Lenny had . . .

Eustace started barking. Judging from the direction, he was in the front garden. Trudy and Lee? I couldn't hear any hooves, but they might not bring their ponies down the path. I got off the bucket and went and stood by the door, heart thumping, desperate to call out, but terrified that Jack would hear me. The barks were getting louder, nearer. The dog let up for a moment and I heard Lee's voice. ''S'all right, mate, wassup, then?'

Thank God. 'Lee?' I whispered.

More barking. Very close, this time.

'Come on, mate, leave it out . . .'

I rapped on the door with my knuckles. Eustace stopped barking. I heard his nails clicking on the cobbles as he padded over to investigate and the scuff of Lee's plimsolls as he followed. The dog sniffed along the bottom of the door, his nose blocking the little strip of light. 'What is it, mate? Wassa matter?'

'Lee,' I hissed. 'Over here.'

'Alice? What you doing in there?'

'Keep your voice down.'

'What's going on? You locked in?'

'Yeah. Lee . . .'

''S a padlock. He lock you in? The bloke off the telly?'

'Yeah. Can you—'

'What you done?'

'Nothing.'

'My mum and dad had a fight once, and Dad locked Mum in the bedroom. We was all laughing, but she was doing her nut.'

'Lee, can you let me out?'

'There's no key. Dad let her out, though. In the end.'

'Lee . . .' *Keep calm, just keep calm.* 'This is really important. The key. Can you see it anywhere?'

''Ang on . . . Dad said he only let her out 'cause he wanted his dinner. He never got it though. Nothing doing. Ain't here. You all right in there?'

'Can you turn the light on?'

'Yeah, course.'

I blinked as the box lit up, warm and orange. 'Thanks.'

'No problem. What d'you want me to do, look in the house?'

'No, wait a sec. Is Trudy with you?'

'Nah, she's gone. That bloke, is he still here?'

'Yes. Just let me think, OK?'

There was silence for a minute, and I heard Lee on the other side of the door, shuffling his feet and fiddling with the padlock. I could imagine him, a suntanned, undersized ten-going-on-thirty with ragged hair and round, boot-polish eyes.

'You scared of him, Alice?' Lee's voice sounded grown-up, sympathetic.

'Yeah.'

'I can tell. You bin crying.'

'Lee, d'you think you can get your dad? Tell him I need some help?'

'Yeah, course. You gonna be all right if I go?'

'Yeah.' The concern in his voice was so touching it almost made me start to cry again. 'I'll be fine,' I croaked.

'I ain't got the pony, Alice. Trudy took 'im back.'

'Never mind, just be as quick as you can.'

''S'all right, I won't stop or nothing.'

'Thanks, Lee. I owe you one.'

'Yeah . . . all right. Cheers, mate,' he said to Eustace. He sounded like his dad.

'Go, Lee. Go quick.'

There was a noise somewhere over to the right. The kitchen door being flung open, banging back against the wall.

Jack.

'He's got a gun.' Lee's voice was a child's again, breathy and terrified. I heard footsteps, heavy, coming towards us. 'A gun on him . . .'

'Just go, Lee!' I shouted desperately, 'Run!' I heard a scuffle – breathing – ripping fabric, then the thud of Lee's small body hitting the stable wall and his voice, shrill with terror, 'Lemme go – I won't grass you up – I won't – lemme *go!*'

I pounded the door with my fists, screaming, 'Stop it! Leave him alone! Leave him!' and heard the boy tearing off across the yard. 'Run, Lee! Run!'

Then a colossal bang.

CHAPTER TWENTY-FIVE

It took a second to register – the sound echoed round the yard – *let him have missed, dear God let him have missed.* I couldn't hear the running feet any more but perhaps he'd got away. Then the echoes died and there were slower, heavier feet, moving away from the stable in the same direction as Lee's, and a moan of pain from somewhere in the middle of the yard.

'Jack, he's a child! For God's sake, he's a baby, don't hurt him, don't—'

Lee's scream, piercing, high and desperate, cut into mine. There was a split second of silence, followed by another huge bang as Jack fired again. 'NO!' I flung myself at the door, screaming, blubbering, trying to beat my way through the wood with my bare hands. 'He's a child, he was trying to help me, only trying to help . . . oh my God . . . Jack . . . *No . . .*' I collapsed in a heap at the bottom of the door.

I don't know how long I was there, what I did . . . any of it. Just clutching my head in my hands, rocking and wailing and moaning and . . . Oh, God. I don't want to remember it, because you can't imagine, you just *can't.* Realising. That was the worst. More, even, than the first shock. The enormity of it. Being part of it. I kept thinking, over and over, if I'd just phoned the police, if I'd told Ted, if I'd tried to warn Trudy and Lee, if I hadn't tried to get the bloody gun, it wouldn't have happened. Lee wouldn't be dead. And then I thought, it can't be true, it's all a mistake, it's not possible. Nobody could shoot a little boy like that, nobody. I lay down on my side and tried to see under the door. Nothing. Just the gutter.

'Lee? Answer me! Lee! Please, answer me . . . please . . . oh, please, tell me you're all right, you're not dead . . . *please* . . .'

There was a noise at the door and for a second I had a wild hope that it was Lee, but it was the dog, whining and scratching to come in. 'Eustace, I can't let you in, baby, I can't. Where's Lee, Eustace, is he all right? Tell me he's all right. I'm coming out of here, I'll be out in a minute, I will . . .'

I clambered back on top of the bucket and tore at the bale, ripping out sections of hay and throwing them down on the floor. The bale in front of the open half-door was wedged horizontally, but if I could just get up into the space I'd made, I'd be able to push it down into the yard.

I grabbed hold of the base of the nearest upright with both hands and put one foot as high up the partition as I could, then kicked off with my other foot. I couldn't get a purchase, wasn't prepared for the pain and I couldn't hold it, I *couldn't*. I hung there for a moment and slid back down the wall and onto the floor. The bucket broke my fall but my lower back hit the floor first and the impact was – well, indescribable. I felt as if someone had whacked the base of my spine with a mallet and driven it straight up through the top of my head. I writhed in agony, stupefied and howling wordlessly, like an animal.

I lifted my head and looked at the partition again. It seemed enormous. Impossible to get off the floor, never mind climb. 'I can't, Eustace, I just *can't*.'

Why had I let Jack stay? Why hadn't I kicked him out, that first night, told him he wasn't welcome? Because . . . because he was a contact with the past, with Lenny, *and I was so tired of being alone.* Just to have someone *there*, even if it meant Jack drunk. And then I was sorry for him, and . . . oh, *God.*

I shook my head violently from side to side. This can't be happening, it can't be, *I can't bear it.* Stupid, so stupid, wanting that excitement, that buzz Lenny'd given me, that feeling of being on top of a great big shout of life. How could I have been so *weak*? I should have told him to go but I didn't, not till it was too late, far too late. And now Lee was dead in the yard and Jack . . . *Jack* . . .

What have I done? My God, what have I done?

I reached out and pulled the scattered sections of hay towards me, teasing them out to make a bed, then rolled myself onto it and curled up, my hands over my ears to block out Eustace's whimpering. 'Stop, please stop. Stop *everything.*'

I don't know how much time passed. I remember being thirsty, and crawling over to where I'd tipped the water out to see if there was any left on the floor. There was a little in a dip by the base of the wall, not enough to scoop with my palm, so I stuck my fingertips in it and sucked them, and it helped a bit, but then at the bottom it was gritty and coated my mouth, and sometime after that I started shaking, and I remember being surprised that I was shaking and couldn't stop, and feeling as if it wasn't me at all but I'd stepped outside myself. My back kept on aching, and I was aware of the pain being there but somehow I wasn't really connected with it, or with anything else, really. I'm not here, I thought. I've gone away somewhere. Cut myself off. Disappeared.

CHAPTER TWENTY-SIX

I heard the padlock being undone and the creak of the door opening. I didn't open my eyes.

'Alice.' Jack's voice from the doorway.

I kept my eyes closed and curled up tighter. I had no will to move, to shout, to fight or do anything. I felt completely empty. I waited for Jack to come in, but he didn't. He said my name again. 'Alice. Look at me.' His voice was flat.

Slowly, very slowly, I raised my head and stared at him. He was standing on the threshold with a blanket in his hand. The gun must be underneath, I thought, dully. The blanket's to silence it.

I pulled myself off the floor into a sitting position. It took so much effort.

'Can you get up?'

'I . . .' The words wouldn't come.

'Let me help you.'

I stared at the blanket.

'It's all right, I'm not going to . . .' He started towards me. 'For you,' he said, holding it out as if he'd brought me a present. 'I brought it for you.'

No gun. He's not holding the gun. In his pocket, the gun's in his pocket. He isn't going to kill me. Not now. But later. Later . . . I've got to talk to him. Make a connection. Make him remember who I am. Say to him . . . what? Say thank you. Thank you for bringing me a blanket.

'Thank you.'

'Here.' He stood over me and draped the blanket over my shoulders. I could smell brandy. He made an odd noise in his throat. Choking. 'I don't . . .' I could barely hear him. 'I don't want to hurt you.'

'You killed Lee. I heard it.'

Jack didn't answer. I looked past him, into the yard. It was dusk. There was a spill of light from the kitchen doorway and halfway across the cobbles a dark, flat shape. Something draped over the top. Cloth. Sacks. Lee. Jack had covered him with sacks.

Eustace came round the corner at the far side of the house, saw me, started to trot towards me, tail wagging, then broke off suddenly and swerved towards—

'No! Eustace!' I meant to shout, but it came out as a croak. The dog looked at me for a moment, then put his head down again, sniffing at the cloth, getting his nose underneath, and . . . 'No!'

I lurched to my feet, pushed past Jack and stumbled into the yard. Eustace had uncovered the top of Lee's head, and I could see his black hair and something – a lump? At the side, near his ear. Yellowish. Dense. Fluid on the cobbles, where Eustace was licking. Blood? Yes, but . . . the stuff . . . the stuff was . . . My God, it was . . .

'No! Stop! Stop it!' I wanted to grab the dog but my body refused to obey me. 'Jack, help me! For God's sake, do something!' Then he was beside me, yanking on Eustace's collar while the dog growled and twisted his head round, trying to bite. 'Get him inside, just get him inside.'

Eustace snarled as Jack dragged him backwards to the kitchen and dumped him inside, slamming the door.

I couldn't move. 'How could you?'

'Alice.' Jack was beside me again. 'Come on. In the house.'

'Twice. You did it twice.'

He didn't speak. I wrenched my eyes away from Lee's head and turned to look at him.

'You didn't have to kill him.'

Jack turned his head away. 'I'm sorry.'

'He was only a *child*. Why, Jack? Why did you kill him?'

'I'm sorry . . . I . . . I'm lost, Alice.'

I suddenly felt completely calm. Shock, probably. 'Jack, we have to call the police.'

He stared at me.

'The police. We've got to tell them about Lee.'

He shook his head. I tried again. 'I know the phone isn't working here, but there's one on the green, and . . .'

'No.'

'Jack, we've got to.'

'I said no, and I mean it.' His hand moved towards his pocket. I took a step back.

'OK, OK. No police. But at least take him somewhere. In the stable. On the hay. Please, Jack. I'll . . . I'll help you.'

He shook his head. 'Go into the house.'

'Wait.' I pulled the blanket off my shoulders. 'Use this. Wrap him. Wrap his head.'

'All right.'

'Will you leave the light on? In the stable. Don't leave him in the dark.'

'If that's what you want. Now go.'

I didn't look back. Eustace greeted me enthusiastically, as if nothing had happened, and I sat on the sofa and stared at the rug and waited for Jack.

He didn't look at me when he came in, but went straight to the sink and washed his hands. When he turned round I saw a dark stain on his jacket and shirt.

'That's tea. You threw it at me, remember?'

'Did I?' I stood up. 'I have to feed the animals.'

'I'll come with you.'

208

I made my way to the barn, Jack beside me, and went through the evening routine in silence, like a robot, and all the time, this other part of me was standing back, watching. Marvelling, almost. As if I'd split into two people. That's the only way I can describe it. The strangest feeling. It must have been exhaustion, because by the time we got back to the kitchen to feed Eustace I was light-headed and swaying, barely able to keep upright.

I refilled the dog's water bowl and sat down at the kitchen table. Jack closed the curtains and sat down opposite me. We stared at each other. I felt as if I would never get up again.

'I'm sorry. About the kid.'

'Lee. His name's Lee. Why didn't you leave, Jack? When you . . . when I was in the stable? Why didn't you just *go*?'

'Nowhere *to* go,' he said, flatly. 'It's the end. Coming here, it wasn't just about the film. I really did want to see you.'

'Why?'

'Last night, you think I don't remember, but when I said I loved you, I meant it.'

I shook my head.

'I'm sorry. It's all . . . out of control. Everything. When Susie died, it was like she was paying for it. Everything I'd done . . . she was the price.' He stopped, ducked his head, and held out his hand. 'Please, Alice. I feel so guilty.'

I didn't move.

'Me and Lenny, we had the lot: money, success, birds, you name it. We'd have made it in America, too, if Lenny hadn't lost his nerve.'

'The film was no good. You said so yourself.'

'Yeah. But if Lenny'd been a hundred per cent we'd have been all right. He was always fucked up – insecure – but he could handle it. Even when we did that run at the Fortune and he was all over the place, we were doing all right. Then sitting there on television telling everyone he

209

was an alcoholic . . . I did my best but I couldn't stop him, he wouldn't shut up. *Jesus.*'

He fell silent, and I thought back. 'That was after . . . after Kitty, wasn't it?'

'Yeah. Couple of months. You'd buggered off and he was falling apart. All hell broke loose afterwards. They asked me for a comment. What the fuck was I supposed to say? "It's a good job we're going to the States because no one in this country's going to give us a pot to piss in"? I told him he'd ruined us. You know why he blamed you? Because he couldn't live with it.'

'I want to know what happened, Jack. With Kitty.'

'Lenny wouldn't take her seriously. The threats, I mean. He thought she was trying it on, that if he bought her a few presents, introduced her to a couple of people who could help her . . .' Jack rolled his eyes. 'She wanted to be an actress. Lenny thought that would do the trick. I kept telling him it wouldn't work but I had no idea he was going to bring her along to that party. I didn't know you'd be there either, come to that. There were people all over the house, you remember, and Lenny and Kitty were in his car, down by the lake.'

'But why didn't anybody see? From the house? There were people swimming, cars everywhere . . .'

'They were on the other side, down the hill. There were trees. Anyway, this was much later, when I went down there. I didn't know where they were. I was in the house and Lenny came and found me. He was in a terrible state. He said . . . he and Kitty, they'd been fooling around in the car and she'd hit her head and he couldn't get her to wake up. He kept babbling away about how he thought she was dead and what was he going to do. For Christ's sake, that was all I could get out of him. I kept telling him not to panic, saying she must have knocked herself out, but when we went down there – to the car – even I could see she'd gone. I couldn't think what to do, so we let the handbrake off, and then . . . that was it.'

'I don't believe you.'

'For Christ's sake, you asked and I told you. That's all there was to it.'

'Why were you so sure she was dead?'

'Alice, she wasn't breathing. I swear it.'

'Why didn't you get a doctor?'

'Just think about it for a minute, will you? Think about that party. The police would have had a field day. More drugs than you've had hot dinners. We'd never have got the place cleaned up, and everyone would have known. The woman was *blackmailing* us, remember?'

'But you said you'd already given her some money.'

'Lenny hadn't. I told you, Alice, he thought she was trying it on. I kept telling him she wasn't like that, but he wouldn't listen. He was all over the place, Alice, you can't imagine . . .'

'So you're telling me it was some kind of weird accident?'

'Yes.'

'And then you got hold of Kitty's keys and sent Val round to her flat to look for copies of the film?'

'Yeah, like I said.'

'So what about Danny Watts?'

Jack was absolutely still. '*What?*'

'His name was on Lenny's list.'

Jack shrugged. 'So was half the entertainment business.'

'You mentioned him. Last night.'

'I thought you might remember him, that's all. He was just someone we used to know.'

'I wasn't born yesterday, Jack. He made that film.'

'What makes you think that?'

'The newspaper cutting.'

'What newspaper cutting?'

'I got it this morning. I told you it was a bill, remember? You know what I'm talking about, Jack. It was like the other one. The one you tried to hide from me.'

'And it was about Danny Watts?' He sounded astonished. I've misunderstood, I thought. I've got it wrong. It wasn't Val . . . or . . . or . . . *he didn't know she knew.*

'Where is it? Give it to me.'

I pulled it out of my pocket. He snatched it and read it.

When he'd finished, I said, 'You killed him. Shot him. You must have taken a gun, you—'

'Fucking *listen* to me, Alice! Just listen to me for a moment. I didn't know what I was doing. When I went there, yeah, I had the gun, but I didn't . . . I don't know, I was angry. I mean, I used to look at him, taking money off me month after month, and I'd think, *why the fuck are you alive?* What gives you the right to be alive when my daughter's dead?' He dropped his head and stared at the cutting again.

'There's no justice. All right, I screwed everything up, but I thought . . . I thought . . . Something I've got to do right, do everyone a favour. Not at the time – I just lost my rag, but afterwards I thought, *what the hell . . .*' He fell silent, then looked up at me, bewildered. 'She can't . . .' he muttered. 'She doesn't know.'

'You mean Val, don't you?'

'Yes.'

'She sent the cuttings, didn't she?'

He nodded.

'Why, Jack?'

'I don't know,' he said, helplessly.

We stared at each other for a moment, then Jack's eyes shifted to somewhere above my head, as if he was talking to someone standing behind me. 'I honestly thought, after that business with Kitty, we were in the clear. Lenny wanted to go to the police, but I kept telling him they'd never find the car. I talked to him, Val talked to him, we kept saying it was just an accident, and we barely knew her, not really. Didn't even know what her name was until Val went to the flat – she'd seen a letter or something, said she wasn't called Kitty at all, but something else.'

'Gail.'

'Yeah, that's right. But we had no idea about Danny Watts until Lenny got a phone call . . . three, four weeks after the party. Danny was asking where Kitty was, then he said he'd got a copy of the film and we had to pay him. A loan, he called it. He wanted to set up a company, making films. Said if we didn't get involved he'd go to the police.

'I got a phone call from Lenny in the middle of the night, that was the first I knew about it. I couldn't get any sense out of him but he kept saying he'd got to talk to me about Kitty, so in the end I got in the car and went over there. He must have been drinking before Danny called, and he was . . .' Jack shook his head and looked at me as if he'd just remembered I was there.

'It was a nightmare. I kept asking him what he'd said to Danny, and he couldn't remember. Or he'd come out with something and then five minutes later he'd say the opposite. It was pathetic – like talking to a child. He'd got me over there to talk about Danny but he kept rambling, mainly about how much he missed you, and how if you came back to him everything would be all right and he'd stop drinking and marry you and it would all be marvellous, and I was tearing my hair out trying to get him to tell me about this phone call.

'I kept asking him what he'd said, but he wouldn't answer, just kept coming out with all this stuff about you, and I knew there was something he wasn't telling me. I mean, all Danny had was the film, and knowing we'd been at that party. Lenny could have denied it but he told him we'd pay. Practically admitted it. He thought we'd give Danny the money and he'd just disappear. He couldn't fucking *see* it! If he hadn't been pissed out of his mind I'd . . .'

'What did you do?'

'I told him he was a stupid cunt and I'd been sorting him out and propping him up for years and I was sick of it. And do you know what he did? He started crying. Saying he was no good and he'd messed everything up and I'd be better off without him. As if I was some bird and he was trying to give me the elbow. I told him not to be so fucking ridiculous.'

'It was his car. In the lake.'

'Danny didn't *know* that. No one saw us, Alice. That was the stupid thing. We could have got away with it. Danny didn't know anything, but Lenny . . . Christ knows what he said to him. He couldn't keep his mouth shut. He was always talking about how we ought to go to the police, how he wanted to tell you. Kept saying if he was going to marry you, you ought to know what you were letting yourself in for . . .'

'He didn't, Jack. I had no idea. I swear it.'

'All the time, in America, I was shitting myself. That's why I used to follow him. He wouldn't talk to me about it any more and I was terrified. I'd imagine him getting pissed in some bar and telling God knows who. I couldn't trust him. For Christ's sake, I didn't even tell Val that Danny was blackmailing us.'

'But then how . . .'

'*I don't know!* I couldn't tell her. After she'd seen that film I'd begged her to help me, and she said, if she helped us, went to Kitty's flat, she made me promise – no more girls. I had to, I owed her that at least, and I couldn't see any way out. She said to me . . . said I'd ruined her life, and I told her I was going to sort myself out, I said we'd go on holiday, Egypt, she'd always wanted to see the pyramids. But this thing with Danny . . . I never told her, Alice, I couldn't.'

'I don't understand. You said you'd left her.'

'I did. When Susie got ill. I don't know what happened, it was . . . I had to get away, I couldn't bear to be there, to look at her, knowing there was nothing I could do and it was all my fault. I know what I said about Val, but I just couldn't cope with it, Alice. I cut myself off. But Lenny'd gone, and there was no one I could talk to. I felt so alone, and just . . . I didn't know what to do.'

'But you've got friends.'

'Not like Lenny. I'd lost him, Alice. Even before he died, he was so out of it. He wouldn't . . . he wouldn't . . . It was all such a fucking mess. The work wasn't there, Alice. Like I told you. Bits and pieces. Nothing that paid. And Danny wanted money, and Val was always ringing me up saying Susie had to have all these treatments: psychiatrists, homeopathy, faith healers. Going from one set of quacks to another, and I couldn't say no. Then Rosie wanted to go to art school, and I was in debt, I'd borrowed off Findlater. I couldn't afford the payments on the flat.'

'Was that why you went back to her? Money?'

'Part of it. And Val. She wanted it. God knows why, but she did.'

'She still loves you, Jack.'

He shook his head. 'That's all gone – a long time ago. My fault. But . . . oh, I don't know. I have this dream, Alice. It's always the same. Lenny, saying he's waiting for me. He looks so happy. Christ, I miss him.'

'So do I.'

There was a moment's silence, and then Jack said, 'Dress up for me, Alice.'

'What?'

'The costume, I saw it in the attic. I want you to put it on.'

'The Bunny costume?'

'Please. Come on.' Jack grabbed my arm and pulled me upright.

'Why?' I said, bewildered. 'I can't.'

'Yes, you can.'

'No, Jack, that's horrible, it's—'

'Do it. For me.'

He put his hand in his pocket and pulled out the gun.

He wants to shut everything out, I thought. Go back to the past. Where he was safe. Successful. Happy. If he was ever happy.

'Have you got any candles?' he asked.

'In the dresser. Do you want one on the table?'

'I want them everywhere. New game, Bunny Alice. We're going to put out the lights.'

He was smiling. I've got to play along, I thought. I don't have a choice.

CHAPTER TWENTY-SEVEN

The bathroom window was too small for me to escape. Jack said he'd wait outside and I had ten minutes to get ready. I could hear him pacing up and down the corridor as I stood in front of the mirror with a mouthful of hairgrips and pinned on the bunny ears. Behind me, on the wall, I could see the shadow of a monster rabbit, thrown there by the row of candles on the basin. You can't do make-up by candle-light, not properly, anyway, and my hands were shaking so much I could hardly get the lid off the foundation, never mind apply it. I've got to cover the bruises, I thought. If I don't cover the bruises, he'll know I haven't tried.

The stuff was all there when we opened the box, even the tights and the rosette with my name on it, but it looked like it belonged in a child's dressing-up chest. The tail was my second-best one, and the collar and cuffs were curling and yellowed. At least the costume still fits, I thought, that's something to be grateful for. But the bow-tie wouldn't stay straight and one of the ears wouldn't stand up properly. It kept flopping forward and I couldn't make it stick. Impossible to believe, now, that this outfit had once made me feel sexy and powerful. I looked like a clown.

I saw Jack in the mirror, pushing open the bathroom door, then felt the gun against the back of my neck. I didn't want to look at his face, or my own, so I looked down at the plug-hole, instead. Big crack in the porcelain. I don't think I'd ever noticed it before.

Jack took hold of my chin and twisted my head so I had to look at him. I closed my eyes and tried not to cry as he rubbed the scar on my cheek – Lenny's scar – with the ball of his thumb. Then he brought the gun round so the muzzle was touching my temple.

'Look at me!' He sounded petulant, like a child. I opened my eyes. His face had no expression and his pupils were tiny. Pinpoints.

He dropped his hands so the gun was pointing at my waist. 'Pick up a candle.'

I did as he said. 'Turn round.' I caught a last glimpse of my broken ear, forlorn and dangling, in the mirror. Almost like saying goodbye to myself. None of it felt real. 'Open the door.' He poked me in the back with the gun. 'Move!'

I tottered down the corridor in front of him, out of practice and crippled by the heels. No chance of running in these shoes, I thought, and wondered how quickly I could get them off.

Jack opened the kitchen door. The curtains were drawn and the room dark except for the table and the worktop, which were dotted with candles in saucers. 'Go on.'

At the club they told us to think of something positive before we went on the floor, but I couldn't. There was only room for one thought in my mind.

I don't want to die.

CHAPTER TWENTY-EIGHT

Eustace trotted over to sniff my shoes. I bent down to reassure him, but Jack took my elbow and propelled me towards the table. The gun banged against the back of the chair as he reached for it and sat down, still keeping hold of me. I stood awkwardly beside him, not knowing what he wanted.

'Say what you used to say.'

'I'm sorry, I don't know what you mean.'

'At the club,' he said, impatiently. 'What you used to say.'

'Good evening . . .' I began, hesitantly.

'Go on.'

'Good evening, I'm your Bunny, Alice.' The words made a strange shape in my mouth. They sounded like nonsense.

'And?'

I looked at him in disbelief. He wants me to do the whole thing, I thought. Serve him a drink.

'Go on. That's what you're here for.'

That's what I'm here for.

'OK,' I said, trying to think. 'I'll need a few things. Can I switch on the lights? To find them?'

'Where are they?'

'In the dresser.'

Jack looked towards it, and then at the back door, and said, 'I'll come with you. Get a candle.'

He stood behind me while I groped around for paper napkins and an ashtray and arranged them on a tray. My hands shook, but my mind was racing, trying to remember what to do next. *Got to get it right. Pretend it's real. Humour him. Be cheerful. Get him to relax.* I forced a smile.

'There was other stuff, too,' I said, 'But it doesn't matter, because this one's on the house.'

He didn't smile back. 'Ready?' he said.

'Yes.'

He gestured with the gun. 'You first.'

Jack sat back down, and I wobbled my way through the Bunny Dip, tail towards the table, back arched, knees bent, and bumped against his shoulder as I put the napkins and ashtray down in front of him. 'Sorry. Out of practice.' He stared at me, waiting for the next thing.

'I ought to ask to see your key now,' I said, quickly, 'but . . .'

'Wait.' Jack fished around in his pocket and held something out to me. It looked like half a cinema ticket. 'There you are,' he said, solemnly.

'Wh . . . ? Oh. Yes.' I pretended to read it. 'Thank you, Mr Flowers. What would you like to drink?'

'Brandy.'

'Brandy,' I repeated, pretending to write it down.

There was only one measure left in the bottle. When I came back with the tray Jack was turning the gun over in his hands, his elbows on the table. I held out the scrap of cardboard. 'Here's your key, Mr Flowers.' He didn't move to take it, so I put it down in front of him with the brandy.

He didn't speak. I wasn't sure what to do next so I perched on the back of one of the kitchen chairs and tried to ease my heels out of the shoes without Jack noticing. There was a long silence while he looked at the gun and then he said, 'When I have the dream about Lenny, and then I wake up, it's like . . .' He shook his head. 'I can't describe it. Do you think I'll ever see him again?' he asked.

'Or Susie? You know, in the . . .' He jerked his head at the ceiling. 'I'd like to say to her . . . both of them . . . tell them I'm sorry. You believe in all that stuff, don't you?'

'Ye-es, but . . . I'm not sure it works like that.'

'How does it work, then?' he asked, plaintively. 'Tell me.' It was like a child asking his mother why the sky is blue. If I just keep talking, I thought, keep him calm, I can get him to give me the gun. If I get this right, he'll do what I say and I'll be able to get out of the house and everything will be all right.

'Well,' I said, carefully, 'I think—'

That was when we heard the car.

'What's that?' Jack jumped up and we stood side by side, listening. The sound was close, and mine's the last house in the lane, a long way past the others. There was nowhere else for the car to be going. Eustace knew it, too. He rushed at the door, barking.

'Get him out of here,' Jack said. The dog growled in protest as I pulled him across the room and into the hall, pushed him into the sitting room, and shut the door on him. When I turned round, Jack was in the kitchen door-way. We stared at each other, listening to the car.

Then the engine stopped. I tried to retreat, but Jack bundled me back into the kitchen, the gun digging into my spine. We stood together, facing the door.

'Who is it?'

'I don't know.'

'*Who is it?*'

'I swear, I don't—'

'Shut up.'

The yard gate dragging across the cobbles. I felt sick. I could hear Jack's breathing, footsteps coming towards the door, knocking . . .

'Alice?'

A man. Fred Boyle?

More knocking.

'Open up!' It wasn't Fred.

The latch moved. 'Don't!' My shout came out as a whisper.

'For Christ's sake, woman, you live in the middle of bloody nowhere and you don't even . . .' *Jeff.* It was Jeff. The door opened wide. I caught an image of him like a snapshot, the tanned, handsome face with the George Best hair, T-shirt, biceps, tight jeans. 'What the—'

That was as far as he got.

Jack shot him.

CHAPTER TWENTY-NINE

I hadn't felt Jack move the gun – seen him raise it – *anything* – but there was an explosion of sound and force that filled the room and slammed right through me, rocking me backwards on my feet. Jeff didn't rock or stagger, he just fell. One moment he was standing in the doorway, the next moment he was flat on his back.

For a split second, I looked at Jack. His face was a furious, meaty slab of flesh and his mouth was working, but I couldn't hear anything, I was in the middle of this world of noise, the room was just full, full of it. Then I got to Jeff somehow, I don't know how, I wasn't thinking, it just happened, and I found myself on my knees beside him, rocking, keening, I don't know what.

The porch light was on and I could see the wound high up in his chest. It wasn't big, but the blood coming out onto his pale T-shirt was so red, so bright, I'd never seen anything so bright, and my one thought was that I must stop it coming out, keep it inside him. I pulled a towel off the rail at the end of the worktop and held it over the place, but I didn't know whether to put pressure on it or what to do, and it was my fault, mine, he'd come because of me and— Jeff's lips were moving. 'What is it?'

'Help . . . me . . .'

'Yes . . . yes . . .' I looked round for Jack, but he'd disappeared.

'Ambulance . . .'

'Yes . . . ambulance . . .' *Get help. Hospital.* I looked round for the phone, remembered it was smashed. No way to get help. 'Sit up, you've got to sit up.'

'No . . . Ambulance . . .'

'Don't talk.' Jeff took another breath, and I stared as bright, frothy bubbles of blood came out of his mouth and then I scrambled up and out into the yard screaming, 'Help me! Somebody – please – help me! Call an ambulance!' Even as I was doing it, I knew it was stupid, there aren't any neighbours near enough, I couldn't even see any lights, but it was just that I didn't know what to do and I felt so responsible . . .

I went back inside. It wasn't bravery, I wasn't even thinking about Jack. He'd vanished, in any case. There was only Jeff. I knew he was going to die. Not because of knowing about medicine or first aid – I don't – but the blood and his face, the look on his face . . . I knew it wouldn't be long, and that even if I managed to get help it would be too late. All I could do was to be with him. I knelt down beside him again. His face had turned grey and his lips were purple, almost blue. There was a noise from his chest almost like whistling, and he started to cough and splutter, like drowning, drowning from the inside.

I wiped the blood with tea towels but there was more and more and it was so *red*. That's what you never see on films, how red it is. And I couldn't do anything, only be there with him and say, 'I'm sorry, I'm so sorry,' again and again. I don't know if he heard me. He never spoke again but his eyes were still open, and I got more tea towels and tried to wad them under his head. I took his hand and stroked it and touched his hair, and then he was making gurgling noises and choking like a baby does, but the blood kept coming out of his mouth . . . I don't know how long, minutes I think, a few minutes, and then . . . then there was one more breath, a sort of long, wet, aaaaah sound, and it was leaving him, the breath – the life – leaving his body, and that was the last, and he was dead.

I didn't let go of his hand. I knew he couldn't feel it any more, but I didn't want to let go. I stared at his face for a long time. A bit more blood trickled out of his mouth and onto his chin. His eyes were still open – huge, black holes. I bent forward and brushed the hair off his face with my fingertips.

'Jeff, I'm sorry. You shouldn't have come. I know, I phoned you, but you shouldn't . . . It was so kind, you didn't have to, you didn't have to come . . . I'm so sorry . . .'

After a while I fetched more tea towels, wetted them under the tap, and tried to clean the blood from his face and neck. Somewhere in the middle of it, it occurred to me about the police – not touching him – evidence. But I couldn't just leave him, lying on the dirty floor, because . . . Well, I'd been married to him, and whatever he'd done to me, when I should never have married him in the first place, I couldn't just walk away from him, and there wasn't anybody else. And that's the thing, you don't know what that's like, what you'll do. And he was so handsome, and he looked – even with all those dirty tea towels round his head, the blood and the mess, he still looked . . . I just couldn't bear to leave him like that.

I wanted to say a prayer, and I started, but then I remembered Jeff hadn't believed, either, like Lenny, and I thought it wasn't right because he wouldn't want it and I'd only be saying it for myself, so I stopped. I closed his eyes, because that didn't seem right, either, leaving them open, and I got a cushion from the sofa and put it under his head, cleared up all the tea towels and put them in the sink to make it more neat, and then came back to him and held his hand again and kissed his forehead. I knew it was pointless because he was dead and he couldn't feel it but I had to do something, and that was all I could think of to do.

Then I heard banging and crashing from the hall and a yelp from Eustace – and then the door was kicked open. 'What the hell was he doing here?' Jack shouted at me. I twisted round to look at him. The gun was still in his hand and he was shaking, furious.

'He's dead,' I said, and turned away.

'What?' I heard a clatter, a chair being pushed over, and the next second Jack was standing over us. I could feel his anger vibrating against my back and head like an electric current, and he was making fidgety, jerky movements as if he didn't know what to do with himself. I looked down at Jeff, lying in front of me, so solid and still. Life and death, I thought. There's so little between them. So very little. A movement, a breath. Life and death, and you are in the middle.

Am I next? I thought. Is it me? Is it now? I wasn't frightened. That was the oddest thing – I ought to have been petrified, but I was calm inside, and silent. Completely silent, and perfectly still.

Jack's roar made me jump. 'What did you say?'

'He's dead,' I repeated, quietly.

'Who is he?'

'Jeff.'

'Who?'

'My husband. Ex-husband.'

'What the fuck was he doing here?'

I didn't answer.

Jack nudged Jeff's arm with his foot. 'You deal with it,' he said coldly. Then he turned and went back to the sitting room, slamming the door behind him.

The kitchen door was still open. I looked out into the

yard, then back at the hall door. Silence. I waited a couple of seconds, holding my breath – *Don't come back, please please don't come back.* Still no sound from the sitting room. I scrambled to my feet, wrenched off my shoes, and ran.

Jeff had left his headlights on, lighting up the gateway and the yard, but the lane was pitch dark. The gravel stung my feet and I got a stitch almost immediately, but all I could think of was keeping ahead of Jack long enough to get to my neighbours at the end of the lane, half a mile down. But I can do it, I thought, I've got to. No noise coming from the house, no shouts. Jack doesn't know I've gone, he thinks I'm still with Jeff, please God, let him not realise I've gone. If I can just get to the church, the Andersons at the Rectory, I can explain, and they'll phone the police and someone'll come and I'll be safe and it'll be all right. Everything's going to be all right as long as I just keep going. Got to keep going, never mind the pain. I could hear my feet, my breathing, my heart, everything, saying, *got to – got to – got to—*

A car. There was a car. I heard it, then saw the lights sweeping through the hedge beyond the bend. Fred Boyle, it had to be. Come for Lee. *Thank God.* I stopped in the middle of the road, clutching my side. The car came round the corner in a blaze of light. Full beam. I raised my arms to wave.

It drove straight towards me. 'Fred!' I shouted. The car didn't slow. He hadn't seen me. He *must* have seen me. But then why didn't he—

The car wasn't slowing, it was accelerating. It wasn't going to stop.

For a second, I stood frozen in the headlights. Move, my brain ordered. *Move!* I dived sideways and landed by the verge, felt my shoulder slam into the ground, the scorch of the gravel skinning my palm and wrist, caught a glimpse of the underside of the car above me and I half crawled, half rolled down into the black ditch while the car ploughed into the hedge above me, and the world was full of the noise of the engine, then a bang and the sound of glass breaking and the trees being ripped apart, grinding and scratching and splintering, and then a thin, high scream, and I thought, it's screaming, the hedge is *screaming*. There was a dark kaleidoscope of branches moving above my head, cracking and tearing and twisting, then the car stalled and there was silence and no movement except a single, spinning tyre, a foot away from my head. I heard a groan from the car as it shifted on the bank. It's going to come down, I thought, land on top of me. I tried to turn round, to crawl out from under it, but the brambles tore at my legs and caught my hair and I couldn't get free and the car lurched again and it was starting to tip and I scrabbled for the bank but I couldn't see, and . . . No! shouted my brain. *No!* Not like this.

CHAPTER THIRTY

The noise came from somewhere above my head. First a creak, then a door slamming. Car door. Car. Car in the ditch. *On top of me, falling, it's falling on top of me and it's going to crush me. GET AWAY FROM IT GOT TO GET OUT OF THE DITCH GET OUT—*

I groped for the bank. Dark, can't see, why so dark . . . got to get the right side for the road – yes – grass, not hedge, good, grass is good, but there's something against my side, my hip – car, it's the car – no – wait, not the car, wrong side, this is concrete – hard – barrier – for the drain, big drain – pull myself onto the verge, hands and knees, yes . . . yes . . .

I found myself flat on my face on the verge. Still here. I'm still here. Still alive. Ha, ha. *Run, run, as fast as you can, can't catch me, I'm the gingerbread man. Oh no. No, no, no, no you can't catch me.* Cold though. I shouldn't be so cold. It's summer. Can't really remember . . . why I'm here. Can't have been taking Eustace for a walk. Not in the middle of the night. That would be stupid.

Twigs cracking. I looked up. It was coming from the direction of the car. Damn thing, trying to kill me. The Andersons, that's who I was going to see, because . . . because . . . *Feet.* I'd heard a door, hadn't I? Car door slamming. Must mean someone getting out. Save me a journey if it's the Andersons, I thought, stupidly. Except he's the vicar, and they don't go around trying to run people over.

There was a light underneath the car. Coming from the other side. Torch. I could make out the shape of a big, dark saloon, its bonnet buried in the hedge and its front wheels overhanging the ditch. The light disappeared for a moment, then re-emerged at the back of the car, blinding me. I put a hand up to shield my eyes, but I couldn't see who was holding the torch.

I got to my knees. Time to go, I thought. Got to see the Andersons. If I could just see them, everything would be all right, I knew it would. Just as long as I arrived. Then I could get it all sorted out in my mind. I'd tell them about the car in the ditch. They ought to know about that. Mr Anderson was in Bomber Command during the war, before he started being a vicar. A car in a ditch would be no problem for him. Or to Mrs Anderson. She wears sensible shoes – probably deals with things like this all the time.

The light was hurting my eyes. It was coming nearer. Why couldn't they turn it off?

It was above me, now. Shining straight down. Dazzling. I couldn't look at it. I ducked my head. The feet were in front of me. Shoes. Pretty. Wedges, with straps. Not Mrs Anderson's shoes, I thought. Or her toenails. She wouldn't paint her toenails red.

'Get up.'

The woman who didn't have Mrs Anderson's feet stood close to me, holding the torch between us, and as I got up I saw her face, illuminated from below in its harsh yellow light. It was sallow and haggard with dark circles under the eyes, as if she'd been ill, framed with wisps of grey, wiry hair. I know you, I thought. You're the gypsy from the picture book, the one who danced on the hill, only now you're old—

'You rang me,' she said. 'That was stupid. But then you never were very bright, were you?'

'Not really,' I said, and then the world disappeared and took the gypsy with it.

CHAPTER THIRTY-ONE

Kitty won't look at me. I can see her through the car window, but she won't look at me. She knows I'm there, but it's somebody else she wants and that's why she won't turn her head. She's waiting for me to go away, but I can't, there's something I've got to ask her, it's important . . . I can see her long arm bones resting on the steering wheel, the skeleton fingers tapping, the bunny ears bobbing on the skull as she nods up and down as if she's listening to music in there, but all I can hear is the fingers tapping, banging, louder and louder . . .

Something was pressing against my face. The car, the window . . . No, not glass, but softer. I opened my eyes. The thumping carried on. My face was pressed against something red. The sofa. I was lying on a sofa, wrapped in a blanket. I was in the kitchen. My kitchen. The curtains were drawn, so it must be night. Why wasn't I in bed?

I was meant to be somewhere . . . The Andersons'. Why hadn't I got there? I turned my head. There was a woman sitting at the table, watching me. Not Mrs Anderson. Wrong feet. It was the gypsy, from the car. The car that chased me and crashed into the hedge. I remembered the wheel hanging over the ditch, spinning, the bonnet tipping down towards me . . . There was something tight around my waist, digging into me, and the blanket was making my skin itch. I shrugged it off and saw that my shoulders were bare and the inside of my wrist and my palm were raw. The other wrist looked all right, except that there was something grey round it, with a cuff-link. Kissing, I thought, vaguely. Your cuff-links should be kissing, the Bunny Mother always checked, didn't she? But there was nothing for it to kiss. The other arm was bare. I had to find the other cuff before I went on the floor, or she wouldn't let me . . . but I wasn't . . . I couldn't . . . I looked down at the flayed skin and suddenly remembered falling on the gravel, trying to get away from the car. Not the club, the Andersons'. But why had I been going there? The question was too difficult. I pushed it away.

The noise stopped, but my head was hurting. Everything was hurting. I wanted to sleep. I stirred, groggily, wondering why I couldn't get comfortable, why the gypsy was there, why Kitty wouldn't look at me, why . . .

'Wake up.' The gypsy was leaning over me, shaking my shoulder.

'You're hurting . . . Leave me alone.'

'Wake up!'

'No . . . go away . . .'

'Come on, sit up.'

I twisted my head round to look at her. 'What time is it?'

'Half-past six.'

I closed my eyes again.

'Wake *up*.' She wasn't going to go away.

'Who are you?'

'Don't you know? You must be even more stupid than you look.'

More stupid than you look. She'd said that before, hadn't she? Said I was stupid. When she'd shone the torch at me. Said I'd done something stupid. Telephoned her, that was it. I'd phoned her.

Val. It was Val. Of course it was. And Jack, he'd been here, and he . . . he . . . what? Where was he? Val stepped back as I swung my legs off the sofa, started to stand up, felt a sudden, dizzying whoosh of blood from my head, and sat down again. Hold on, I told myself. Don't panic. You'll get there in a minute.

I stared hard at a pair of legs – mine, apparently – in sheer black tights, spider-webbed in a mess of ladders down both sides. Then I examined the backs of my hands. Dirty knuckles. Mud under the fingernails.

'Having a little game, were you?' I looked up. The room, and Val, came back into focus. 'Or was it a lovers' tiff?'

'I was wearing jeans,' I said, confused.

'Not now, you're not.'

'No,' I agreed. 'I'm not. How did I get here?'

'Jack carried you.'

'I don't remember. Where is he?'

Val shrugged. 'No idea.'

I looked round the room. The empty brandy bottle was on the table, the glass, the napkins, candles in saucers . . . Cautiously, I put a hand on the top of my head. Bunny ears. I pulled out the grips, took them off and sat fingering the torn, muddy black satin. They were mine, weren't they? I'd kept them, put them away. *The gun.* Jack had had a gun.

Everything came back in a rush: the newspaper cuttings, the film, Jack threatening to kill Eustace, locking me in the stable, and Lee . . . and then . . . then Jack made me dress up in all this stuff and then . . . *Jeff had arrived.* He'd been here. His body. Lying on the ground by the door. I'd tried to wipe the blood off, kissed him, put a cushion under his head. I turned to look at the sofa. Something was different. The throw had gone. But five cushions. That was the right number. I would have used a plain one, not one with embroidery and bits of mirror. I picked up the brown one and turned it over. Nothing. The green one had a dark patch in one corner. Blood, I thought. From Jeff's mouth.

But where *was* he? I knew he was dead. I'd seen him – *heard* him – die. Jack must have moved him, but there weren't any marks on the lino. Easy to wipe off. Perhaps Val had helped.

I sat with the cushion on my lap. If Val knows Jeff is dead, I thought, she must know that Jack has a gun and he's dangerous, so . . . But she might not know any of it. Jack might have moved him before she arrived. I watched her cross the room, turn on the tap and pour a glass of water. She's bringing it to me, I thought. If I can just keep her calm, perhaps I can talk to her, explain. Persuade her to go to the police.

Val stopped a couple of feet away from me. 'Here,' she said, and with a flick of her wrist chucked it straight in my face. I was too surprised to duck and the water hit me full on, making me gasp.

I groped for the edge of the blanket and wiped my eyes, blinking, too stunned to speak. It wasn't going to work. The woman had crashed her car trying to run me over. Whatever she'd seen in the headlights, I thought, it wasn't just me, it was all the women Jack had ever slept with, including Kitty. No wonder she'd put her foot down.

What had Jack said to me? *Val's always had a thing about you.* I'd belonged to the other bit of Jack and Lenny's lives, hadn't I? And she'd been shut out, excluded. Sending the newspaper cuttings, what was that about? To frighten me, hurt me? To get even? She probably didn't know herself. But the business with Kitty, and then Jack just disintegrating in front of her and leaving her to cope with Susie, and Susie's death. Her world had fallen apart, too.

Still, she'd got me where she wanted me, hadn't she? Sitting here in this stupid costume, looking like something the cat dragged in. She wasn't going to listen to me now.

I measured the distance to the back door with my eyes

and wondered if I could get past her. She was shorter than me, smaller, but I felt so weak and achy. She saw where I was looking. 'It's locked,' she said, scornfully. 'So's the front. I don't know what you think you're playing at, but I've got a few things to say to you, and you're going to hear them whether you like it or not.'

OK, I thought, willing myself not to panic. There's no choice. Listen to her, then get her on your side. Make her give you the key. I looked up at her, standing in front of me, the empty glass in her hand, and tried to read her face. She seemed calm. Controlled, even. I won't mention Jeff yet, I thought. Don't panic. Don't say anything. Wait for her to speak.

'Your dog stinks.'

'Where is he?' I asked.

'I shut him in the dining room.'

'Is he all right?'

'Far as I could see.' She shrugged and played with the glass for a moment, rolling it between her palms. 'Do you know what my daughter said to me? She said she was so ugly it didn't matter what sort of person she was inside because no one was ever going to bother finding out. She really believed it. She said, "Dad doesn't know what you're like. He doesn't know what any of us are like." And do you know why that was? It was because he was never at home. Because there was always some . . . slut – like you – making herself *available* to him.'

'It . . .' I wanted to say, 'It takes two,' but I stopped myself. 'It wasn't like that. I know you don't believe it, but I loved Lenny.'

'I loved Lenny,' she repeated, mockingly. 'But of course you didn't let a little thing like that stop you sleeping with my husband, did you?'

'I . . . I don't know what to say, except . . . I'm sorry.'

236

'No, you're not,' she said, evenly. 'You couldn't care less. I don't imagine anything much matters to you unless you can get something out of it, but then the world's your oyster, isn't it? You just take anything you want.'

I shook my head. 'That isn't true.'

'But Lenny didn't come to you, did he? He didn't come to you and say, "I'm in a mess, help me." No, he didn't. Him and Jack, they came to me.' She stabbed a finger at her chest. '*Me*. They knew who'd help them. Who they could trust. And it wasn't you, was it?'

'No,' I said, quietly. 'It wasn't me.'

'That's why I'm here. To help Jack. Like I've always helped him. That's what love is, you stupid little tart. I knew you wouldn't be any use. A fuck, that's all you are to him. Nothing more than that. You and all the others.'

'Val, *don't* . . .'

'Not very nice, is it, the truth?'

She gave me a contemptuous look, then went over to the sink and stood with her back to me, smoking. I stood up, keeping hold of the arm of the sofa. 'Val?' She didn't turn round. Shakily, using the furniture for help, I went and stood next to her. She carried on looking at the curtain as if she could see through it into the yard.

'I'd like to rinse my arm,' I said. 'It's bleeding.'

She stood aside.

I held my arm under the tap and tried to sluice out the dirt. The tea towels, the ones I'd used on Jeff and put in the sink, were gone. Had Jack moved them, or had Val? I kept my head down and looked at her sideways, through my hair.

She stared at the cigarette in her hand. 'I'd given up. Three years ago. I started again after Susie died.'

'I don't . . .' I said, 'I can't imagine . . .'

'Don't try,' she said. 'I don't want your sympathy.'

'Can I get you something?' I asked. 'A cup of tea?'

She looked at me in surprise. 'Yes. If you want.'

'I could do with one,' I said, filling the kettle. We stood in silence, waiting for it to boil. I looked out of the window. It seemed to be taking for ever.

'I found a diary Susie'd written,' said Val, suddenly. 'It was from one of the places she went to. They had to do it as part of the therapy. There was a photograph stuck in the back. You and a lot of others, standing on a staircase. It was glamorous, bright colours, everyone smiling. I suppose she must have thought that was the way to be. I told her she was beautiful, but she didn't believe me. All the stuff she'd written in the diary was about how ugly she thought she was, how much she hated herself. The things we'd said to her, trying to make her feel better, she'd put them down but they'd be . . . twisted round. Hideous. That was the word she used. *I am hideous.* Over and over again. *Pages* of it. It just . . .' Val faltered, and then said, 'It broke my heart.' We looked at each other, tears in her eyes, tears in mine.

I heard the hall door open and turned round. Jack was standing in the doorway. No gun. It must be in his pocket, I thought. 'Come here,' he said. He was speaking to Val, not to me.

'Don't . . .' I started, but she looked straight through me and went to him. I looked away as he kissed her – stared at the back door. Val had said it was locked, but there was no way to tell. Even if it wasn't, there were two of them now, I thought. I wouldn't get past both of them. I don't think I've ever felt so alone in my life, so helpless, as I did then. I looked down at my ridiculous, filthy clothes, and sank to the floor, my back against the sink unit.

I heard Jack say to Val, 'Are you all right, sweetheart?'

'Where's Jeff?' I shouted. 'What have you done with him?'

'Who's Jeff?' Val asked.

'It's all right,' Jack said, softly. 'Don't listen to her. Everything's going to be all right.'

'How can you say that?' I screamed. 'You killed him!'

'What's she talking about?' asked Val.

'Nothing. She's mad. Ignore it.'

'No! You shot him! And Lee, and . . .' I couldn't get any more words out. 'Let me go,' I whispered. 'Just – let – me.– go.'

Jack looked at me for the first time. 'No,' he said. The top of the kettle started rattling. 'What's that?'

'She was making tea,' said Val.

'Would you like some?' he asked.

'Yes,' Val said. 'That would be . . . I'd like some.'

'You heard,' Jack said to me. 'Make her some tea. I'll be back in a minute.' He disengaged himself from Val. 'You'll be OK, darling. I'm coming right back.' He patted her on the bottom and disappeared into the hall, shutting the door behind him.

Do what he says, I thought. Don't think about it, just do it. You don't have a choice. Val came back and leant against the dresser, arms crossed, and watched as I got to my feet and reached over to turn off the gas. Boiling water was slopping down the sides onto the hob.

I could feel her eyes on me as I assembled the teapot and mugs, and got the milk out of the fridge. Willed her to say something, anything, just to let me make contact. It has to come from her, I thought. I've got to let her be in charge. I mustn't panic her, or she'll call Jack.

I noticed her cigarettes by the sink. 'Do you mind if I have one?' I asked.

She shrugged again, then fumbled in her skirt pocket for a lighter and handed it to me. 'Thanks.' I passed it back to her. She motioned with her hand for me to give her the packet, as well, and she then lit one, too.

She smoked it in silence, then said, 'Susie thought you were beautiful. I remember, a few years ago, she must have been eighteen, nineteen. She was looking at some snaps Jack had taken of you and Lenny, and she said, "I'd give anything to be like that, but I never will." You don't look so great now, do you?'

I shook my head.

'I wish Susie could see what you look like now. I wish I could tell her.'

There's no answer to that, I thought. I handed her a mug of tea. 'Do you take sugar?'

'No. Did Jack do that?' She gestured at my face.

'Yes.'

'He's never laid a finger on me,' she said, '*Ever.* What happened?'

'He thought I'd phoned the police. I told him I hadn't, but he didn't believe me. Then some kids came to the door, and he thought that's who it was, and he just . . . lost it.'

'I see. Who's Jeff?'

'Jack shot him.'

'*Shot* him?' Val shook her head.

'Killed him. He's dangerous, Val.'

'Rubbish. He's fine.'

'He's off his head! He's been drinking – taking pills. When Jeff came in here—'

'You mean your husband? The photographer?'

'Ex-husband. He didn't even get through the door. Jack just—'

'Why would Jack want to shoot *him*? It doesn't make any sense.'

'I told you, he doesn't know what he's doing. And he didn't know it was Jeff. He had no idea, not when he . . . I told him afterwards. I think Jack . . . It was an impulse. Like . . . When Jeff arrived, he saw it as, sort of, another

240

problem, and he just . . . *did it.*' It was coming out all wrong and I could tell she didn't believe a word of it. 'Jeff came because I rang him. He wasn't there but he's got a machine where you can leave messages . . . I was frightened, Val. Jack broke the phone – my phone – so I went to the one on the village green. That's when I rang you. From the call box. I didn't know what to do. And when I told him this morning – yesterday – that I'd phoned you, he went mad. Threatened me, said he'd shoot the dog, and then he locked me in the stable, and when Lee came back . . .'

'Who's Lee?'

'A kid from the village. Ten years old. I'd asked him to go for help, and Jack came out, and he . . . Shot him.'

'You're telling me he killed a *child*?' Val shook her head. 'You'll say anything, won't you? You're the one who's mad. I'm calling Jack.' She took a step forward and I put out my hand to stop her. 'Don't you dare touch me!' She beat me away with her hands. 'You've ruined my life – my family – you get my husband down here and you . . . you . . .' She twisted away from me and ran towards the hall door.

'No!' I grabbed hold of her wrist and she turned on me, slapping, spitting, clawing at my face, while I clung on, desperate not to let her go. 'You can't go out there, you don't know what he's doing, you don't understand, he'll kill us!'

'Let go of me, you mad bitch! Nobody's killed anybody. You're making it all up. Let *go*!'

'It's true!' I caught her other arm, pulled her towards me, and held on for dear life. 'You have to believe me. There are two – people – dead. Lee's in the stable, and Jeff . . . I don't know. He was here, right in this room, when I left. I know how it sounds, but I'm not making it up, I am telling you the truth. Jack has got a gun, and you know what he's capable of, because you know he killed Danny Watts.'

She stopped struggling and glared at me. 'You know that.' I said. 'You sent the newspaper cuttings.'

'Yes,' she said. 'I did. I wanted you to know what your precious Lenny'd been up to.'

'All right,' I said. 'But Lenny didn't kill Danny Watts. That doesn't matter. Not now. What matters is Jack. He's off his head, upset about Susie. He said—'

Val jerked her head up. 'He talked to *you* about Susie?'

'Yes.' I let go of her hands and took a step back. 'He said . . . He said it was his fault she got ill, and he couldn't cope with it, the guilt, seeing her like that. And that was why he went away, in spite of . . . Kitty . . . and everything you'd done for him, he couldn't . . .'

'He didn't say that to me. Any of it. He wouldn't talk about it. She was our daughter, and she was *dying*, and he wouldn't bloody talk to me!' She was shouting. Jack would hear, I thought, desperately. He'd come in before I'd had the chance to explain to her. I kept my voice as calm as I could. 'I know,' I said.

'How can you *know*? You're just . . . just . . .'

'You can call me anything you want, but we have to get the police. We've got to, Val. If we're quick, we can go—'

'But why would he talk to you and not to me?'

'Sometimes,' I said, slowly, 'it's easier, talking to someone who's not, well, who's not close to you. Someone you don't care about.'

'Jack told *you*,' she repeated, as if she was trying to get it to sink in. Her eyes widened and she put a hand up to her mouth. '*My God*. You've been seeing him, haven't you? Don't tell me he just came down here to see you, out of the blue, some half-forgotten fuck – don't tell me he just came down here and talked to you about us. You've been seeing him all the time, haven't you?'

'No. He just turned up here. Two, three nights ago. I

242

wasn't expecting him. I hadn't seen him since Lenny's funeral.'

'Then why did he come *here*? Why didn't he come home?'

'He was frightened. When they found Lenny's car . . .'

'But I wouldn't have gone to the police. He knew that! He knew I wouldn't . . . I'd never . . . surely he knew that?'

'I think he just panicked,' I said, helplessly. How could I explain something when I didn't understand it myself? 'He's in a terrible mess, and sometimes people just *run*, don't they? They feel trapped and they can't deal with it, and . . . That's what's happening now. That's why we have to—'

'But why would he come to you, unless—'

'No! I told you. You know that isn't true,' I said. 'Look. How did you find out about Danny Watts? Jack didn't tell you, did he?'

She looked at me for a moment, almost as if she was weighing something up, then shook her head.

'So how . . .'

'I got someone to follow him. They read the name on the doorbell when Jack went in to see him.'

'I don't understand,' I said, suddenly puzzled. 'How did you know who he was? I mean, that it was connected to Kitty. If Jack didn't tell you . . . Danny Watts could have been anyone.'

'I recognised his name. He'd phoned the house. Left messages. Then I saw in the paper that he'd been killed, and it said that he was a cameraman, and he'd worked on those films, those smutty things. After what happened with Kitty, I asked Jack – both of them – if there was anyone else involved. Because I thought, how could she do all that on her own, set it up? But they kept saying no and I had to believe them, believe Jack, because . . .' She looked at me, bleakly. 'Because I had no choice.'

'Listen,' I said. 'If you got someone to follow Jack, and he'd been seeing me, this investigator, or whoever he was, he'd have told you, wouldn't he?'

Val looked at the floor. It flashed through my mind that there was something she wasn't telling me. Not now, I thought. Later. 'So you know Jack wasn't seeing me,' I said. 'You know that.'

Val looked up. 'But you've slept with him. While he's been here.' It was a statement, not a question.

It threw me, and I hesitated a second – a fraction of a second – too long.

'Don't bother,' she said, wearily. The hurt on her face was unbearable. There was nothing I could say. I was responsible, that was the truth. I could have said no to Jack, but I didn't. It was pretty ironic that we hadn't because he couldn't, but I could hardly say that to Val.

'I'm glad you think it's funny,' she said.

'No, it's not that,' I said, appalled. 'I didn't mean . . .'

'I wasn't born yesterday, you know. Leopards don't change their spots. My family's destroyed because of women like you. My daughter's dead. So don't stand there, wearing that . . . *thing* . . . and tell me it isn't true.'

'Jack made me put it on,' I said.

'Oh, and he raped you as well, did he?'

'No. I went to bed with him. Not my idea, but . . . I did. That makes it just as much my fault as his, I know that. I'm sorry. And I'm sorry for you. About Susie, and . . . all of it, I really am. But I didn't ask Jack to come here, and I'm not responsible for his . . . his *behaviour*, or for what Kitty did, or Danny, or for the fact that he left you when Susie was ill. I didn't do any of that. I am not a threat to you, Val. But Jack *is*, and that's why we've got to get out of here.'

She crossed her arms. 'Why should I believe you?'

I looked round the room. Proof. I thought, I need proof. 'Let me show you something,' I said, and went back to the sofa to fetch the green cushion. 'Look,' I said, holding it out to show her. 'Blood.'

'Could be anything. Red wine. You said he'd been drinking.'

'No. I put this under Jeff's head. When he was dying.'

She turned towards the window and drew back the curtain. It was almost light. 'Take it away.'

I put the cushion back on the sofa. 'Look,' I said, desperately. 'Even if you don't believe a word I've said, you know Jack's in trouble. You know the police want to talk to him about the car, but they don't know about Danny Watts. I mean, they know he's dead, but there's nothing to connect him to Jack, is there? All right, they worked on the same films, yes, but there must be hundreds of people like that, and it's not as if they were friends or anything. So why don't you just give me the key to the back door, and I'll go down to the green and call the police. They're bound to catch up with him sooner or later, and it'll be better if . . . if it's *now*, than . . . He needs help, Val. He really does. Running away from everything isn't going to do any good.'

I went over to the back door and tried it. It was locked, like she'd said. 'I can't give you the key,' Val said. 'Jack's got it.' Her voice was expressionless. I had no idea what she was thinking.

'The window,' I said. It was just about big enough for me to squeeze through. 'Will you come?'

She shook her head, but she didn't move to stop me. I hesitated for a moment, then leant across the draining board to undo the latch.

CHAPTER THIRTY-TWO

The hall door burst open and crashed against the wall. I whirled round. Jack was standing on the threshold. He had the gun in one hand and the urn – Susie's ashes – in the other.

'My God . . .' I heard Val whisper behind me. 'Oh, my God . . .'

'Close the curtain.'

Neither of us moved.

'Close it!'

I reached over and tugged it shut. We watched in silence while Jack went to the table and positioned the urn very carefully in the middle. He stood back for a moment and looked at it, then lifted it up and slid one of the napkins underneath. 'Good. Now we're all here. Except Lenny.'

He lifted the empty brandy glass and mimed drinking. 'Absent friends. And Rosie.' He looked at Val. 'Why didn't you bring Rosie? She ought to be here.'

Val stood petrified, staring at him with enormous, terrified eyes. 'She . . . she was . . .'

'What? What was she?'

'She was going off somewhere with Nick. I didn't think . . .'

'No,' said Jack. 'You didn't think, did you? You just charged down here and left *my daughter* with that evil-minded thug. I want her *here*!' he shouted, banging the table with his fist. Val was shaking. She looked as if she was about to pass out. 'Anything could happen! She could get pregnant, for Christ's sake!'

'She won't, Jack. She's grown up, she knows what she's doing.'

'*You* didn't.'

Val's whole body seemed to shrink, and she half turned towards me, her face in her hands.

'You bloody didn't, did you?' Jack shouted. I put my arms round Val. She didn't resist me, just stood there sobbing like a child, her shoulders heaving.

'It's all right,' I whispered, 'it's all right . . .'

Jack turned his back on us. I watched him over Val's shoulder. He was looking round the room as if he was trying to work something out. Then he spun round and pointed at the chest of drawers beside the back door. 'Move that,' he said. 'I want it in front of the door.'

That's what the thumping was about, I realised. The noise I'd heard when I came round. He'd been moving furniture. Barricading us in.

The chest was wooden. Solid. 'I can't,' I said. 'Not by myself.'

'She can help.' The smell of his sweat, strong and stale, like onions left in a frying pan, hit me as he came towards us, and I recoiled as he grabbed Val round the waist, wrenching her from me and pinning her against his body. 'That's what you came for, isn't it?' he shouted. 'To help. And you're going to. Go on, help Alice.' He pushed her away. '*Go on!*'

I did my best, but it took a long time to move the chest. It was too heavy, impossible to lift, and Val wasn't much use. She was still shaking, too shocked to do much more than go through the motions. Jack stood a few feet away from us, fiddling with the gun.

When we'd finished, he jerked his head towards the

middle of the room. I limped over to the table, head down, clutching my side. Val followed, and then Jack. We each pulled out a chair and sat down. No one spoke. Jack's leg jigged up and down as he fidgeted with the gun, opening and closing it, pulling out bullets and looking at them, then putting them back again. His pungent, unhealthy smell hung in the air over the table.

Val sat with her head bowed, not looking at either of us. I was numb – my brain, anyway. My body was aching so much and felt so weak that after about five minutes the sheer effort of keeping myself upright on the hard chair was all I could think about. The costume dug into me, and my lower back and legs felt as if they were about to dissolve. I held onto the edges of the chair seat and braced my arms to try and take the pressure off them. A minute at a time, I thought. Just one more minute, I can do that. Someone will come, something will happen, if you hang on for *one more minute.*

Then another minute, then another, and another . . . I don't know how much time passed. I wasn't wearing my watch, and I couldn't see anyone else's. Val was sitting with her hands in her lap, and Jack's was covered by his sleeve. His other hand, the one with the gun, was down by his side.

I heard Pablo whinny from the field. I'll need to feed the animals soon, I thought. If Jack'll let me. I glanced at him. He seemed to be staring at the urn. Val was rocking backwards and forwards, her head down. After a while, she began to make a moaning noise, a thin, pitiful sound like a wounded animal. I could feel the anguish of it right inside my heart, and it went on and on until I couldn't bear it any longer. I slithered sideways off my chair and went to her. Jack's eyes followed me, but he said nothing.

I put my hand on her shoulder. 'Don't,' I said. 'Please don't.' She didn't turn round, but she fell quiet, and after a moment she lifted her arm and put her hand on top of mine.

Pablo whinnied again, louder this time, more urgent, and we heard hooves thudding across the field. They've seen somebody, I thought. In the lane. 'Someone's coming,' I said.

There was a clunk as Jack brought up the gun and put it down on the table, and Val's fingers tightened over the back of my hand. Jack got to his feet and stood staring at me. I stared back, over Val's head. 'Don't move, Alice,' he said. His voice was flat. 'Don't even think about it.'

The front doorbell rang.

CHAPTER THIRTY-THREE

Eustace, shut in the dining room, started to bark. The bell stopped and then rang again. Val hunched over in her chair as Jack came towards us, letting go of my hand and folding her arms over her stomach, but I knew he wasn't going to touch her.

I clenched my teeth and forced myself to keep still as he walked round behind me, raised the gun, and pressed it against my right temple. I could see it out of the corner of my eye, a black, fuzzy shape, and behind it part of Jack's face, so close to me that I could feel his breath on my bare shoulder. I jumped as his free hand touched my back, and it took me a couple of seconds to register what he was doing . . . rubbing my skin, caressing the nape of my neck.

I felt sick. 'Please . . .' I whispered to Jack. 'Please don't.'

'Don't move, Alice,' he muttered into my ear. 'Just don't move.'

We both jumped slightly as the bell rang again, three short bursts this time, followed by shouting. 'Alice? You in there? Open up!'

'Who is it?' whispered Jack, hoarsely.

'Lee's father.'

'Alice!' shouted Fred. 'You all right, girl?'

'Hello!' Another voice, male. 'Anybody there?'

'Who's the other one?' Jack hissed.

'I think it's Mr Anderson.'

'Who's he?'

'The vicar.'

Eustace gave one last, hoarse bark and fell silent. Fred and Mr Anderson were talking, but we couldn't hear the words. I concentrated as hard as I could, picturing them standing together on the front step, trying to communicate with them in my mind. *Don't go. Help us. We need help.* I repeated the words over and over again, like a mantra.

Val stayed hunched over, her whole body quivering. She's doing the same, I thought. She must be doing the same. I shut my eyes. *Please God, make them help us. Make them not go. Please . . .*

The voices stopped. There was silence, then footsteps, two sets, crunching the gravel by the side of the house, turning the corner by the window, then a different sound as they walked across the cobbles. Jack shifted his weight slightly beside me, banging the gun against my head. We stared at the door.

'. . . quite a mess . . . didn't recognise the car . . .' Mr Anderson's voice, outside the window. 'Alice's car's here, in the yard.'

'I come looking for my boy,' said Fred. 'He's not been home since yesterday. His mum's worried sick. He come up here with Trudy. Alice asked them to get her a paper, and Lee come back with it, like she said. We thought he'd gone to his mate's for the night, but he's only been on the phone this morning, where's Lee, he's never turned up. So I come up here. That car . . . I thought that was him, run over.'

It's worse than that. I felt tears welling up and closed my eyes.

'No,' whispered Val. 'No, no . . .'

She tailed off in a whimper as Jack made a noise in his throat like a growl and caught up a handful of my hair, jerking my head back and pulling me towards him so I lost my balance and bumped against his chest. He dug the gun

251

under my chin, forcing my head up even higher. My neck was agony. I'm going to choke, I thought, as saliva ran back into my throat. I know I'm going to choke.

'. . . must have happened last night.' Mr Anderson again. 'Can't have been earlier, or we'd have heard it. Would have made a fair bit of noise, going into the hedge like that. They must have been on their way here. Mary's reported it, of course, but I thought I'd better nip over to see if they were still in one piece.'

'There's got to be somebody here,' said Fred. 'What about the other car? And she's got all the curtains closed. Trudy said she wasn't feeling too clever.'

'Perhaps they're still asleep.'

'What, with that racket? And she'd be out for the horses, wouldn't she? It's gone nine.'

'She might be in the barn.'

'No chance. She'd have heard us.'

'All the same, best to make sure.' Footsteps crossed the yard, out of earshot.

Fred banged on the door. 'Alice! You there?'

I'm here. I'm here. Help me. The pain was spreading across my shoulders and down to my chest. I swallowed painfully, trying to ease the pressure, but it didn't help. Let go, I begged Jack, silently. *Let go.*

We listened to Fred moving around the yard, and then Mr Anderson came back.

'You'd better take a look at this.'

I heard Fred say, 'You all right?' then two sets of feet crossing the yard, very fast.

A body, I thought. Lee was in the stable, so it's Jeff. He's found Jeff.

I started to choke.

CHAPTER THIRTY-FOUR

I felt Jack's grip loosen, and he shoved me forward and pushed me into a chair. I sat with my head down and my arms on the table, retching and trying to catch my breath.

When I looked up, coughing and wiping my eyes, Jack was standing over me. 'They're coming back.' The gun poked the back of my head, pushing me down until my cheek was squashed against the table top. I was facing Val, who was staring straight ahead. She looked exhausted, finished – like a shell – two empty eyes embedded in a grey bag of skin. She must know now, I thought. She must know I was telling the truth.

We heard the footsteps again, then Fred's voice, '*Jesus* . . . My boy could be in there.'

'We don't know that anyone's in there.'

'I'm going to have a look.'

'I think that's best left to the police. They'll be sending someone anyway, for the car, but I'll go and phone. Mary's up there now, so . . .'

'I'm not hanging about. If Lee's in trouble—'

'I really don't think . . .'

'Well, Alice ain't out here, so where is she? And where's my boy?'

'He may not be . . .' I couldn't catch the rest of it. We heard footsteps moving away, then the sound of the gate opening, then closing. Then silence. They'd gone.

I took a deep breath, in . . . and out. The police are

coming, I told myself. Soon. Very soon. Just keep calm. Keep Jack calm. It's only a matter of time . . . Whatever you do, stay calm.

'How could you?' whispered Val. 'How could you?' Her expression hadn't changed, and she wasn't looking at Jack. She seemed to be talking to herself. 'The boy. She said he was ten years old.' Dear God, I thought, *Oh, dear God . . .* 'She said you killed him.'

'Shut up.'

'Tell me it's not true. You didn't . . . Tell me . . .' She sounded bewildered. She knows, I thought. She doesn't want to believe it, but she knows. 'She said you killed him, and those men out there—' She broke off suddenly and lunged forward, taking hold of the urn in both hands and clutching it to her chest.

'Put it down,' Jack muttered. 'Leave it alone.'

'No.' *Stop it*, I screamed, inside my head. *Let go of it.*

'Do you want me to kill her?' asked Jack.

Val didn't answer him. 'Please,' I whispered. '*Please . . .*'

'Is that what you want?' shouted Jack. 'Is it?'

Our Father, which art in heaven . . . Our Father . . . can't remember, Christ, I can't remember it . . . I saw Val's hand twisting the lid of the urn, her bracelets scraping against the metal, and I thought, is that the last thing I'll ever see, her hands? But what was she doing? What . . . ?

She was taking the lid off.

'No!' Jack shouted. 'I'll kill her. I'll—'

'Haven't you done enough?' She stood up and the lid dropped out of her hand and clattered on the floor, then I felt the gun lifted away from my head as Jack lunged towards her and tried to pull the urn out of her hands. She wrenched it away from him and he overbalanced, falling across the chair. Then I was on my feet and backing away, appalled, as Val's hands jerked the urn upwards and the ashes flew out in a cloud. They settled on the table and chairs and clung in a sticky film on the empty glass.

'It's too late now, isn't it?' she shouted at him. 'Go on, take it! That's what's left – have it! Have what's left!'

She stumbled over to the sofa and sat holding the empty urn, rocking back and forth. She looked . . . I can't describe it. Destroyed. Beyond tears. Beyond everything. Jack was sitting on the floor by the chair, the gun loose in his hand as if he'd forgotten it. His face was rigid with horror. 'Pick them up,' he mumbled. 'Put them away. Just . . . get them away.'

'How?' I asked, helplessly.

'Just do it!'

I looked around the room. A cloth, dustpan, what? I caught sight of *Charley's Aunt*, lying on one of the chairs. Scarcely knowing what I was doing, I picked it up and started trying to scrape the ashes into a heap, but it was impossible. They puffed up into the air and settled back on the cover, the edges of the pages, on my skin . . . After a few attempts I put the book down and turned away from the table, my hands shaking. 'I can't do this,' I whispered. 'I'm sorry, I can't. It's horrible. I can't . . .'

I looked at Jack. He was trailing his free hand aimlessly back and forth across the lino, staring down at it as if he was mesmerised. In spite of the gun, he looked docile, stupefied, almost babyish. It was grotesque. 'Jesus,' he muttered. 'Jesus Christ . . . I need a drink.' He looked up at me. 'Get me a drink.'

I went to the cupboard and pulled out the nearest bottle, then fetched a glass, poured – most of it went in – and handed it down to Jack.

'What is it?'

I looked at the label. 'Cointreau.'

He shrugged, drank it, and held up the glass for more.

'For Christ's sake, sit down,' he snapped.

Do what he says, I thought, lowering myself onto the floor. Keep him calm. The police'll be here soon. Just be . . . normal. What's normal? I thought. Nothing's normal. Val was still cradling the urn, head down. Jack stared at his drink. Three separate people, isolated in their own worlds. How could he have done this? I thought. How could we have got here?

'You'd have been all right with Lenny,' Jack said, suddenly. His voice too loud, slurred and sentimental. He's drunk, I thought, looking at him in surprise, then realised that I'd got no idea how much he'd put away during the night, and the Cointreau must have topped up his alcohol level.

'Yeah . . . You'd have been all right. Not like us.' I glanced at Val, but she didn't seem to have heard him. 'He was very kind, you know. We took my old man off on holiday once, years ago, just after my mum died. Spain. Just Lenny and him and me. I thought my dad would enjoy it, because he could be a bit flash, and it was unusual back then, going abroad, but it wasn't his patch and I think he was a bit overwhelmed by it all.

'The second day we were there, he lost his top set in the sea. All the local kids piled in trying to help us find them, but they must have floated away or something. All the rest of the week we had these boys coming up to us with teeth they'd nicked off their grandmothers, or it was the same set and they were passing them round, I don't know. Either way they weren't Dad's, but everywhere we went there was some kid chasing us with these bloody snappers, asking for money.

'I said to Lenny, "We've got to make something out of this," but he wouldn't. I kept saying to him, "It's great, really surreal, and no one's going to know." He said, "Your dad'll know. He'll think we're taking the mickey."'

'Dad hadn't said much about it, and I didn't think he was that bothered, but the day after that we'd arranged to go sightseeing or something, and he wouldn't come. Said he didn't want to leave his room. I tried to get him a new set when we got back – private dentist – but he wouldn't let me. Just wanted to forget about the whole thing.

'I hadn't realised how upset he was, but Lenny had. He was concerned about things like that, not hurting people's feelings. He was a good person, Alice. Decent. Fucked up, but decent.' He nudged my arm with his empty glass. 'Go on . . . He was good, but . . . Shut me out . . . I couldn't . . . this is fucking evil stuff, Alice . . . fucking poisoning me with this stuff.' He drained the glass again and held it out for me to refill. 'Christ, I wish I'd seen him.'

'You mean . . . before he died?'

'Yeah. I should have gone down there. I knew he was in a bad way, but I was angry with him. I thought he'd fucked everything up. Drinking, letting us in for it with Danny Watts, then saying he wanted to tell you, tell the police. I couldn't deal with it. And then when I found out about you two . . . engaged . . . He never bloody told me, not even afterwards.'

'So that wasn't you?'

'What are you talking about? What wasn't me?'

'It wasn't you who went to see him. At Ivar.'

He shook his head. ''S what I'm saying, Alice. Should have. Wish I had.'

I thought back. *Not you as well.* That's what the man said when I went to the house. Not you as well. Perhaps he'd meant . . . Not another *woman.* I looked at Val. 'It was you, wasn't it? You went to see him.'

She raised her head. 'Yes.'

CHAPTER THIRTY-FIVE

'It was the day before we went on holiday,' Val said. 'We were supposed to be happy, Jack. We were going on holiday, and there you were, a black cloud. You wouldn't talk to me, or Don, or anyone. It was ruining everything for the girls, and I thought, if I just talked to Lenny . . . Yes, I know, I was trying to help, and it didn't work. *As usual.*'

'What did you do?' I asked.

'I went there.' Val shook her head. 'Lenny wouldn't let me in at first. I could see him through the window. He wasn't doing anything, not even drinking, he was just sitting on the bed. It must have been ten minutes before he came to the door. I tried to talk to him, but it was useless. Even if you had gone down there, Jack, it wouldn't have made any difference. He'd given up. There was nothing I could do. I persuaded him to get into bed, I sat with him for a bit, and then I left.'

'Did you think he was going to kill himself?' I asked.

Val hesitated.

'You did think that, didn't you?'

'Didn't *you*?'

'Val, the last time I saw him I was terrified. He was so . . . abusive. Violent. I had to get away from him. I didn't think he'd . . . I was too scared, too mixed up. But if you thought – if you *knew* – he was going to do it, why did you leave? Why didn't you help him?'

'Why didn't *you*?'

'I didn't know! I went back because I was angry, not because I thought he was going to kill himself. You knew about the film, I didn't. All I knew was, I was engaged to him and he hadn't even asked me. A friend rang up and told me she'd seen it in the paper. And he'd hit me, Val, banged my face into a door. How was I supposed to feel? Why didn't you get help? A doctor, or . . . You could have told someone. You just let it happen. You let him *die*.'

'I was frightened, too,' said Val. 'Not like you, but . . . what he might say.'

'About Kitty?'

'Yes. Because of Jack.'

'But Jack hadn't . . . I mean, it was Lenny, wasn't it?' I glanced at Jack, then Val. Neither of them looked at me. 'It was Lenny's car, he'd taken her to the party, everyone saw them together—'

Val interrupted. 'Danny Watts had the film, remember?'

'Yes, but you didn't know that *then*. You didn't even know Danny Watts existed until . . . Wait. You did know, didn't you? Lenny told you, didn't he? That day?'

Val's eyes flicked towards Jack, and she hesitated for a moment and then said, quietly, 'Yes.'

'And two years later, when Susie got ill and Jack abandoned you, you started following him, didn't you. And you found out where Danny lived. It wasn't some private investigator.'

'I did have to employ someone to find out the address, but . . . yes. I followed Jack.'

'Why didn't you tell me all this?' Jack shouted.

'There was no point,' said Val, calmly.

'Of course there was a fucking point! I could have gone to see Lenny, talked him round. I don't know. *Something*.'

'It wouldn't have made any difference.' Val's voice was flat. 'He was going to do it anyway. Besides,' she added, dismissively, '*we* weren't exactly communicating, were we? You didn't tell me about Danny Watts.'

'I told you about Kitty.'

'Only because you needed my help.' She gave a breathy, bitter laugh. 'That was why I didn't say anything – because I was thinking about *you*. Lenny'd have done it anyway, sooner or later. I thought it was better, safer, for all of us if I just let things take their course.'

'But you're not *God*. You can't just—' I started, but she cut me off.

'I found this.' She put a hand in the pocket of her skirt and pulled out a cassette. 'Lenny had a tape recorder by his bed. It's a confession. For you.' She nodded at me.

For me. I looked at the cassette in her hand. Inside was Lenny's voice. Talking to me. What had his note said? *Don't blame the camels. I have tried . . .* And then that last, illegible line. I'd been wrong. Lenny hadn't been telling me he'd tried to blame the camels, he'd meant he'd tried to explain, and it was on the tape . . .

'Why didn't you give it to me?' I said.

'What, so you could take it to the police?'

'I wouldn't . . .' I stopped. I didn't know what I would have done.

'I took his tape recorder,' said Val. 'I stopped on the way home and listened to the tape.'

I stared at her, appalled. 'Then why didn't you go back?'

Val looked at me for a moment and then said, wearily, 'If you had any idea of what my life's been like, you wouldn't need to ask.'

'Of course I need to ask! All that stuff you came out with about helping Jack and Lenny when you just calmly sat there and listened to a tape of him saying he was going to kill himself and then drove home and went on holiday and . . . and . . . I'm just . . . I don't know what to say.

How could you just leave him like that?' I jumped up, shaking. 'Even if you didn't care about Lenny, what about Jack? What did you think it would do to him?'

'I did it for him.'

Jack lurched to his feet beside me. 'You did it for yourself, you selfish bitch.'

Val looked up at him and said calmly, 'I'm not the one who's selfish. Everything I've ever done has been for you. And for the girls. Every single thing.'

Jack banged his glass down on the table and swayed towards her, clutching the back of a chair for support. 'St Valerie the Martyr,' he snarled. 'Do you want me to pray at your shrine, is that it?' She shrank back against the cushions as he tottered towards the sofa, slumped on his knees in front of her and fell forward. One hand was clamped round her thigh, the other held the gun in her lap, pointing at her crotch.

'You didn't go to Ivar to keep us together. You wanted us apart.'

'That isn't true, Jack.'

'Yes it is.'

'I wanted to persuade him. I couldn't bear to see you so unhappy. The whole time, when I was driving down there, it was the only thought I had, to get you together again. But when I saw the state he was in, I *knew*, Jack. I had to think what was best for everybody.'

'It wasn't best. Not for Lenny.'

'Yes, it was. Believe me. You didn't see him.' Val looked at me. 'You know. You saw him.'

I remembered Lenny's glazed, empty eyes. 'Yes . . .'

'Don't blame me,' Val said to Jack. 'What about *her*?'

'But you had the tape,' I said. 'I didn't know—'

Jack raised his head. 'Both of you!' he shouted. 'You left him. You just fucking left him! She did it because she's all cunt and no brain, and you,' I saw Val wince as he jabbed her with the gun, 'because you've always been jealous. You wanted Lenny out of my life for years and it was very fucking convenient, wasn't it? You could say you were doing it for me.'

'I went back,' I whispered. 'I did go back.'

Jack pulled himself round to face me, using Val's legs for support.

'When it was too fucking late.'

'Don't, Jack.'

'Don't, Jack,' he mimicked me. 'You're nothing, Alice,' he said, viciously. 'We had women like you crawling out of the woodwork.' The gun swung away from me as he turned back to Val. 'And as for you, like some vicious old bitch at the guillotine with your fucking knitting . . . Saying what was best for everybody, like . . . organising some fuck-ing . . . gymkhana . . . Lenny was my friend, the only . . .'

'You haven't heard the tape,' said Val. She held it up. 'Lenny's last words. Don't you want to hear them?'

'No!'

'Alice does.' She looked at me over Jack's head. 'Don't you?'

I shook my head.

'Why not?' asked Val.

'Not here,' I said. 'Not now.'

'Afraid of what you'll hear? Jack is, aren't you? You're afraid of what she'll hear. Or did you tell her the truth?'

'Give me that.' Jack made a lunge for the tape, slipped, and collapsed across Val's lap. As she bucked her hips and tried to stand up, unbalancing him, I saw the gun hit the arm of the sofa, bounce, and fall out of his hand. I leant forward to grab it and saw his body jackknife as he scrabbled across Val's legs and crashed against me, knock-ing me backwards into the table.

I got myself onto my hands and knees, reached the gun just before he did and felt it under my palm for a second before Val stamped on the back of my hand. I screamed and tried to pull away, and then her knee smacked into the side of my face. As I fell sideways I saw Jack's hand shoot forward and pick up the gun, and as he straightened up Val flew at him. Her weight caught him off balance and he fell onto his back with her on top in a frenzy of flailing arms. As I scrambled to my feet I caught a glimpse of his face over her shoulder – his eyes were round with astonishment and fear – then, as he put his hands up to protect his face, Val knocked his arm, hard, and the gun shot out of his hand, hit the floor and skidded under the table towards the back door.

I went after it, got there as it fetched up against the chest we'd put in front of the back door, bent down for it and felt my fingertips brush against the metal before Val cannoned into me like a rugby player, knocking me sideways. We rolled over, kicking and clawing, and then I was on my front, stretching for the gun with her on top of me. I felt her knee in the small of my back and then she had it, and we were both dazed and panting on the floor. I lunged forward and closed my fingers over hers, and for a second I thought I had it but she flung herself forward and my arm was being twisted round and I couldn't hold it and I felt my head crack against the sharp wooden corner of the chest and found myself sprawled on the floor.

When I opened my eyes the first thing I saw was the lino, a threshing pattern of waves and spots underneath me like a sea, and when I looked up, there were two fuzzy, flesh coloured columns in front of my eyes. Legs, I thought. Val's legs.

I felt the back of my head, wetness in my hair, sticky, then saw blood on my fingers, and through them, the moving floor. I shook my head dizzily and looked up at Val. At first her head seemed terribly far away and small, but then her body folded over and slid down towards me and suddenly her face was a foot away and all I could see was flesh. Tiny hairs in the nostrils, and on either side a sweep of pores like little pocks, sharp for a moment and then blurred as she leaned closer, and all I could see was eyes, two blurring into one. No lashes, no colour, just a big, soft, black dot. Then the face receded and the dot wasn't an eye any more, it was the gun, a dark, round O. She's got it, I thought, she's the one with the gun, she took it away from me, pushed me, but that was better than Jack. Better than if Jack . . . And we could go, but I had to get off the floor, get away from it, it wouldn't keep still, waves of lino coming up to meet me.

I heaved myself into a sitting position. Beyond Val, I could see a weaving thicket of wooden table legs and Jack, kneeling, slumped over the seat of a chair behind them. It crashed to the floor as he pushed himself away from it and began crawling towards us on his knees and elbows, head down, clutching the cassette. 'It's mine.' I held out my hand. 'Please, Jack . . .'

He stopped a few feet away and looked up at me. 'You're not having it,' he said. 'No one's having it.'

'Jack . . .' I leant over to reach it but Val grabbed my arm and held me back.

'Let him.'

Jack examined the cassette with drunken, squinting concentration, turning it over in his hands, then stuck a finger in the base and hooked out length after length of tape.

'No,' I whispered. 'Please. It was Lenny's. For me . . .' Jack smiled with childish triumph before he reeled out the last of the tape, stretched it taut and jerked it viciously until it broke. 'That's it.' With a flip of his hand, he sent the empty cassette skidding along the floor to me. 'Had to consider what's best for everybody,' he said in a shrill, high voice. 'That's what you said, isn't it?' he asked Val. 'The best thing. Now everybody's happy.' He started to laugh.

'What did he tell you?' Val asked me. 'An accident?'

'For Christ's sake,' said Jack. 'Lenny was fucked. He'd had it. You said so yourself. Better for all of us . . .' He looked down at the snarl of tape in his fist. 'Don't tell me you believed this.'

Val got to her feet and stood over him, the gun by her side. 'I believed it.'

'No you didn't. You kept it as a hold over me . . . Thought I'd do whatever you wanted. Do you know what Val wants, Alice? *Do you?*'

I shook my head.

'Shall I show you?' He raised himself to a kneeling position, held up his hands like paws, made an eager, panting noise like a begging dog and buried his face in her crotch. 'That's what Val wants,' he said, shaking his head from side to side, his voice muffled by her skirt. 'That's what you want, isn't it?'

'Not any more.' Val raised the gun and clouted him, hard, over the ear. He sprawled on the floor, clutching his head. 'Christ, that hurt . . .'

She bent down and caught hold of the collar of his jacket, tugging him towards me. He shuffled beside her on his knees and slumped down beside me, his back to the chest of drawers. 'Hello, Alice.' He peered at me, blearily. 'Poor bunny, you've lost your ears. Never mind.' His head drooped against my shoulder. 'I've got a present for you,' he said. 'Make it better.' He dropped the mess of tape into my lap. 'Here you are. All better now.'

Val stood over us. 'We can go,' I said to her. She looked down at me, her face unreadable.

'All better,' mumbled Jack, stroking my leg. 'Make every-thing better . . .'

There was a sudden, volcanic growl from Eustace at the front of the house, followed by footsteps and the sound of something being scraped along the gravel. Then more growling and a burst of frenzied barks. Not police, I thought, we'd have heard the cars. Fred. He hadn't gone with Mr Anderson. He was coming to find Lee.

I pushed Jack away from me and started to get up. 'The other door,' I said to Val. 'The front way. Through the hall.'

Val pointed the gun at me. 'No,' she said.

'But we—'

'*No.*'

Jack slumped against my shoulder. 'Best,' he muttered. 'All for the best . . .'

CHAPTER THIRTY-SIX

'Was that why you killed a child, Jack?' asked Val. 'For the best?'

I sat like a rag doll, arms at my sides, not moving, Jack's head a dead weight against my chest. I shouldn't be here, I thought, dully. This has nothing to do with me, now. It's about them. I shouldn't be here at all. I'm just a body in a room, taking up space.

'Alice told me.'

'Alice . . .' Jack gave a snuffling laugh. 'Alice doesn't know what the fuck she's talking about.'

'Yes, she does.' Val bent down and nudged his cheek with the gun. 'Look at me.'

'I told you,' Jack mumbled into my cleavage, 'she doesn't know . . .'

'Look at me!' Val's voice was shrill and urgent. 'Look at this.' She poked the gun in his face. 'You said I wanted Lenny out of your life. You were right. I knew the only way I could get him out was if he died. That's why I didn't go back to the cottage. That's why I went round and gathered up all the pills and booze I could find and dumped them by his bed, and God knows he had enough to kill an elephant. *I did it because I wanted him to die.*'

The gun quivered in her hand, an inch away from Jack's temple. 'I always thought you'd be better off without him. Always drunk, always letting you down. But you couldn't see it, could you? And even when he gave you the chance,

when he said he didn't want to work with you any more –
you wouldn't let him go. Don't tell me you weren't relieved
when he died. I was with you, remember? I saw your face.
I'm sure you had a great time telling Bunny Rabbit here
how sad it was and how much you miss him, but I know
how terrified you were that he'd blow the gaff, get drunk
and tell someone, say it on television. That *Close Up* show
was bad enough, and I remember what you said afterwards,
"I don't know how long I can go on with this," that's what
you said. I *know*, Jack. You're just lucky I picked up that
tape instead of Danny Watts. Or *her.*' Val gestured at me
with the gun. 'Don't you understand, Jack? I made you free
of him. Oh, he'd have done it anyway, it was just a matter
of time – but there wasn't time, was there? Because he'd have
told *someone*.

'I was the only one you could trust, Jack. Not Lenny, not
her, *me*. And you couldn't see it. I did everything to make
it work between us, and I thought, without Lenny . . . I
thought there might be a chance, because you might as well
have been married to him for all the time you ever spent at
home. God knows why, because right from the first you
made it blindingly obvious you'd rather be with him than
me. Do you know, at one point I thought you must be a
queer? In spite of all the evidence to the contrary, and
Christ knows there was enough of it, I even wondered
about that. And then after I saw your little home movie I
thought, perhaps I was right. Was I, Jack? Was that what it
was all along? A bit of both?' She turned to me. 'There's a
thought for you, your wonderful Lenny was a nancy boy.
What about that?'

'You're talking rubbish,' growled Jack. 'Leave her alone.'

'That got your attention, didn't it? You bastard. I might
as well have been your housekeeper! After everything I
did . . . What do you think my life's been like, Jack? Have

you got any idea? Sitting up waiting for you night after night, everyone knowing what you got up to, never having a bloody holiday. What do you think it's been like?' she screamed at him.

'I stayed with you, didn't I?'

'You stayed with me so you could screw around and then make an excuse and run back to your wife! We were your insurance policy, Jack. Me and the girls. Oh, I know exactly what you thought. I heard you once, talking to Lenny. You were too much of a bloody coward to do it any other way. Even after Kitty, when you promised, and then Susie got ill and you . . . you just . . . Don't you understand *anything*, Jack? There are some things you can justify, and some things you can't. Like abandoning your daughter when she needed you. Like killing a ten-year-old boy.'

'Stop it.'

'After you left, when Susie was ill, I thought about taking that tape to the police, Jack, I really thought about it. But I didn't, and you know why? Because of the girls. You might not have cared about them, but I did.'

'That's not true.'

'No? You don't remember, do you? You really don't remember. Do you know what he said?' she asked me. 'Susie was eight. We were having a row, shouting, and we thought she was in bed, but she must have come back down. Jack said he'd only married me because I was pregnant. I said, "I didn't do it on my own," and he said, "No, it takes two to make that much of a mistake." We didn't know she was there. Standing in the doorway. First I thought she couldn't have understood, but she had. I'll never forget the look on her face. She ran away from us – upstairs – tripped on her nightdress and cut her knee. I got a plaster for her and put it on and I was trying to tell her it was all right, that Daddy didn't mean it, but she just sat there, stiff, like . . . like . . . wood. I tried to cuddle her, but she pushed me away, and she wouldn't say "good night", or . . .'

Val faltered and stopped. The pain in her face was awful. 'You don't know what it's like,' she said to me. 'You don't know. Susie never forgot it. Last year, when she was in hospital, the first time, she said to me, "It's my fault you and Dad aren't happy." She said she was sorry. She never felt loved, Jack. I did everything, everything I could, to try and make up for it, but you . . . You didn't even try. Never, not once. You didn't even try.'

'I wish . . .' Jack cleared his throat. 'I wish it hadn't happened.'

'Is that all you can say?' Val shouted. 'Is that it?'

'Yes,' said Jack, dully. 'Yes.'

Val stepped back, the gun at her side. 'Fuck you, Jack,' she said, coldly. 'Fuck . . . you.'

Jack gestured weakly at the table. 'Fuck you, too. Don't respect . . . ashes . . . can't even . . . that . . . fuck you.'

'You killed her, Jack.'

'You asked me . . . come back . . . that's what you said . . . you wanted it . . .'

'I thought you needed me.' Her hand shook as she raised the gun and pointed it at Jack. 'But you don't. You don't care . . . You don't care.'

There was a sudden eruption of sound from the front of the house – the dog, barking hysterically, and a second later, the jagged crash of a window being broken. Val looked wildly round the room, the gun jumping in her hand. Jack leant forward as if he was going to stand up, and Val took a couple of steps towards him.

'I love my girls, I love Rosie . . .' Jack made a grab for her leg, unbalancing her, and she tottered above us, ankles wobbling, and for a moment I thought she was going to fall over, but she steadied herself and kicked out at him. 'Get back,' she shouted, against a background of baying from Eustace, punctuated by smashing noises and clattering glass as whoever it was knocked out the rest of the window. 'Get away from me! Rosie hates you! She never wants to see you again. She told me.'

'You're lying.'

'No.' Val shook her head violently. 'You don't care, you don't care . . .'

Through Eustace's din, I heard a door open, footsteps in the hall . . .

'Lying . . . bitch . . .' Jack's feet slipped from under him as he tried to stand up. I clung onto his arm. 'Stop it, Jack, *don't* . . .'

'She hates you!' screamed Val.

Footsteps closer now, outside the door. Val looked up. Her skirt whirled next to my face as she swung towards the door. Jeff fell through my mind, the hole in his chest, and I shouted, too late, 'Don't! Don't come in!' and then the door was kicked open, and there was Fred holding up a spade like a weapon. He looked at us and we looked at him and he said, 'Oh, Jesus,' and Eustace started barking again and Val turned, but this time like slow motion, she was pointing the gun at us, Jack or me, I couldn't tell which, and Jack turned to me and she was shouting his name over and over, 'Jack! Jack!' and then he said in my ear, 'I'm sorry,' and yanked my arm so I was in front of him like a shield. I saw the muzzle of the gun come towards me in a big black blur and closed my eyes, and then Val shouted again and Jack shoved me down across his lap.

Then everything was blasted apart in a deafening explosion and Jack's body bucked and then slackened underneath me and the only thing I could hear was the ringing in my ears.

CHAPTER THIRTY-SEVEN

I don't know how long it was. A minute, two minutes at least before the ringing subsided, and then I opened my eyes and the first thing I saw was my hand curled into a fist. There were spots on it like freckles and all down my arm where none had been before and I blinked and saw they weren't brown, but red – blood – Jack's blood spattered on me and I thought, *I'm alive, I'm alive*, and then I felt something wet on my other shoulder and Fred's voice came from miles away saying, 'Don't turn round, Alice, don't turn round . . .'

It sounded as if he was choking, and I raised my eyes and saw Val's face white and shocked and her mouth gaping open and Fred said, 'Oh Jesus, oh Jesus Christ . . .' As I crawled off Jack's lap I heard Val making sounds, mewing and wordless, and I stood up, swaying, and saw she had the gun by her side and she was looking down at it and knew I must take it away from her and make her safe because her distress was so terrible. That was the only thing that mattered.

I had to keep looking at her, not at Fred, not Jack, *no don't look at Jack don't turn round*, just concentrate on her and connect with her, *keep looking at her make her look away from the gun.*

I wasn't afraid, I felt no fear or shock but just an overwhelming need to reach her. I could feel Fred's eyes, his concentration on us, but he was outside, somehow, as if the two of us were sealed together by the intensity of her pain and that was the only thing. I felt nothing but the need to reach her, somehow, just to speak her name.

'Val.'

Her eyes, huge, muddy and lost, stared into mine. I felt, rather than saw, her bend her arm and bring the gun up so it was clutched against her stomach . . . her chest . . . *Talk to her.* My brain felt paralysed. *Say something, anything.*

'Val,' I repeated. The word seemed to take a long time to reach her, as if it was hovering in the air between us. 'Val, it's all right, it's going to be all right . . .'

She took a step back and I saw her hand shift and her finger tighten around the trigger. Now the gun was tilted upwards, to her chin. She blinked, then squeezed her eyes shut.

'Rosie,' I said. 'Your daughter Rosie. What about her?' The gun twitched against the cords in her neck. 'Rosie needs you, Val.'

'She . . . she . . .' Her voice was so quiet I could barely hear it.

'Rosie,' I repeated. 'Your daughter. She needs you.'

Another whisper. 'Rosie.'

The gun – and Val – started to shake, the muzzle banging against the point of her chin.

'Think about Rosie.'

She opened her eyes and I held her gaze as she slowly lowered the gun, and then I extended my hand and felt her push it, still warm, into my palm and release her grip on it. I closed my fingers over the handle and felt her fingertips graze my knuckles and I knew she wanted something to hold, so I transferred the gun from my left hand to my right and let her have that one, instead.

And that was how we stayed, side by side, quite still, holding hands, not speaking, until the police arrived.

EPILOGUE

Maynard's Farm, Duck End, Oxfordshire
Friday 3 September, 1976

It's rained. The first time in two months, according to the radio. And then it goes and does it on Bank Holiday Monday. The garden needed it, though. There's only so much you can do with bathwater.

I got a cassette in the post this morning with a note.

Dear Mrs Jones, I am a neighbour of Valerie Flowers. She has requested that I send you this article in confidence. Yours sincerely, Felicity Manville.

I suppose she must be the neighbour that Lenny told me the story about on our first date – the one with the burning dildo. Obviously a better friend to Val than Jack thought. It's a home-recorded tape with Donna Summer written on the card and a list of the songs. It must have been Rosie's, and Val must have swapped them. But it's odd – she must have taken it from the car after she'd tried to run me over, because she didn't have a bag or anything. Perhaps she wanted to taunt Jack with it. She didn't come here intending to kill him, I'm sure of that. But this tape, if it's what I think it is because there's no label on the cassette, then the ruined one the police have must be just music. That must be why they haven't asked me about it.

I'm lying in bed looking out of the window. I shouldn't be up here at all. It's the middle of the afternoon and there's lots to do, but I get so tired. I've been spending a lot of time in bed recently. Sleeping, or just lying here thinking. It feels like a safe place to be. Like when I had chickenpox as a kid. That was in summer, too. Granddad used to come and read to me in the afternoons, and I'd lie there, listening, getting drowsy. Lovely clean white sheets.

I wish he was here now. I've tried to tell him about it in my head, but I keep getting muddled. I don't remember the end part at all, just the sirens and cars and shouting, then seeing the policemen in the doorway and coming towards us and Fred behind them and Eustace barking and barking . . . That was when I saw Jack. When they banged on the back door, that's when I turned round. She'd shot him through the mouth. I mean that quite literally, in one cheek and out the other side. Jack was slumped against the wooden chest with his legs out in front of him. His head was drooping, turned to one side, and I could see the wound where the bullet had gone through his face. His mouth was just a red, blasted hole, slack and open with skeins of blood and saliva hanging down onto his clothes, and blood all over his shirt and jacket. It was on me too. I didn't realise, but later . . . Not just the drops on my arms, but the wetness I felt on my shoulder, his blood, when they cleaned me up I saw . . . and on the floor and soaking into the wood of the chest, blood and pieces of his teeth and jaw, little fragments everywhere, that side of his face, that I couldn't see because it was against the chest, it was just . . . disintegrated. Bone is so hard, you wouldn't think . . . but they found it embedded in the chest, bits of his face, and the bullet . . .

I could hear the shouting, outside, 'Open up, open the door!' and I was staring at this great red hole that was his mouth and it went on and on and Eustace was barking and I was still holding Val's hand – or she was holding mine, I don't know – but I couldn't let go, even when they came in I couldn't let go of her hand.

They told me Jack would have died almost immediately: the wound and the shock. They took the chest of drawers away for evidence. I don't want it back. I never want to see it again.

Val told the police straight off that she'd shot Jack, before they even said anything, and they took her away. They took Fred, too. I thought I was going with them but they took me to hospital, I suppose because they didn't know whose blood it was. When I tried to move my legs just collapsed underneath me. I remember looking over at the door and wondering if I'd ever get there because it seemed such a long way away, and then not much else after that, really, until we got to Casualty.

The police questioned me for ages. I told them about Jack and Lee and Jeff and Val and . . . They asked me about Kitty, because of Lenny's car, and I told them what Jack had told me, that it was an accident. I told them about Danny Watts and the film as well, but I don't know if they believed me. They took me back to the station and asked more questions and in the end they said I could go and someone brought me home. Mrs Anderson was here. She said Mr Anderson had gone to fetch my mum so I wouldn't be on my own. He'd found the address in my book. I don't know how he managed to persuade her, but she's downstairs now. She hasn't come up much, except to bring food. Tomato soup, mostly. I'll turn orange if I have much more of it.

I don't feel like going down to talk to her but I'm glad she's here. I'll have to go through it all again at some point, because of the trial. They've charged Val with murder. There's no date yet. Too soon, I suppose.

I don't want to talk to anyone at the moment, except Granddad, and that's only in my head. And Eustace, of course. He's here now, lying under the window in a patch of sun. He only leaves the room to use the garden, then he's straight back. The doctor gave me some pills to help me sleep, and that's really all I want to do. Without the dreams, though. I don't have the dream about Kitty any more, thank God, but the new ones are horrible, everything mixed up – Jack trying to tell me something about Lenny, only he can't talk because his jaw's hanging off and he's trying to hold his face together with his hands, but it keeps slipping and his voice is like a record getting slower and slower and his mouth is coming apart at the corners and disintegrating into a red mass . . . Lee's there too and I can hear him screaming but I'm behind the stable door and I can't help him because I'm locked in and I know he's dying and I can't get to him . . . Then I wake up and it's me who's screaming.

It must be loud. Loud enough to wake me up, anyway. And Eustace. Mum's never come in, though. Perhaps she doesn't hear. I'm glad. I don't want to have to explain. It's a good job she's here, though, because of the animals. I tried to get back to normal, but I couldn't manage it. I wanted to. I'd get started on something, then I'd find myself doing something else when I hadn't finished the first thing. Just drifting, really. Hopeless.

I did talk to Mr Anderson a bit, though. I was worried they'd charge me with killing Jeff or Lee because my fingerprints were on the gun. But when I told him he said that was why they'd done the tests on my hands, because they'd still have powder on if I'd fired the gun, even if I washed them afterwards, there'd be traces, and they'd be able to tell . . . I couldn't bear that, if Fred thought I'd killed his son. He's not been in touch. I've been telling myself it's because the phone's not repaired yet, but he could have come round, and he hasn't. I tried to write him a letter, but I couldn't concentrate. I don't know what to say. Lee's dead, and he was only a child. He'd had no life at all. He didn't do anything wrong, just tried to help me. If I hadn't called out to him, if he'd just left the paper and gone, then he'd still be alive.

There was nothing in that paper about Kitty, that's the stupid thing. Jack hadn't even looked at it anyway – he can't have done, because they found it when Fred moved the furniture away from the front door to let the police in. There was a note from Trudy saying *Get Well Soon* scribbled across the top. I know because the police asked me about it. I suppose they must have spoken to her as well, poor kid.

I keep going over it all in my head. What if, what if, what if . . . Sometimes, usually at night, I start crying and I can't stop. Other times I just feel numb.

I went downstairs just now – Mum's gone out to the shop – and got my tape recorder. It's on the chair by the bed, all plugged in and ready. All I have to do is put the tape in and press the button, but . . .

Lenny wanted me to know. He wouldn't have made it otherwise, would he?

If I listen to this tape, I know that'll be it. I won't be able to keep my Lenny, my memory, any more. I didn't believe Jack's story about how Kitty died – a drunken accident – but the real thing might be worse . . .

Lenny wanted me to know. He wanted it to be like this. Like that thing I read: you live your life forwards and understand it backwards, and that's how it works. But somehow, I don't know how, I know I'll survive. Maybe it does come down to love. It does for me, at any rate. After all, love is the only thing we've got. And hope, of course. Love and hope.

Lenny didn't survive, and Jack didn't, but I will. It might take a long time, but I will. I know that. But first, I have to do this.

I'm putting the tape into the machine, like *so*, and now I'll turn it on. The wheels are turning. Faint hissing . . . background . . . that's all I can hear. Still time to turn it off. Take it downstairs and burn it, like I did with the film. But as I put my hand out, I hear Lenny's voice.

'*Alice* . . .'

Too late.

'*Alice* . . . *I want to tell you* . . .' Lenny's voice is loud, incoherent, sometimes urgent, rambling, tailing off, and sometimes he turns the tape off and puts it back on again halfway through a sentence.

'I did see Kitty. Didn't mean anything, it was Jack as well, just fooling around . . . I took her to the party, wanted to make you jealous . . . only reason . . . Kitty said she wanted to do it some more . . . said she'd bring some other girls . . . Told us to meet them at the lake, so we got my car and went down there . . . She was on her own, and that's when she said . . . told us she'd got this film of the three of us and we had to pay her . . .

'We had no idea, neither of us . . . We'd just been larking around, chasing through the wood, and when she said it, I didn't think she meant . . . I just thought it was funny, we'd been drinking and the idea of it just struck me as . . . I was sitting under a tree, laughing, and Jack caught her round the waist and she was struggling and he said "Get her legs." I still thought . . . just messing about . . . thought Jack was going to chuck her in the lake or something, so I got hold of her legs and we all sort of fell over and I was sitting on her, Jack was by her head, he started hitting her and she was yelling so I said something, I don't know, "Steady on," or something like that, "You'll hurt her and she won't want to play any more," but I was laughing so much I couldn't catch my breath and Jack said, "She isn't playing now." She was

279

trying to get up but he wouldn't let her, she said she'd go up to the house and tell Marcus and she got to the car, the driver's seat . . .

'I was hanging onto her legs but she got in and it wouldn't start and that was funny, too, women drivers . . . I was leaning on the car, I couldn't stop laughing . . . Jack went round the other side and he was banging her head on the steering wheel and I said, "Don't," because I didn't want him to hurt her, then I was on the ground by the door stroking her legs and her head was jerking backwards and forwards. I asked him to stop, begged him . . . but she went all floppy and Jack said, "That's it." I said, "What do you mean?" and he said, "We've got to get rid of the car," because there was blood, blood on the steering wheel and all around . . . dashboard . . . and I said, "She'll be all right," or something, and I went over to get her a drink but I must have fallen over because next thing I knew Jack had her bag out of the back and her clothes and he was saying, "It's in here, the bitch, she's got it in here," and he showed me the films – two of them – and he said, "We've got to do this," and I asked him why we can't just take the films and he said, "They won't be the only ones."

'I went to look through the window again and I could hear this funny noise, like a calf or . . . moo-ing . . . and I opened the door but Jack leant over me and took the handbrake off and said, "Help me push," and I said, "She's alive," but he wouldn't listen and he started pushing and the car was moving down the slope and bouncing and I could see her face at the window, up and down, and her hands against the glass, and I said, "She's not dead . . ." . . . told me not to be so fucking stupid, "Of course she's dead," and I said, "No." Told me I was hallucinating but she was alive, I know she was . . . and just before it went down in the water, I could see her . . . Jack says I imagined it but I know . . .

'I get dreams – nightmares – her face behind the glass . . .
unbearable . . . can't pretend any more. I thought . . . you
were my future, but now I can't . . . Jack says we mustn't tell
anyone, but . . . doesn't matter now . . . only for Jack, if
he . . . but I know you won't . . . I had to tell you, Alice, so
you know . . . better without me . . . We took her bag and
dumped it, and Jack sent Val round to her flat to get the
other tapes, but then I got a phone call asking where she
was . . . a man, wanting money, he knew about the party,
and when Kitty didn't come back he must have put two and
two together . . . threatening us . . . we've paid him, but he
won't leave us alone . . . Why I accepted the cottage . . . so
I could go to the lake – thought I could get through to Kitty
somehow, make her leave me alone, but it's worse here, the
nightmares are worse, and Danny knows . . .

'Can't remember . . . what I told him, but something . . .
Jack says, live with it, but I'm a coward, Alice . . . I can't be
with you and not tell you but now I know you won't want
me . . . I love you but I keep seeing her face in my mind . . .
always there, so this is . . . I love you so much, Alice . . . I
love you . . . I love you . . . I love you . . .'

Nothing more. I turn off the tape. I shan't give it to the
police. That won't bring anyone back, and besides, there's
Rosie. I can't.

That's my decision. I won't go back on it.

I lean over, rewind the tape a very, very little, and press
Play. Then I turn onto my back and close my eyes.